‘Why?’ She looked panicked. ‘What does he want with me?’

He wishes for you to marry again.

The answer sprang to his lips, but the obvious fear in her voice made him hesitate. With his hand gripping her arm he felt suddenly irrationally protective. It wasn’t his place to tell her the Earl’s plans, but she was watching him, no longer defiant but frightened, asking him a question. He felt a stirring in his chest—something he hadn’t felt in a long time—as if something were shifting inside him. Damn it all, how could such a small woman have such a powerful effect on his senses?

‘He intends for you to marry again,’ he said softly, surprising himself.

‘Marry a *Norman*?’

Author Note

The early years of William the Conqueror's reign in England were marked by instability and rebellion. Some of those Saxon nobles who had survived the Battle of Hastings had their lands confiscated, but others were offered a chance to keep their homes in exchange for their allegiance. Most, however, such as the infamous Hereward the Wake in East Anglia, chose to rebel against the oppressive new Norman regime—though this generally took the form of stubborn resistance rather than outright warfare.

The description of William's treatment of the rebels in this story is based on real-life events, most notably those that occurred during the brutal Harrying of the North in 1069. By this point the King had abandoned any attempt at compromise, to the extent that, according to the Domesday Book, by 1086 only five per cent of English land still remained in Saxon control.

This story, however, is set in Mercia in 1067—less than a year after the Conquest—when it might still have been possible to gain favour with the new King. William did reward his supporters with English land, and encouraged intermarriage between Norman and Saxon as a means to secure property and lend legitimacy to his Kingship. In order to control a large, rebellious Saxon population he also started a campaign of castle-building almost immediately upon arriving in England, so although the stone castle described in this story is slightly ahead of its time, its presence is still plausible during a time of tumultuous political unrest and upheaval.

MARRIED TO HER ENEMY

Jenni Fletcher

MILLS & BOON™

HarperCollins
PUBLISHERS
Since 1817

Published in Great Britain 2016
by Mills & Boon, an imprint of HarperCollins*Publishers*
1 London Bridge Street, London, SE1 9GF

ISBN: 978-0-263-92555-5

Our policy is to use papers that are natural, renewable and recyclable products and made from wood grown in sustainable forests. The logging and manufacturing processes conform to the legal environmental regulations of the country of origin.

Printed and bound in Spain
by CPI, Barcelona

Jenni Fletcher was born on the north coast of Scotland and now lives in Yorkshire, with her husband and two children. She wanted to be a writer as a child, but got distracted by reading instead, finally writing down her first paragraph thirty years later. She's had more jobs than she can remember, but has finally found one she loves. She can be contacted via Twitter @JenniAuthor.

Married to Her Enemy
is Jenni Fletcher's gripping debut for
Mills & Boon Historical Romance!

Visit the Author Profile page at millsandboon.co.uk.

To my wonderful family,
because you always said I could do it.
And to Andy, my best friend.

Chapter One

Etton, near Peterborough, Mercia,
August 1067

Aediva shoved the full weight of her body against the heavy wooden gate, skidding in the mud as she finally dropped the iron locking bar.

Then she turned and ran. Back up the hill, back past the abandoned houses and scattered belongings dropped in the desperate rush to escape, back towards the Thane's hall that stood, circular-shaped and slightly raised on a mound in the centre.

At the entrance she stopped, windswept hair tumbling over her face like a hazel and honey-flecked veil, glancing fearfully over her shoulder as if expecting to find an arrow aimed at her throat.

How long did they have? How long before the Conquest reached their door?

An hour if they were lucky.

Not long enough.

Then she blinked and the fear was gone, replaced by a steely determination. The Normans might be coming, but she had another, more urgent crisis to deal with first.

Breathless, she charged into the hall, skirting around the still-smoking central fireplace before bursting headlong into the birthing chamber.

'How is she?' She dropped, panting, into the straw by the bed. 'Is the babe any further along?'

Eadgyth, the midwife, shook her grey head sadly. 'Not yet. She needs to push.'

'But she's been pushing for hours!'

Aediva chewed her lip anxiously, still weighing their chances of escape. How could it be taking so long? How much more could Cille's small body take? Every moment of delay brought the Normans closer towards them. Every moment increased the risk of capture, or worse. But Cille's baby seemed in no hurry to be born.

'What can I do?'

'Nothing. All we can do is wait.'

Wait! Aediva caught her breath, trying to stave off the rising tide of panic, the feeling that her whole world—the Saxon world that she knew—was collapsing around her head. First Leofric, then her father and now Cille. Not to mention Edmund. The last year had brought so much heartache and suffering, surely she couldn't lose her sister as well?

She squeezed her eyes shut, trying to banish the memory of that morning: the dull thud of Cille's swooning body, the terrible slow spread of blood through the rushes. News of the Norman soldiers' approach had finally shocked her into labour, albeit not before time. The babe was already dangerously late, but Aediva had thought her older sister still asleep, not listening as she'd ordered their people to pack up and flee east, towards the Fens, one of the last strongholds of Saxon resistance. If it hadn't been for that shock, they might all have escaped.

'They've gone, then?' Eadgyth handed her a cup of mead.

'Aye.'

She took a long draught, listening to the heavy rumble of carts in the distance, wondering if she'd done the right thing. She'd made the decision on Cille's behalf, just as she'd made every decision since their father's death that last winter, taking over the day-to-day running of the village while her sister prepared for her confinement. Not that Cille had shown even the slightest interest in her inheritance. Since her unexpected arrival in the spring she'd seemed a mere ghost of her former self, barely talking let alone taking charge.

Which had left *her* to do it, acting as Thane in deed if not name, doing her best to behave as their father would have wanted. But then he'd never faced a Norman invasion! How could she know what he would have done? Would he have run away or simply refused to leave, like Eadgyth? Or put up a fight, defending Etton to the bitter and bloody end? Her heart suspected the latter, but her head had prevailed. What chance did Saxon farmers have against Norman soldiers?

Her gaze slid towards the leather curtain that separated the birthing chamber from the hall, as if she were expecting a horde of Normans to burst through at any moment. What chance did three women have?

She only hoped she'd done the right thing.

She leaned over and stroked the side of Cille's face—*her* face, so like hers that they might have been twins, not sisters born two years apart. Every small feature seemed to mirror her own, from the sharply arched brows to the slightly pointed chin. Only their eyes told them apart. Cille's a warm forget-me-not blue, soft and gentle as a summer's sky, and her own a fiery brown with gold flecks flashing like lightning across them.

A tear seeped from the corner of one of those eyes now and she brushed it aside, reaching across to clasp Cille's trembling hands between her own. The fingers felt damp and clammy, as if she were sweating and shivering at the same time. In mercy's name, how much more could either of them take?

'Take care of the baby.'

The voice was faint, but Aediva jumped, afraid that she might have imagined it. But, no, those were Cille's eyes staring up at her, black orbs ringed with crimson shadows so large they seemed to drain the life from her small, sunken face.

'Hush.' She smiled reassuringly. 'You need to save your strength.'

'Please…' Cille's voice was ragged, but the look on her face was deadly serious. 'Promise me. Take care of my child.'

Aediva caught her breath, hot tears scalding the backs of her eyelids. 'I promise.'

'There's something else.' Cille heaved herself up on her elbows, ignoring Eadgyth's grunt of protest. 'Something I need to tell you.'

'Later. You need to…'

She left the sentence unfinished as she heard a noise outside—a faint rumble at first, building steadily to a thunderous crescendo. The unmistakable heavy pounding of hooves, and lots of them.

Warhorses!

A jolt of panic tore through her body. She'd thought she could control her emotions, but now that the time had come and all hope of escape was lost all she could feel was the rush of blood in her ears and the terrible, deafening thud of her own heartbeat.

Not yet! The plea echoed in her head. Not before the baby was born! They needed more time!

Cille sank back onto the bed with a gasp, her body convulsing with pain. Had she heard it too?

Aediva exchanged a look with Eadgyth, an unspoken message passing between them, and then reached under the bed and drew out a long iron broadsword. It was almost as tall as she was, and heavy to boot, but it was a formidable weapon. She only hoped she could wield it.

Briefly she glanced down at her dishevelled appearance. She'd barely had time to dress that morning, throwing on a simple homespun tunic that was already mud-stained and tattered. Her hair was even more unkempt, coiling down her back in a mass of tangles. She hadn't had time to put on a headdress. Not that it mattered. What the Normans thought of her appearance was the very least of her worries.

She dropped a kiss onto Cille's forehead and pulled back the curtain to the deserted hall. Now that the first rush of panic was over, she knew what she had to do.

She took a deep breath, willing her heart to stop racing. She couldn't help Cille give birth, but she could keep the Norman invaders away until the baby was born. No matter what, she wouldn't let them into this chamber.

No matter what. Or who.

* * *

Sir Svend du Danemark ran a hand through pale blond hair and swore fluently under his breath.

'It looks like they knew we were coming.'

His squire, Renard, had a habit of stating the obvious.

Steel-blue eyes narrowed, taking in every detail of the terrain with the experienced gaze of a professional soldier. The base of the valley was a craggy gorge, split down the middle by a meandering river that carried water from the high hills to the east. There was no sign of habitation, just gorse and a scattering of twisted hawthorns, but as the river curved to the south, the land rose and flattened out into a ledge, revealing the stockade of a small, almost completely hidden settlement. No wonder it had taken so long to find.

Svend swallowed another oath. At this time of year the villagers should have been busy harvesting their crops, but the long strips of farmland were deserted. Instead he could see fresh furrows in the mud, tracks left by horses and carts. If they'd put out a banner the residents couldn't have made their departure any more obvious.

'Ten shillings if she's still here?' Renard persisted.

'Twenty,' Svend murmured, resisting the urge to knock his squire into the mud.

In truth, he would have paid a lot more to get

this over with. Hunting a woman was no honourable task for a knight and he resented his orders—even if they did come from the King via his cousin, William FitzOsbern, the new Earl of Hereford.

Hawklike, his gaze narrowed in on the meagre earthen defences. What in blazes was Lady Cille doing *here*? The village was well hidden, but hardly a stronghold. What had made her flee a fortress like Redbourn and take refuge in such an isolated place? And why the hell was he wasting his time finding her? Surely the future of the Conquest couldn't depend on one Saxon woman! There must be something more important he could be doing!

He kept his thoughts to himself. He'd learnt to keep his own counsel a long time ago, preferring to live up to the reputation his men had ascribed him of being inscrutable, keeping his emotions well hidden.

'Take the men and surround the palisade.' He rubbed the light blond stubble on his chin with irritation. He needed a bath and a shave. 'Let's get this over with.'

'You're going alone, sir?'

Renard's expression was anxious and Svend raised an eyebrow, not sure whether to be amused or insulted. 'She's only one woman.'

'But it might be a trap. The Saxons might be hiding.'

'Perhaps.' He bit back a sarcastic retort. 'But

she's more likely to come peacefully if we don't scare the wits out of her.'

'She might be armed.'

'I'm certain of it.'

He placed a reassuring hand on the younger man's shoulder. Renard was a good squire, and would make a fine knight one day, but he could be annoyingly over-attentive at times.

'Don't worry. You'll be close by if she overpowers me.'

He winked, spurring his destrier forward before Renard could detect the sarcasm. The hill was steep but he surged fearlessly ahead, trusting his mount's training and his men's obedience as they thundered towards the stockade, his blond hair, worn to shoulder-length rather than in the cropped Norman fashion, streaming behind him like a banner of white gold, as if he were charging headlong into battle.

The wind tore at his face and he grinned, sharing his mount's exhilaration. Talbot was a fine specimen, sixteen hands high at his grey shoulder, and worth every bruise it had taken to win him. Svend's grin spread wickedly as he recalled the French Baron whose haughty dismissal of a fifteen-year-old farmer's son had cost him his finest warhorse—not to mention his dignity before the then Duke William of Normandy.

It was the same day that he'd been plucked from a life of brawling in tournaments and offered training as a household knight—been given a sense of focus and purpose, a way to vent the anger of his past. His low rank hadn't made him popular with the rest of the high-born squires at William's court, but thick skin and quick fists had earned him a position he could never have dreamed of. Knighthood and a place in the King's personal guard. It was no mean feat for the fourth son of a Danish farmer.

Not to mention an outlaw.

He drew rein in front of the wooden palisade and dismounted, tossing his cloak aside and drawing his sword from its scabbard in one fluid movement. The ground was muddy—hardly surprising after a week of near constant rain and mizzle—and it covered his boots in a cloying, sticky mess. Not for the first time he found himself wondering why they'd left Normandy for this fogbound, rain-soaked isle. He was heartily sick of the rough terrain, the appalling weather and, most of all, this search for a woman who seemed more phantom than flesh and blood.

Phantom. His mouth curved in a mirthless smile. That was what his men called her. Impossible to find, let alone to capture. They'd spent two weeks travelling in circles, searching for Etton's hidden valley. And now, from the look of things, she'd eluded them yet again.

He muttered another imprecation. The Earl had promised to reward him on the King's behalf upon his return to Redbourn—some share in the spoils of conquest for ten years' loyal service—just as soon as he found the woman.

At this rate it would take another ten years.

He took his frustration out on the gate, shattering the wooden frame with one kick and sending the locking bar spinning ten feet into the mud. He frowned at the sight of it. If the gate had been barred from the inside there might still be a chance she was there. Foolish of him not to have checked, letting frustration get the better of caution, but no matter. The village was clearly deserted, the wattle-and-daub dwellings empty and abandoned.

He stalked between them, past broken pots and dropped blankets strewn haphazardly over the rough ground, as if the inhabitants had left recently and in a rush. He felt a now familiar twinge of unease. Clearly the fearsome Norman reputation had preceded them—bloodthirsty tales of retribution and punishment. The thought made him uncomfortable. Rule by fear was no just way to govern a country, but the King was implacable towards those who resisted his rule.

Svend wanted no part of it. For the first time in his career he found himself questioning his King's methods. How could the Conquest ever be peaceful when Normans were so hated?

He reached the Thane's hall and thrust his sword point-first into the mud. No matter what

Renard's concerns, if by some unlikely chance she were still hiding inside, there'd be little enough room for swordplay and he had no desire to fight a woman. He still carried his sax on his belt, but he had no intention of using it. He'd bring her by force if he had to, but he wouldn't hurt her—not if he could help it.

Unlike a Norman fortress, there was no wooden door, just a heavy oxhide draped over the entrance. Cautiously he pulled it aside and stepped over the threshold. A shaft of light filtered in through a hole in the centre of the thatched roof, helping his eyes adjust to the half-darkness. As he'd expected, the hall was deserted—and yet something about the scene wasn't right. The room was empty, not abandoned. And there was a strange sound coming from behind a partition at the back, like an animal whimpering in pain.

He took a step towards it and then stopped, realising his error a split second too late as the blade pricked the back of his neck.

'Don't move!' The voice was soft but determined, and unmistakably female. More surprisingly, it was speaking in perfect French. 'Raise your hands!'

He did as he was told, annoyed by his own complacency. He'd been caught out like some raw, callow recruit—but then he'd never expected to find her completely alone. Where were her men? Surely there was somebody here to defend her?

He put his hands on the back of his head, starting to turn. 'You're a difficult woman to find, Lady Cille.'

'Stop! Stay as you are!'

The blade pressed harder against his skin, but he detected a faint tremor. She was afraid.

Briefly he considered disarming her. The position of the sword told him everything he needed to know about her combat skills. A more practised opponent would have pointed the blade to his throat. But he decided to try diplomacy first.

'My name is Sir Svend du Danemark. I mean you no harm.'

There was a lengthy pause as he waited, inhaling the sweet, heady scent of summer flowers, which reminded him of his home in Danemark.

Fool. He didn't have a home. He'd left his parents' farm half a lifetime ago.

'My lady?' He prompted her, pushing the memory aside.

'How did you find me?' She spoke slowly, as if choosing her words with care.

'With difficulty. Etton isn't an easy place to find.'

'And what do you want from me?'

He felt a flash of irritation. If she thought to interrogate him she'd be swiftly disappointed. Even so, the hint of steel in that soft voice was intriguing. 'The King's deputy sent me to find you.'

'The King's deputy?' She sounded genuinely surprised. 'Why?'

He paused, having considered the same question at length over the past weeks. It couldn't simply be her value in marriage. As a Saxon noblewoman, and widow of ealdorman Leofric of Redbourn, she'd lend legitimacy to a Norman husband's authority, but it was unlike FitzOsbern to expend so much time and effort on one who'd proved so troublesome. There had to be something else—something special about her.

He'd hardly been in Redbourn long enough to hear any rumours. The Earl had summoned and then dispatched him almost as soon as he'd arrived. But there had to be a reason. Somehow he'd hoped she might be able to tell him.

The blade pushed harder. 'Have you lost your tongue, Norman whoreson?'

He grinned, having heard the insult numerous times over the past few months, though rarely spoken with such venom. Clearly Saxon ladies weren't as sheltered as their Norman counterparts.

'I'm not party to the Earl's thoughts, my lady,' he answered with exaggerated courtesy.

There was another cry from the back—less like an animal, more like a woman sobbing. His brows snapped together.

'You can't come in here!'

By the note of panic in her voice he could tell his assailant had heard it too.

'I can't?' His voice was low and dangerous, all trace of humour extinguished.

'You have to leave!' Her voice rose higher, becoming hysterical as the blade shuddered against his neck.

It was time to end this.

He moved so fast that she had no time to react. In less than a heartbeat he was facing her, clamping his hands together over the flat sides of her sword and hurling it easily into the floor rushes, then hooking a foot expertly around her legs, knocking them out from under her so that she tumbled backwards, straight into his waiting arms.

It wasn't a manoeuvre that he'd ever used before, usually preferring that his opponents stayed down when he disarmed them. But then none of his opponents had ever been a woman...and none so light and willowy as the one now cradled in his arms, the dark honey waves of her long hair rippling over his hands almost to the floor.

For a heart-stopping moment he thought he might drop her. It wasn't because she was pretty, though she undoubtedly was. Her small face was that of a woman in her late teens or early twenties, lightly tanned with smooth, round cheekbones and a pair of pink bow-shaped lips. It was her eyes that held him. Unlike any he'd ever seen before, so wide and lustrous he might almost fall into them. What colour were they? A swirl of copper and gold, fringed with long black lashes, strange and beguiling as jewels.

He shook his head, trying to break the spell. He didn't know what he'd expected, but the roundabout journey to Etton had hardly disposed him to think charitably of his quarry.

The change as her face contorted into an expression of implacable fury, was enough to render him speechless.

The knife was flicked out of her sleeve so fast that he was almost caught off guard. But a lifetime of fighting had honed his reflexes to the point that he caught her wrist instinctively, stopping the blade a hair's breadth from his chest.

'Norman pig!'

She shrieked in her anger and he heard voices outside, followed by footsteps running in their direction. He called out, ordering his men to stop even as she screamed and hurled herself bodily against him, sending both of them sprawling into the rushes.

Svend landed heavily, trying to shield her from both the fall and herself as she thrashed recklessly against him, heedless of the blade still between them, pummelling at his chest as if she wanted to pound him into the ground. The scent of flowers filled his nostrils—honeysuckle and daisies, like a meadow he wanted to bury his face in. He tossed the weapon aside and captured her arms above her head instead, clamping his hands over her wrists like iron manacles.

Still she refused to yield, flailing against him like a cornered animal, fists beating impotently at thin air. He felt a vague sense of surprise. Pretty she might be, but she was also half wild, with an impressive temper to boot.

He rolled on top of her, pinning her legs to the floor with his own, struggling to keep his weight on his arms. She wasn't the sort of woman he was accustomed to having beneath him, so slight and slender he was almost afraid he might break her.

Then he waited, letting her fury wear itself out. Trapped beneath him, she flung herself from side to side, arching her back and squirming as she tried to escape. Her small breasts heaved against his chest and he felt a stirring in his loins, quickly suppressed. This was hardly the time for such thoughts, but her endless writhing was bringing to mind other, more enjoyable pursuits.

'I'm not going to hurt you!' he muttered through gritted teeth, dragging his mind away from the snug fit of her body beneath his. He'd never taken advantage of a vulnerable woman before and he wasn't about to start now. If she'd only stop wriggling...

'Scum! Son of a Norman bitch!'

She kept on thrashing against him, venting her anger in a torrent of what he assumed was Anglo-Saxon abuse. Long hazel hair tumbled over his chest like a silken blanket, stirring his senses, and his gaze fell to her lips. They looked full and soft and suddenly desirable. But her eyes…

If looks could kill he'd be dead a hundred times over. Her eyes were aflame with anger. He couldn't blame her. He was a Norman and she'd lost her husband at Hastings. He'd seen the same look of raw loathing in the faces of her countrymen every day for months, and yet it unsettled him to see it so close. He wanted her to look at him with something other than hatred, with a very different emotion…

Damn it, he must have been without a woman too long if he was drawn to this Saxon wildcat.

With an effort, he steered his thoughts in a different direction. Why was she still resisting? He felt an unwanted flicker of admiration. From long experience he knew that most opponents would have surrendered by now, but by the determined gleam in those fiery eyes it was clear that she'd never submit. She would fight to the bitter end.

And he didn't want to fight her. She was just one of the Conquest's many victims—a woman whose whole existence, like that of her people, had been overturned by the Norman invasion—but at that moment he was the one holding her down. And he didn't want to.

Something inside him rebelled. He'd seen enough injustice in his life, didn't want to be a part of any more. He was a warrior, but he was also a man, and something about this felt wrong. He wouldn't be the one to defeat her.

He released her abruptly, letting her push back against him until their positions were reversed and she was sitting astride him, legs straddling his thighs, her whole body coiled to attack. With a cry of triumph she snatched up the knife and swung her arm back, as if making ready to plunge it into his heart.

Then she froze, her expression suddenly stricken as the knife hung motionless in the air.

At the same moment, the curtain swung open and Renard stood framed in the doorway, his jaw dropping at the sight before him.

'Sir? Should we come in now?'

Svend's gaze remained fixed on the woman looming threateningly above him. He flexed a wrist, ready to deflect the knife, but he didn't think he would need to. She was panting heavily, her chest rising and falling as if she'd been running, but she looked dazed, as if she were only seeing him for the first time.

'Renard.' He addressed his squire as if there were nothing unusual in the scene. 'It seems you were right to be cautious. We've found our phantom. This is Lady Cille.'

Chapter Two

'How long has she been like this?'

Aediva bristled. Bad enough that he had dared to enter the birthing chamber, but now this Norman invader was insolent enough to ask questions, as if Cille's condition were *any* of his business. This wasn't his place. It was no man's place.

'The pains started early this morning,' Eadgyth answered. 'She's sleeping now, but it won't be long.'

Aediva threw Eadgyth a worried glance, willing her not to call Cille by name. She'd taken her sister's identity on the spur of the moment, without considering the consequences if her deception were uncovered. Now she had to maintain the pretence at least until the baby was born. Cille was in no condition to deal with Normans, let alone this warrior whose wintry blue gaze seemed altogether too perceptive. She had to warn Eadgyth before she said something to give them away...

Her mouth fell open. Eadgyth had spoken to him! Which meant…

'You speak Saxon?'

Pale eyebrows arched upwards. 'As you speak French.'

'My father thought it important. Besides, that's hardly uncommon. Not many Normans speak Saxon.'

'Fewer than you think. I'm not Norman.'

She tilted her head towards him enquiringly but he was already looking at her, his gaze wandering over her face as if a new idea had just struck him. She fought the urge to take a step backwards. Such intense scrutiny made her uncomfortable. What was he looking at?

His gaze dropped. Slowly, almost leisurely, it travelled down over her neck and breasts. Lower. And lower. Past her waist, lingering over the curve of her hips, down to her toes and back up again, as if memorising every inch of her body. She flushed, her skin tingling wherever his eyes rested, as if they might strip away her gown and see the nakedness beneath. Instinctively her hands coiled into fists. Conquering warrior he might be, but she was a Thane's daughter! How *dared* he insult her so brazenly?

He jerked his head towards the bed. 'She's your sister?'

She nodded cautiously. The question was casual—too casual. She felt a cold sweat break out on the back of her neck, hardly trusting herself to speak. It was obvious that they were sisters. Was he suspicious? Had he guessed who she really was? She had the discomforting feeling that he was testing her.

'You're very alike.'

'I've noticed.' She bit her lip instantly, regretting the sarcasm. She should try to ingratiate herself, not insult him.

His eyes flashed with something like humour. How could eyes be so intensely blue? she wondered. It was a blue that seemed to change every time she looked at them, sometimes so pale as to seem almost white, sometimes a vivid, piercing turquoise. People said that her eyes were unusual, but his were almost hypnotic. When they demanded she meet them, there was no way to refuse.

Like now. What did his scrutiny mean? What was he thinking?

He turned towards Eadgyth abruptly. 'Is the baby moving? And facing the right way?'

'Yes, but the mother is weak. She can't stand much more.'

'How close together are the pains?'

'Close enough.'

Aediva looked between them, feeling suddenly out of place and excluded. Not many men had more than a vague idea about the mysteries of childbirth, preferring to leave such matters to their womenfolk, but this man seemed to know more about the birthing process than she did.

'Is there anything you need?' He sounded genuinely solicitous.

'Something hot to eat wouldn't hurt.'

He strode purposefully out of the chamber, leaving Aediva open-mouthed. Had this Norman warrior really just taken orders from an old Saxon midwife?

'Not a monster after all,' Eadgyth muttered.

She closed her mouth with a snap. 'He's still a Norman.'

'Be glad you're still alive to say so.' Eadgyth looked her up and down critically. 'What on earth happened to you, girl?'

Aediva turned her face aside, cheeks flaring anew. Eadgyth was right. She was lucky not to be in chains. What had she been thinking? She'd armed herself with no real intention except to warn the Normans off, but far from bartering with them, or pleading for mercy, she'd clambered on top of their commander and aimed a blade at his heart, channelling the full force of her fear and anger into one frenzied, pointless attack. For certes, Cille would never have done such a thing.

And what had she hoped to achieve? She couldn't possibly have fought off a whole Norman battalion. She hadn't even stopped one man. Fighting her off had caused him little more effort than batting away a troublesome fly. And now it seemed she didn't even matter enough to be punished. She didn't know whether to feel relieved or insulted.

The sound of footsteps brought her back to herself.

'He thinks I'm Cille,' she whispered hurriedly, throwing a worried glance over her shoulder as Svend reappeared in the doorway, bearing a thick, fur-lined cloak in one hand and a wineskin in the other.

For the first time she looked at him properly, free to do so now that his attention no longer held hers. Strange that she hadn't done it before, but somehow those blue eyes had made everything around them seem like a blur.

He was unlike any man she'd ever seen before—like a Viking from one of the old stories, a dangerous warrior from a wintry land across the sea. He was young, still in his mid-twenties, but there was no doubting his air of authority. His taut, muscular body was clad in a simple leather gambeson and dark hose, shunning armour except for a top of light chainmail.

Eadgyth was right; he wasn't a monster. Far from it. If he hadn't been her enemy she might have called him handsome. No, she corrected herself, that word was too bland. His features were too rugged to be called simply handsome, his jaw too squarely set, those glacial eyes too piercingly, disconcertingly blue.

Why did she keep coming back to his eyes?

She watched him cross the room, remembering the feel of his muscular body over hers, the vivid sensation of strength held in check. She'd aimed a dagger at his heart and yet he hadn't fought back, hadn't lain so much as a finger on her except in restraint. And then he'd let her go. Why? She could never have beaten him and yet he'd let her reclaim the knife. Had he been toying with her? Or had she really found a chink in his defences?

'One of my men is preparing broth,' he murmured, passing the wineskin to Eadgyth. 'This contains feverfew. It should ease the pain.'

He moved to the far side of the bed and raised Cille gently, draping the cloak around her shoulders and holding her steady as the midwife pressed the spiced liquid to her lips.

Aediva stared transfixed at the scene before her. *He is our enemy!* she wanted to scream to the rafters. *A Norman, or as good as!* Had the world turned upside down? Normans were cold-hearted, ruthless invaders! They'd killed Leofric in battle, murdered her father in cold blood, driven Edmund away—destroyed the very fabric of their lives! So why was he helping them and not punishing her? And how could they possibly accept help from such a tainted source?

Cille's flickering eyelids gave her the answer. She was gulping the liquid down greedily, as if she hadn't touched a drop for days, seeming to gain strength with every mouthful.

'Here.'

Without looking up, Svend shifted aside to let her take over and she brushed past him warily, careful not to make contact as she slid an arm under his and around Cille's narrow shoulders. She was uncomfortably aware of his proximity, of the heat radiating from his broad chest, reminding her that less than an hour before, she'd thrown herself against it in an abandoned murderous frenzy. Wanton or murderess—which would he think was worse?

And why should she care?

He moved around the bed, apparently oblivious to her discomfort, and crouched down on one knee, bringing his face level to Cille's.

'My lady, in the name of King William, I promise that no harm will come to you or your child.'

Even through the heavy cloak Aediva could feel some of the tension ease from Cille's trembling shoulders. She gaped at him in amazement. The unexpectedly gentle, reassuring tone of his voice, so utterly at odds with his warrior-like appearance, was having a similar effect on her own tattered nerves. How could this man, their enemy, be inspiring such confidence?

He glanced up suddenly, then away again, as if he hadn't seen her, and her anger reasserted itself. He might be helping them now, but if it hadn't been for this Norman's arrival, Cille would still be safely awaiting her baby. Offering his protection was the very least he could do!

Cille groaned and Eadgyth stooped to feel her swollen stomach, nodding with satisfaction. 'It's time.'

Svend nodded and strode briskly to the doorway, pausing briefly on the threshold. His broad shoulders filled the space easily.

'If you need anything, one of my men will be waiting outside.'

Then he was gone, leaving Aediva staring at a swinging curtain, emotions in turmoil. Of course she was glad that he'd gone, and yet his presence had been inexplicably reassuring—as if Cille had been safe when he was close by. Typical of a Norman to inflict himself upon them and then leave…

'Are you going to help me or not?'

Eadgyth's shrill voice interrupted her thoughts.

'Fetch some water, girl!'

She leapt to her feet, smitten with guilt at neglecting Cille, if only for a moment. Her distraction was his fault too.

Never again, she promised herself.

Svend du Danemark wouldn't distract her again. Not ever.

Aediva stumbled out into the courtyard, gulping mouthfuls of air like water. After the stultifying atmosphere of the birthing chamber it was a relief to be out in the open.

It was twilight. But on what day? An eternity seemed to have passed since she'd last felt the cool breeze on her skin.

She leaned back against the timbered wall and looked up at the first scattered sprinkling of stars, letting the tension ease from her tired limbs. It was over. Cille had a son, a tiny red bundle with powerful lungs that had already made more noise than his mother had in her whole life.

She smiled, recalling the blissful look on Cille's face as she'd cradled her newborn baby to her breast, so happy even after so much pain. Cille had defied their worst fears, her small body proving stronger than they'd dared to imagine. Aediva had known that childbirth was dangerous, but she hadn't realised it could be so brutal.

Tears welled in her eyes. Was that how it had been for their own mother? Had she suffered so much?

'Lady Cille?'

She jumped, dismayed to be caught at such a vulnerable moment. She didn't normally let down her defences so easily, but her emotions were still raw and the stress of the day had made her careless.

She hadn't heard him approach, but Svend was already standing beside her, barely an arm's length away, pale eyes glinting like twin crystals in the near darkness. He must have shaved, because his stubble was gone and his jutting cheekbones were even more prominent in his tanned face, his blond hair slicked back as if he'd just finished bathing. She'd never seen a man without a beard before. His skin looked smooth, the strong line of his jaw soft and almost strokeable. She found herself wanting to reach out and touch it. Instead she scowled deliberately.

'Forgive me.' He bowed stiffly. 'I didn't mean to startle you. Is there news?'

'What do you care?'

She tossed her hair and stared into the distance, reluctant to meet his gaze until she had her tumultuous emotions under control. After his too intimate assessment of her in the birthing chamber, he'd barely glanced in her direction, but now his scrutiny was back—too close, too penetrating. Why did he have to stare at her again now, when she wanted to be alone? How long had he been watching her?

She thought she heard a sigh, but when she looked back his expression was blank, impenetrable.

'You should eat,' he said finally.

For a moment she thought of refusing, but the very idea of food made her ravenous. A curl of smoke twisted up from a chimney in one of the abandoned cottages, accompanied by a strong smell of cooking, and she felt her stomach tighten with hunger.

Svend gestured towards it and then stepped aside, letting her precede him across the courtyard. It was another thoughtful gesture, but she refused to acknowledge it. Now that the crisis was over, her nerves felt stretched to breaking point. She felt utterly drained and exposed. Why was it proving so hard to pull herself back together?

She looked around, trying to clear her befuddled head, and experienced a vague sense of surprise. She'd assumed that the Normans would take over the Thane's hall, but they were scattered throughout the village, billeted in the recently vacated dwellings. Damn them, *why* were they being so reasonable? She didn't want to feel indebted.

Not looking where she was going, she tripped and stumbled headlong into the cottage, a foot catching in her tunic and dragging her down. At once a strong hand gripped her elbow, but she shied away, hitting the ground with a thud, preferring to sprawl in the dirt than accept any further help. If he did one more honourable thing she would scream.

Svend stared down at her for a long moment, his expression set hard as tempered steel as she glared defiantly back, ignoring the pain in her hands and knees where she'd grazed them, daring him to help her up.

'As you wish,' he commented icily, striding to the central fireplace and ladling out a bowl of steaming broth. 'Will you deign to eat Norman food or would you prefer dirt?'

Aediva struggled to her feet, abandoning the last shreds of her dignity as she snatched up the bowl and drained the contents in a few short gulps. The warmth coiled through her limbs, giving her strength, but she still couldn't bring herself to thank him.

Instead she licked her lips, savouring the last taste of broth, delaying the moment when she'd have to face him again. The fire flickered and crackled between them, casting eerie shadows along the walls and filling her nostrils with woodsmoke. She looked around the room and felt a shiver of unease. Aside from a few cracked earthenware pots and a straw mattress it was completely empty, when just this morning it had been a home.

She could sense his eyes on her, but when she finally looked up they were hooded.

'It's a boy,' she said finally. 'Eadgyth says he's a reasonable size.'

'That's a good sign.'

'She said so too.'

She hesitated, loath to tell him any more, but somehow it seemed ungrateful not to.

'My sister's asleep, and her breathing's steady.'

Aediva, she told herself. She should say *Aediva.*

But she couldn't trust herself with the lie. Not yet—not when he was standing so close.

'I'm glad of it.'

'And the babe is called Leofric after h… my husband.'

She bit her lip, mortified that she'd almost given herself away. But this Norman's proximity was unsettling. It distracted her. The cottage seemed too small with him in it, as if the walls were closing in on her. Or was he too big? She hadn't noticed how tall he was before. The top of her head barely grazed his shoulder. Not to mention his chest. If both she and Cille stood together behind him no one would guess they were there.

Suddenly she wished she were back in the birthing chamber, back in the open air—anywhere but there.

She gave him a searching glance but he seemed not to have noticed her slip. Still, it would be too easy to give herself away. Perhaps it was time to tell him the truth, to admit who she was and that she'd been pretending to be her own sister. After all, he'd been unexpectedly kind to Cille. If she admitted the truth now he might let the lie pass, but the longer she deceived him the worse it would surely be. He didn't look like a man who'd take kindly to being deceived. He would be angry… furious, even.

But at least he couldn't blame Cille…

No, she decided, she wouldn't tell him the truth just yet. She'd bear the brunt of his anger when it came, but it was too soon for Cille to be burdened with questions. Eadgyth had said she'd recover, but she was still weak. And she needed time with her baby. Whatever this warrior wanted could wait.

She peered at him from under her lashes, but his expression was closed, revealing nothing of the thoughts underneath. What *did* he want? Whatever it was, he looked like a man accustomed to getting his own way.

Well, that didn't mean she would give it. And before she said anything—before she simply turned her sister over to him—she ought to find out what it was…

Svend stayed silent, unwilling to intrude upon her grief. The mention of her husband seemed to have upset her and he knew better than to offer sympathy.

What the hell had he been thinking, trying to offer solace at all? She'd looked so upset outside the hall that he'd assumed the worst, had felt drawn to comfort her despite himself. *Why?* What did it matter to him if she was upset? Women cried every day—their reasons for doing so were none of his concern. The world was a hard place, and the sooner everyone learned that, the better. No one had comforted *him* when he'd been forced to leave his home and family. So why did the sight of this woman crying bother him so much?

He frowned, trying to unravel the skein of his own tangled emotions. It was this place. He hadn't noticed it at first, but something about it felt strangely familiar, stirring memories he'd thought long since forgotten. He'd seen villages enough since his arrival in England, but this one felt different. This one might have been his village in Danemark, one of these houses his home. The woman in the bed might have been one of his sisters, Agnethe or Helvig—young girls when he'd left them, probably mothers themselves by now. The feeling had been so striking that he'd felt bound to help her.

As for Lady Cille… Nothing about her was sisterly at all. Quite the opposite. So why was he still trying to comfort her?

He watched her out of the corner of his eye, studying her silhouette in the firelight, her slender figure still obvious and enticing despite her tattered tunic. Her waist was so small that his hands would probably meet if he wrapped them around it—which he realised he wanted to, and badly. He wanted to slide them down the slender curve of her hips, over her thighs, up and under her tunic, between her legs…

A surge of desire coursed through him. Was that all his concern meant, then? That he was attracted to her? The idea was…surprising. He was no stranger to women, nor was he easily swayed by feminine charms. And she was nothing at all like the kind of woman he was usually drawn to. She was too small, too delicate-looking—as if a strong wind might carry her away. A tender reed with a temper too big for her body.

Clearly he'd been in the company of men for too long. He desired a woman, that was all, and in the meanwhile he had no time to soothe tender feelings—especially those of a prisoner who'd just tried to kill him.

Besides, she was hiding something—he was sure of it. Just as he was certain that a pack of rabid wolves wouldn't drag it from her. In the birthing chamber, he'd let his eyes rake her body deliberately to unsettle her, to undermine whatever premeditated answers she might have intended to give him. The fact that he'd wanted to look was simply a bonus. And she'd definitely been unsettled. The flicker of panic when he'd asked if they were sisters had been fleeting, but unmistakable.

He'd assumed that she was Lady Cille because she had answered to the name and fitted the description he'd been given exactly. But then so did the woman in the bed… Quickly, he filtered through the few details he'd been given. Lady Cille was the young widow of the ealdorman of Redbourn, hazel-haired, slight of build, kind and virtuous. But weren't *all* wives described as virtuous? No one had mentioned golden eyes or a violent temper. And he found it impossible to believe that anyone could describe the woman before him without mentioning her eyes.

On the other hand, surely someone would have told him if Lady Cille had been with child!

He pushed his suspicions aside. As usual he was being too analytical, too thorough. This was no military campaign, to be examined from every angle, just a simple assignment. Find the woman and take her back to Redbourn. Whatever she was hiding was none of his concern.

'What do you want from me, Norman?' She spun around suddenly, interrupting his musing.

He ignored the question, absorbing her anger impassively, vaguely impressed. At least she didn't try to inveigle him with sweet words, or try to flirt her way out of trouble, like most women of his acquaintance. He doubted this one knew how to do either. She was clearly overwrought and exhausted. But he had his own questions—ones that couldn't wait. And besides, he had to prepare her for what lay ahead—though, judging by her temper so far, he ought to arm himself first.

'She's alone here, your sister?'

Her face clouded instantly. 'Yes, apart from Eadgyth and me. I ordered our people to leave for their own safety.'

He ignored the jibe. 'And her husband?'

She blinked, as if the question surprised her,

and he raised an eyebrow. 'She has a husband, I presume?'

'Of course! Edmund.'

'But he's not here?'

'No.'

She didn't elaborate and his eyebrow inched higher. 'No?'

'He joined the rebellion.'

'And left his wife with child?'

She shrugged. 'I came to look after her.'

Svend stared at her incredulously. What kind of a man abandoned his pregnant wife, rebellion or no? Small wonder that Lady Cille seemed reluctant to talk about him. On the other hand, at least it explained what she was doing here—though not why she'd left Redbourn so suddenly and secretly.

'You ask a lot of questions, Norman.' Her expression was guarded.

'I'm simply confused. Since the death of your husband, you've inherited his lands, have you not?'

'No. Leofric had a younger brother. He's the ealdorman now.'

'He forfeited that position when he refused to swear fealty to the King and joined the rebels. Surely you knew that?'

'Forfeited under *Norman* law. I don't have to accept it.'

'It would be wise if you did.' His voice was low, but the veiled threat was unmistakable. 'In any case, you're now mistress of one of the largest estates in England.'

She looked less than impressed. 'What of it?'

'You left Redbourn in something of a hurry, my lady. It's time for you to return home.'

She froze instantly. If he'd told her Redbourn had burnt to the ground she couldn't have looked more horrified. 'And if I don't wish to go?'

'Your people are vulnerable and afraid. As the ealdorman's widow it's your duty to take care of them. Or did you forget that when you ran away?'

'I told you—I came to look after my sister. I have a duty to her as well.'

'And yet you ran away by yourself, without telling anyone where you were going. That doesn't speak of a particularly clear conscience.'

'How dare you? My reasons for leaving are none of your concern.'

'You still have a duty to come back.'

'Duty?' She gave a brittle laugh. 'Ironic for a Norman to be worried about Saxons!'

She whirled away but he caught her wrist, pulling her back again. 'Even a Norman understands duty.'

'Let me go!'

'Forgive me.' His tone was anything but apologetic. 'But my orders come from the King. He was most displeased to hear that you'd left Redbourn.'

'The Conqueror is at Redbourn?'

'The King,' he corrected her. 'King William

was crowned in December. But, no, he returned to Normandy in the spring. He left his half-brother Bishop Odo in charge, along with his cousin William FitzOsbern. He's the one waiting for you at Redbourn.'

'The King's cousin wants to see me?'

He nodded slowly. His fingers were still wrapped around her arm, but he felt strangely reluctant to pull them away. He'd held her wrists before… The memory of her writhing beneath him flashed through his mind, heating his blood. He could feel the quickening of her pulse against his thumb and fought the urge to caress it.

'Why?' She looked panicked. 'What does he want with me?'

He wishes for you to marry again.

The answer sprang to his lips, but the obvious fear in her voice made him hesitate. With his hand gripping her arm he felt suddenly, irrationally, protective. It wasn't his place to tell her the Earl's plans, but she was watching him, no longer defiant but frightened, asking him a question. He felt a stirring in his chest—something he hadn't felt in a long time—as if something were shifting inside of him. Damn it all, how could such a small woman have such a powerful effect on his senses?

'He intends for you to marry again,' he said softly, surprising himself.

'Marry a *Norman*?'

She staggered backwards, the colour draining

from her face, and he dropped her wrist instantly, the protective urge evaporating.

'That is something I wouldn't say to FitzOsbern, my lady.'

'But I've no wish to marry again! The King has no right to force me!'

Svend held his temper with an effort. Was she determined to fight him on *everything*? This wasn't the way he'd intended their interview to go. He hadn't even got to the part that was bound to provoke her more.

'That's no longer your choice. You're a vassal of the King now, not a freewoman. Your people need you.'

'They're not my people any more—they're his.'

'You don't think they'll take comfort in having a Saxon mistress?'

'False comfort!'

'Perhaps, but this marriage will permit you to keep your lands. I'd have thought you'd be grateful.'

'My *lands*?' She gave a hollow, derisive laugh. 'Is that all you Normans think about? Land?'

Svend's patience snapped, and his voice was coolly insulting. 'Aye. Land, money and tupping Saxon women!'

This time he didn't even try to stop her hand. He didn't flinch as she slapped him hard across the face, her outstretched fingers connecting violently with the side of his jaw.

There was a long silence, broken only by the crackle of wood in the fire and the sound of their combined breathing. Svend rubbed a hand over his chin. He supposed he'd deserved that. Normally he prided himself on his self-control, on not showing what he was thinking or feeling, but this woman pushed the very limits of his self-restraint. Something about her unsteadied him. She was dangerous, somehow. He'd known her for mere hours and already she was under his skin.

He looked down at her glowering face, at her slender chest heaving beneath it, and felt the sudden urge to grab her around the waist, pull her towards him and…what? His lips curved slowly. Do something that would wipe the defiant look off her face for certain.

What would she do if he kissed her? he wondered. Stab him in his sleep, most likely. Well, he could keep a guard outside his door. It might be worth it.

'Sir?' There was a discreet cough from the doorway.

'Come!'

Svend beckoned to Henri, his second-in-command, relieved at the interruption. One more second and he might have done something he'd regret.

'Are the men settled?'

'Aye, sir. I've set shifts for guard duty—not including the men riding tomorrow.'

'What happens tomorrow?' Lady Cille eyed the new soldier suspiciously.

'We leave for Redbourn in the morning.' Svend met her horrified gaze squarely.

'But Aediva cannot travel tomorrow!'

'No… *She* cannot.'

'You're leaving her behind? After you promised she'd be safe! What kind of a man lies to a vulnerable woman?'

'Enough!' His temper flared again. 'Before you offend me! We're *not* abandoning her. Henri will stay with half of my men until she's recovered. I gave my word that she and the babe would be safe, and they will be.'

He folded his arms across his chest, deliberately intimidating.

'Now, are you satisfied? Or have you any more insults to hurl at me?'

She opened her mouth and then closed it again, as if trying to think of an argument or excuse—anything to cause a delay. 'I… I'm satisfied.'

'Good. I see that Saxon manners are overrated. You're welcome.'

He turned away from her, suddenly eager to put some distance between them. She was maddening. Stubborn, insulting and ungrateful to boot! Not to mention determined to turn every conversation into an argument. She was the most infuriating woman he'd ever met!

Except one.

He pushed the thought aside and strode purposefully towards the door, Henri following like a wolf at his heels.

'Get some rest.' He hurled the words over his shoulder. 'We're leaving at dawn. I've no more wish to be in this situation than you, but like it or not I'm taking you home.'

'So I'm your prisoner?'

He stopped in the doorway, his jaw clenched so tight he could feel his teeth grind together.

'I'd rather be your escort, but if you want it that way then, yes, you're my prisoner. I suggest you don't try to escape. Believe me, I'll drag you to Redbourn in chains if I have to.'

Aediva watched him go, feeling the final remnants of her old life collapsing around her.

How dared he? She marched up and down inside the empty cottage, struggling to contain her anger. The arrogance of the man! How dared he talk about her—*Cille*—as if she were some commodity to be passed from man to man? As if she had no mind, no heart, no choice of her own. He was an insensitive monster! Just like every other Norman!

At least she'd shown him how she felt and left a red hand-shaped patch on his cheek to prove it. There'd be a noticeable bruise there tomorrow. Whatever happened afterwards, she'd have that satisfaction at least.

So *this* was why the Normans had come! The truth was even worse than she'd imagined. They wanted Cille as a bride—a prize for some grasping Norman interloper. But what kind of husband would such a man be? What kind of stepfather to Leofric's son…the son she'd promised to protect?

She clenched her hands into fists. It was cruel—barbaric! It would break Cille's heart. She couldn't let it happen!

But what could she do? She could hardly go to the King's cousin and pretend to be Cille. Someone would be bound to recognise her and reveal the truth. And yet… From a distance, she and Cille were almost identical. And surely Cille's own people would keep her secret.

She stopped dead in her tracks. *Would* they? Svend's criticism of Cille was all the worse for being true. Cille *had* fled her home in the spring—five months after Hastings and Leofric's death. And he was right, as the ealdorman's widow she should have stayed—should have remained to take care of her people. Would they be angry with her for abandoning them? Would they keep such a dangerous secret to protect her?

Svend had been right about Edmund too, and the disgust had been writ plain on his face. Now she wished she'd made up a name—not reminded herself of the one man she wanted to forget. They hadn't actually been married, but the lie hadn't been so far-fetched. Her father had wanted it, even if Edmund himself had shown no sign of caring for anything except her dowry. Worse still, he'd been rougher than she'd expected a suitor to be. His kisses had been too demanding, and he'd pressed her for more—far more—than she'd been willing to give. For her father's sake she'd tried to accept him, but in truth his violence had frightened her.

But he was a Saxon—part of her old life—and the thought of him still hurt, like a bruise she'd inadvertently pressed too hard. He'd abandoned her just when she'd needed him, running off to join the rebellion despite her entreaties. Let Svend draw his own conclusions about such a man. They couldn't be any worse than her own.

A sense of isolation swept over her, leaving a hollow sensation like a gaping pit in her stomach. Since her father's death the feeling had become all too familiar. There was so much she felt responsible for, but there was no one—not a single person—she could turn to for help. And there was no one to protect Cille and her baby either. If *she* didn't, who would?

She crouched down by the fire, trying to warm the chill in her heart, trying to work out a plan. *Could* she pretend to be Cille? It was possible. Surely Cille's people would support *her*, a Saxon, over the Norman usurpers? And the Normans themselves had never met Cille…had they?

Now that she thought of it, Cille had been

strangely unforthcoming on that subject. She hadn't even said whether she'd left Redbourn before or after the Normans had arrived. On the other hand, what did it matter? After this many months who would remember the colour of her eyes?

She rocked back on her heels, making her mind up. If this was the only way to protect her sister and nephew then she'd do it—and gladly. The Normans might have invaded her country, but *she* wasn't conquered yet. If she took Cille's place she could find a way to stop the marriage. In the meantime, who knew what might happen? The rebels might gather an army and overthrow the Conqueror, or Cille and the babe might escape. Any risk would be worth that.

She glanced towards the open doorway with a new sense of resolve. She could do it. After all, she'd already fooled Svend du Danemark. And if she could stay one step ahead of *him*, she had a feeling the rest would be easy.

Chapter Three

Svend tightened the bridle on his destrier with a snap. The sun was casting a pink glow on the horizon and a dozen soldiers were mounted behind him, ready and awaiting his order to depart.

Where *was* she?

He looked towards the Thane's hall, his scowl deepening from dark grey to black. He'd slept badly after their confrontation the previous night, angry at himself for losing his temper and at her for provoking it. And now she was late, after he'd told her they'd be leaving at dawn! Damn it, they should have left already!

'Sir?'

He turned to find Henri at his shoulder. While he was in his present temper, only his battle-hardened lieutenant dared to approach.

'We're ready to go after the villagers.'

'Good.' Svend nodded with satisfaction. At least *one* part of the morning was going according to plan. 'Their tracks head east. They took carts, so they can't have gone far or fast. Bring them back. Use persuasion if you can, force if you have to, but I don't want anyone hurt—understood?'

'Yes, sir. And the woman?'

'I'll deal with her.'

Henri grinned. 'Her new husband might not appreciate you manhandling his bride.'

'Then he should have come himself.'

Svend tightened his knuckles instinctively. For some reason the mention of her future husband made him irrationally angry. Not that he knew who it was. FitzOsbern had been unusually taciturn on the subject.

'I'll see you in a few weeks. Just make sure the villagers are settled before you join us in Redbourn. I don't want them running away again.'

'Yes, sir.'

'And, Henri? As far as anyone else is concerned they never left.'

'Understood. There's just one other matter, sir. The new lad—Alan—I found him in the hall an hour ago.'

'Looting?'

'Searching the rafters.'

Svend's expression hardened. He didn't give his soldiers many orders to follow, but when it came to those he did he was inflexible. No stealing, raping, brawling or looting. Most of his men had sense enough to obey. Alan obviously thought he knew better.

'I'll deal with it.'

Henri mounted his horse. 'He's still a lad… just seventeen.'

Svend didn't answer, his mouth set in a thin, implacable line as Henri and his men thundered out of the gates. *Seventeen.* When he was that age he'd been in exile for three years already. Seventeen was more than old enough to learn that actions had consequences.

'Alan!'

'Sir?' A young soldier came running at once.

'You were in the hall this morning?'

'I… Yes, sir.' Alan flushed guiltily. 'I was searching in case they'd hidden valuables. The King gave us the right of plunder, sir.'

'Do you see the King now?'

'No, sir.'

'Have we conquered this village? Did you fight anyone for it?'

'No, sir.'

'Would you like to?'

The boy gulped and Svend brought his fist up quickly, knocking him to the ground with one swift, decisive blow.

'We raid only where we conquer, we don't steal from farmers, and under my command you follow my rules—understand?' He turned away brusquely, shouting over his shoulder at his men. ‘Wait outside the gates! This won’t take long.’

He stormed into the hall, barely resisting the urge to bellow her name. That whole incident had been her fault too. If she’d been ready when he’d told her the boy might never have been tempted to go looting. Was she obstinate on principle or just naturally infuriating? Either way, his patience was worn out. No matter how desirable she might be, her attractions were more than outweighed by her character. Thane’s daughter, ealdorman’s widow, nobleman’s future bride—whoever she was, she was under *his* command now. He’d meant what he’d told her last night. He’d drag her to Redbourn in chains if he had to.

His step faltered momentarily. What would the Earl make of her? What kind of maelstrom would this Saxon wildcat unleash in the Norman court? He’d been deadly serious in his warning. FitzOsbern wouldn’t tolerate disobedience or insults. Nor forgive them either. And Lady Cille seemed the kind of woman to learn lessons the hard way.

That strange protective feeling was back and he pushed it aside irritably. He’d warned her. That was all he could do. He wasn’t responsible for her temper—only her safety until they reached Redbourn. Once they were there she could do and say as she pleased. If she insulted FitzOsbern that was her mistake and not his problem. He certainly wasn't about to risk his hard-earned reward for a woman who made the whole Saxon army seem welcoming.

'Shh!'

He halted mid-stride, caught off guard as she stepped out of the shadows, the babe cradled in her arms.

For half a moment he wondered if he were imagining the vision before him. With the child in her arms she looked calmer, softer, a completely different woman from the spitting wildcat of the previous day. She'd changed her clothes too. Her mud-splattered tunic had been replaced by a woodland-green gown. He ran his gaze appreciatively over the close-fitting contours of the fabric, his body reacting despite himself. She was swaying from side to side, cooing gently as she tried to soothe the grumbling child, slim hips rolling in a slow and alarmingly distracting rhythm.

He forced his body back under control. This was the second time she'd caught him by surprise in this very hall. What was the matter with him? She seemed to undermine all his defensive instincts. What was it he'd wanted to tell her? Something about his authority…

'You almost woke him!' She hissed through her teeth. 'You were stamping like a whole herd of cattle!'

Svend raised an eyebrow, the vision of loveliness dissipating before his eyes. It was her, no doubt about it. That fiery glare would have given her away even if her adder's tongue had not.

He cleared his throat deliberately loudly. 'It's time to go. My men are waiting.'

'I can't.' She shook her head so vigorously that tendrils of hair broke free from the sides of her headdress. 'Not yet. It's taken me half the night to calm him. If I stop moving he'll wake up for certain.'

Svend narrowed his gaze critically. Her face looked wan and drawn, her eyes circled with dark shadows. Had she slept at all?

'Have you been pacing all night?'

'No!'

Her denial came too quickly and he scowled ferociously. 'I told you to get some rest! For pity's sake, woman, we have a day's ride ahead.'

'I *did* rest!' Her chin jutted upwards unconvincingly. 'But Eadgyth needed some sleep too.'

'Then you should have asked one of my men for help!'

'Ask a *Norman*?'

Her voice dripped with scorn and he clenched his teeth, trying to restrain his temper. 'Is it too much to hope that you've packed?'

'No.' She gestured towards a sack by the door. 'I did it last night, if you must know.'

'Well, that's something.' He scooped up the bag and untied the leather cords, ignoring her shocked intake of breath as he rummaged inside.

'What are you *doing*? Those are my things!'

He bit back a smile with effort. It was quite a spectacle, watching her lose her temper and try to comfort a baby at the same time. He wouldn't have thought such an endeavour were possible.

'You'll have to forgive me for searching for weapons…' he paused meaningfully '…under the circumstances.'

'I'm not a fool!'

'I never said that you were. Now, say goodbye to your sister. We should have left an hour ago.'

'I can't wake her. She needs to rest.'

'Then don't say goodbye—let her sleep. Either way, leave the baby with the old woman and let's go.'

He fixed her with a hard stare, challenging her to argue. She was nearly trembling with anger, every muscle in her body taut with tension, eyes sparking so brightly he could almost feel the heat. If she'd been holding anything other than a baby he was quite certain she'd have thrown it at him by now.

He swung her bag over his shoulder, deliberately relaxing his stance to present an open target. Her eyes flashed and he found himself smiling sardonically. She was a wildcat, in truth. Surely any man would enjoy taming her—or at least trying to.

'I need a few moments.' Her voice was clipped with anger.

'A few,' he agreed, turning his back and strolling casually towards the door, not even bothering to turn for his parting shot. 'Just be quick or I'll come and carry you out myself.'

'Cille, wake up!'

Aediva shook her sister's arm urgently, wondering how much she should tell her about what had happened. The truth was impossible. She didn't want to frighten her. And, besides, there was so little time. How could she possibly tell her everything in a few minutes?

Nervously she glanced back over her shoulder. She'd no wish to be carried anywhere over any man's shoulder, let alone a Norman's, but she'd believed this warrior when he had threatened to drag her outside. Something in his face told her he wasn't a man to make threats lightly.

'Aediva?' Cille's voice was groggy with sleep. 'What's the matter? Is the baby all right?'

'Yes, he's here. But I have to go.'

'Go?' Cille sat up in alarm. 'What do you mean?'

Aediva perched on the edge of the bed, trying to find words to reassure her. 'I have to go with the Normans. Not for long, but it's important. We'll be together again soon, I promise.'

'What do they want?'

'Nothing to worry about. And some of the

soldiers are staying to make sure you're safe, so there's no need to worry. Just get better.'

The baby stirred in her arms and she passed him carefully to Cille, smiling at the sight of his round pink face.

'His hair is so dark,' she mused aloud. 'Darker than either Leofric's or yours. Maybe he takes after someone else in the family…?'

She stopped mid-sentence, taken aback by the horrified expression on her sister's face. 'What's wrong?'

'I wanted to tell you…' Cille's eyes brimmed with tears. 'I tried to, but I didn't know how…'

'What?' Aediva felt a shiver of panic ripple down her spine and pool in her stomach, hardening there like a lump of ice. What was the matter? What could possibly be so bad?

'You'll hate me…' Cille's voice was almost inaudible.

'No! You can tell me anything.'

'She's delirious.' Eadgyth bustled between them suddenly, taking charge of the baby as she jerked her head towards the curtain. 'You should be going.'

'But—'

'I'll take care of her.' The old woman gave her a pointed look. 'You do *your* part. Before he gets suspicious.'

Aediva leapt up at once. Eadgyth was right—there was no time to talk. If she didn't hurry

Svend would be back. And this time he might pay closer attention to the resemblance between the two sisters. Whatever Cille wanted to tell her would have to wait. Right now she had to get Svend away from Etton before he guessed the truth.

'I'll be back soon.' She forced a smile, already hastening towards the curtain. 'You can tell me what it is then.'

'Wait!'

She ignored the plea, scooping up a cloak and flinging it around her shoulders as she flew through the hall, trying to shake off a vague sense of unease. What had she said to upset Cille? She struggled to remember, but her memory felt as wrung out and weary as the rest of her body. Something about the baby's hair...?

Clearly she was more exhausted than she'd realised. Her thoughts were in chaos. She'd have to think on it later, after she'd had some rest...

She stepped outside and the cold air hit her full in the face, sending her reeling backwards. The evening before had been mild and still, but this morning she could almost believe it was winter again. She clutched the cloak tightly beneath her chin, wishing she could turn around and go back inside.

'Just in time.'

She frowned at the sound of Svend's voice. He was standing to one side, arms folded as he leaned against a towering grey destrier. From a distance his posture looked relaxed, but close to, she could see there was nothing casual about him. He was watching her as a falcon might size up its prey, as if half expecting her to run, his whole body poised and ready for pursuit.

She caught her breath. The rest of the stockade was empty, so that for a moment it seemed as if they were completely alone—the only two people left in the world, facing each other across a deserted, windswept village.

'Where are your men?' She glanced around nervously. 'Surely we're not travelling alone?'

He grimaced. 'Believe me, I find that idea as appealing as you do. My men are waiting outside the stockade.' Blue eyes had frosted to ice, hard and unrelenting. 'I take it that you're finally ready?'

She inclined her head. From the tone of his voice it wasn't a question. She wasn't about to dignify it with an answer.

'Good. Raise your arms.'

'What?'

He ignored the question, closing the distance between them in a few swift strides.

'What are you doing?' she spluttered as his fingers tightened over her forearms.

He was standing so close to her that their chests were almost touching. If she took a deep breath, surely they *would* touch. Not that she could.

Something about his proximity made her breathing too shallow, too rapid. Could he tell? Towering above her, he seemed to be watching, waiting for something. For a fleeting moment she thought he was going to lean closer, and yet her body seemed to be frozen, unable to pull away…

Suddenly he hoisted her arms out to the sides, running his hands along their length, all the way from her shoulder blades to her wrists.

She felt her cheeks flush scarlet, too shocked even to protest. What on *earth* was he doing? Did he think he could insult her just because she was Saxon?

His hands swooped around to her back and she jerked against him indignantly. 'Let me go!'

'As you wish.'

He released her at once and took a step backwards, scrutinising the rest of her body.

Comprehension dawned at last. 'Weapons again? There isn't much room to hide a sword.'

'You'd be surprised. Show me your feet.'

She stared at him, tempted to laugh, though judging by the look on his face he wasn't joking. Far from it. With or without her help, he was going to see her feet. Tentatively she lifted her gown, just enough to reveal brown leather boots.

He crouched down, frowning with concentration as he felt around the rims of the leather. For a moment his fingers brushed against her bare skin, and she shivered as a new, tingling sensation raced up her legs and between her thighs. This was intolerable. What could she possibly hide in her boots? It would serve him right if she kicked him full in the face.

'I wouldn't.'

His voice was barely a murmur and she stiffened guiltily.

'Wouldn't what?'

'I wouldn't do it.'

He sat back on his haunches, catching her eye with a look that she couldn't interpret.

'If I were you.'

She squirmed uncomfortably. He was still crouched down beside her, the top of his head level with her waist, his eyes speaking a language her brain didn't understand. Only her body… Somehow her body wanted to respond.

She shrugged her shoulders, feigning innocence. 'I don't know what you mean.'

'No?' He cocked an eyebrow as he stood upright again. 'I'm glad to hear it. I had a feeling my head was about to be used as a football.'

She pursed her lips, swallowing an insult. 'I thought you said we were in a hurry?'

'We are, but I've found it best not to take chances where you're concerned, Lady Cille. I never knew Saxon women were so violent.'

'And *I* never knew Norman men were so easily frightened.'

His eyes flashed, though whether with humour or anger she couldn't tell.

'Can you ride?'

'Yes.' She blinked at the abrupt change of subject. 'That is...'

She peered around him, past the grey destrier to an only slightly smaller brown palfrey, and her mouth turned dry. She'd never been much of a horsewoman and the animal was substantially bigger than the mounts she was used to.

'Our horses are smaller.'

'It doesn't make much difference. The basics are the same. Here.'

He offered a hand but she ignored it, lifting her chin as she brushed past him and grasped hold of the reins. It was a long way up, but she wasn't going to show fear—not to him or any other Norman. And she wasn't going to accept help either. Not if she could help it.

She took a deep breath and heaved, hoisting herself up, and almost into the saddle before she stopped abruptly, feeling the tug of her skirt trapped beneath her boot in the stirrup, holding her back. Desperately she tried to scramble upwards, but it was no use. The horse was shifting impatiently and she could feel herself sliding.

'Aren't you going to help me?' She swallowed her pride, squealing in panic.

'Aren't you going to ask?'

'Help me!'

'Please…?'

'Please!'

At once she felt his hands around her thighs, lifting her up and depositing her in the saddle with an inelegant, unladylike thud.

'Thank you.' She tossed her head, refusing to look at his face, vividly aware that her own was flaming red. This was mortifying. Even her thighs felt red-hot where he'd touched her, as if she were blushing all over.

'My pleasure.' He swung up onto his destrier, his voice brimming with wicked amusement. 'I've never seen anyone mount a horse like that. Is it some kind of Saxon custom?'

She rounded on him fiercely. How dared he? After everything else that had happened over the past twenty-four hours, how dared he make fun of her too? Anger, hot and raw, coursed through her veins as her taut emotions finally snapped.

'What do *you* know about Saxon customs? What do you *care*? All you want is to destroy them! Isn't that what Normans do? Destroy anything, *anyone*, who gets in their way!'

There! She felt a surge of triumph. *That* had wiped the smile off his face. There wasn't a single trace of humour left in it now.

'It's not what we all do.'

His voice was dangerously quiet but she kept going, unable to stop herself from venting her anger.

'You only want us to lie down and surrender!'

'It would be best if you did.'

'Well, we won't! We might have been beaten, but it doesn't mean we've surrendered. We'll rise up again and fight!'

'Do you think that you'll win?'

She inhaled sharply. His voice was expressionless, but the quiet certainty behind his words made them all the more chilling. He wasn't really asking her a question, he was giving her an answer. For a moment she felt as though she were facing the whole Norman army—one that the Saxon rebels could never hope to defeat.

'And as I've told you before…' his voice held a note of warning '… I'm not Norman.'

'You're still with them. What's the difference?'

'We're not all the same.'

'If I had my way I'd plunge a dagger into your heart—into every single Norman heart!'

She gasped, surprised by her own vehemence as he regarded her sombrely.

'That's quite a threat. And not one to make lightly.'

'You think I don't mean it? After everything your Conqueror has done?'

She lifted her chin defiantly, too angry to back down, thinking of her father, of Leofric and Edmund—of all the men who hadn't come back from Hastings. The Normans had destroyed her world. Of *course* she wanted them to pay for it! She *should* make them pay!

He held her gaze for a moment before reaching down to his belt, fingers closing over the hilt of his dagger. Slowly, inexorably, he drew the blade from its sheath, weighing the metal in his hands as if he were considering something.

Aediva felt her heartbeat accelerate wildly. What was he going to do? Punish her on the spot? Her stomach lurched. Of course he was going to punish her. He was a Norman and she'd just threatened to kill him. He couldn't let such a threat go unanswered.

'Go ahead.' He flipped the knife in his hand suddenly, grasping the blade between his fingers as he held the hilt out towards her. 'Do it.'

'What?' She gaped at him, uncomprehending.

'Unlike my King, I don't believe in revenge, Lady Cille. But if you do, if you think it will make one tiny scrap of difference, then go ahead. You have my permission.'

Aediva stared at the knife, dumbfounded. Was he serious? He *looked* serious. But surely he wasn't going to hand her a weapon just like that? She couldn't win so easily…could she? It must be a trick.

Her gaze locked with his, shock mingling with suspicion. 'Your men would arrest me.'

'Renard!'

She jumped as his shout broke the stillness. Her already ragged nerves were in tatters. What now? Was he going to offer her a lance too?

'Sir?' His squire came running through the gates, stopping short as he saw the blade.

Aediva blanched. Hadn't they acted this scene before—just yesterday in fact? She hadn't been able to stab Svend then. What made her think she could do it now?

'Renard will act as witness.' Svend threw a glance at his squire. 'Whatever happens here is an accident, understand? No one should be punished for it.' Then he looked back towards her, lowering his voice as if imparting some secret too intimate to be shared. 'Will that satisfy you, my lady?'

Aediva licked her lips, trying to moisten them, her mouth too dry to answer. This wasn't what she'd intended. In her wildest imaginings she'd never thought that he'd simply hand her a blade. She'd been angry, upset at leaving Cille, lashing out without thinking. Surely he didn't expect her to go through with it? Wouldn't actually let her attack him? But he was watching her steadily, waiting for her to do something. Was he testing her? Because if this was a challenge, she had to meet it. She couldn't, *wouldn't* let him win.

Slowly, she nodded.

'Good.' Svend jerked his head towards Renard, though his gaze never left hers. 'You can go.'

Carefully she wrapped her fingers around the hilt of the blade, grasping it tightly to stop her hand from shaking. He relinquished his hold at once, letting her take possession as he pulled his leather gambeson swiftly over his head.

Out of the corner of her eye she saw Renard cast a last anxious glance towards them, and then they were alone again. Why was he doing this? What was he trying to prove? Except for a thin tunic, his chest was now completely unguarded. She could see the flex of his powerful muscles beneath the linen, the sculpted hard lines of his chest.

'So…'

His eyes seared into hers and she felt a jolt like a flash of blue lightning pass between them.

'You have your wish, my lady.'

Her wish? She could hardly breathe. He was close—close enough for her to reach him if she dared. All she had to do was lunge forward. Just lunge and in another second it would be over. She tightened her grip, trying to strengthen her nerve. He was one of them—a Norman! She hated them! She should seize this opportunity, should avenge her people while she had the chance.

Except… It was too brutal, too barbaric. She couldn't do it. Not like this—not with him offering her the knife as if it were some kind of favour. If she did she'd be no better than a Norman.

She shook her head, turning the hilt back towards him, feeling as if she'd both passed and failed the same test.

'Good.' He took the knife and stowed it away quickly. 'I have enough on my own conscience, Lady Cille. I've no wish to be a burden on yours.'

She stared miserably at the ground, hardly noticing as he took up her reins, leading her towards the gate. Somehow the world seemed to have shifted beneath her. She felt numb and weary and overwhelmingly tired. She'd failed. At the moment of crisis she'd failed her people. And yet she couldn't help but feel that he'd been right. What good would it have done?

'I don't have to be your enemy, Lady Cille. Believe it or not, I've no more wish to see bloodshed than you do.'

'No?' She couldn't keep the bitterness out of her voice. From what she'd heard about Normans, she found that hard to believe.

'No. I wouldn't have harmed your sister's people. You shouldn't have sent them away.'

She looked up at him sharply. 'How could I have known that?'

'You couldn't. But what kind of life did you think you were sending them to? Do you know what the King does to rebels?'

Her scalp tightened. 'I've heard rumours.'

'Believe them. And how far do you think they'll get without provisions? They haven't brought in the harvest yet. What are they going to eat?'

'They'll survive.'

'Will they?' His voice hardened. 'How?'

She twisted towards him, battling a tidal surge of panic. 'What if they come back? What if I go after them, persuade them to return?'

'Too late. My orders are to return you to Redbourn as soon as possible. Besides, if the King ever hears that they ran he'll tear down the village, destroy their tools and poison the earth. Etton will be naught but a ruin. Trust me—I've seen it.'

Aediva gaped at him in horror. How could he describe such an event so calmly? It was horrific! And it would all be *her* fault. She was the one who'd sent them away. She'd been trying to protect them, but she'd sent them to their destruction instead. The pit in her stomach was so deep she felt as though it were swallowing her up from the inside.

'So they're doomed either way?'

'No.'

'No?'

'Henri went after them this morning. He speaks some English and he knows what to say. If anyone can persuade them to come back, it's him.'

'You did that?' She sagged forward, breathless with relief. 'Why?'

'Why wouldn't I? I told you—I don't believe in revenge.'

'And you won't tell the King?'

'No.'

'What if someone else does?'

'Who? My men know better than to spread rumours. Unless *you're* planning to?'

She shook her head vehemently and he gave a dismissive shrug.

'Then there's nothing to worry about.'

'Nothing to worry about?' Anger took over again. 'Then why did you scare me like that? How could you be so cruel?'

'Because you need to understand what you're dealing with! You can't go to Redbourn and threaten the Earl. You can't speak of rebellion so lightly. Whether you like it or not, Lady Cille, the conquest is over and we have won. And I'm not your enemy—not unless you want me to be.'

He spurred his destrier forward then, cantering away as she stared helplessly after him, trying to make sense of her jagged emotions as they veered from anger to gratitude and back again. She was still furious, but if he'd sent Henri to rescue her people then she was in his debt too. Indebted to a *Norman*! The very idea made her blood run cold. How would she ever repay him? How *could* she repay a Norman?

She sat completely still, looking around at the narrow confines of her world, at the village and the valley where she'd spent most of her life. Etton and England would never be the same again. She hadn't wanted to believe it, but it was true. The

Conquest was over and the Normans had won. Even if she came back—even if her people came back—nothing would ever be the same again.

And if Svend du Danemark wasn't her enemy, who *was* he?

Chapter Four

Svend galloped to the head of the valley, trying to outrun his bad mood. She was maddening! Barely a slip of a woman, but what she lacked in size she more than made up for in temper. She hated Normans, that was obvious, but why couldn't she understand that he was simply her escort, not her enemy? All he wanted was to get her to Redbourn as quickly and uneventfully as possible. Was that too much to ask, or was she going to argue with him all the way?

He placed a hand on his chest, vaguely surprised to find himself still in one piece. Had he taken leave of his senses, handing her a knife? What had made him so certain she wouldn't use it? He grimaced. He hadn't been certain at all, but something in her face had made him want to find out. The desire to test her had outweighed everything else, even self-preservation.

Well, now he knew. She didn't want to kill

him—not today at least. That was a minor improvement.

He rubbed a hand over Talbot's neck, slowing the destrier to a trot. On the other hand, her anger that morning had been largely his fault. He shouldn't have mocked her as she'd tried to mount the palfrey, shouldn't have deliberately provoked her temper, but it had been easier than admitting the unwelcome urges she'd aroused in him. Those eyes…even when she was in a temper they lit up her whole face. He could hardly keep his own off her. Checking her for weapons had been harder than he'd expected—in more ways than one. When he'd finally lifted her up, wrapping his hands around her waist and feeling the soft pliancy of her body beneath, it had taken all his self-control to release her again.

He clenched his jaw, resenting his orders anew. He was a warrior, not an escort. He ought to be hunting rebels, not escorting Saxon ladies! Women had no place in his soldier's world—especially this woman, who somehow angered and appealed to him in equal measure. He couldn't help but admire her feisty spirit, the way she flared up like a spark catching light, but she was more than infuriating. If she were anyone else he might enjoy watching the sparks fly, but she wasn't. She was his prisoner, and if he had any sense he'd keep as far away from her as possible.

If it were only that easy… Redbourn was still three and a half days' ride away. And suddenly that seemed like a very long time.

Aediva awoke with a jolt, catching her breath as the earth swayed and then righted itself in front of her. Quickly she hauled herself upright, half amazed, half alarmed to have fallen asleep in the saddle, the night's exertions finally catching up with her.

Blinking rapidly, she glared at the back of Svend's broad shoulders, easily visible at the head of their small procession. He hadn't so much as glanced in her direction since they'd left Etton. Not that she cared, but he was supposed to be her escort. He might have checked that she was all right—not left her to fend for herself. It would serve him right if she fell off her palfrey and broke a leg. Let him explain *that* to FitzOsbern!

She stole a furtive glance at the rest of his soldiers. There were around a dozen of them, most as grim and indomitable-looking as their commander, though a few were younger. One of them had a swollen eye, she noticed. It looked a fresh wound too.

She put a hand to her mouth, stifling another yawn. If she could only rest for a while… Her head lolled and her eyelids drooped. *No!* She mustn't fall asleep. If she fell from this height it would be a lot more dangerous than from the ponies she was used to. She had to stay awake… even if she just dozed for a moment…

She felt a sudden strong grip on her arm, snatching her back to consciousness.

'I told you to get some rest last night!' Svend's voice was low and furious. 'You should have slept!'

'What?' She looked around, disorientated, cheeks flushing self-consciously.

What was *he* doing there? She'd been dreaming of a man with white-yellow hair and a smile so mesmerising it took her breath away—a man bearing so little resemblance to the one looming beside her now that she wrenched her arm out of his grasp indignantly.

'Let me go!' She tossed her head, trying to salvage some small shred of dignity. 'I'm perfectly all right.'

'Good.' The ice in his stare could have caused frostbite. 'We've a long way to go and we're not stopping for *you* to sleep.'

'I didn't ask to stop! I told you I'm all right.'

'Have you eaten?'

'What?' Now that he mentioned it, she hadn't eaten anything since the broth he'd given her last night. Her mouth watered at the memory. No wonder she felt so light-headed.

'I asked if you'd eaten.' He sounded impatient.

'I'm not hungry.' She grasped her stomach quickly, stifling a growl. Why had he made her think of food? Now it was *all* she could think about!

'Really?' He raised an eyebrow sceptically.

'It's your fault for mentioning food!'

Glaring, she turned her attention back to the road. They'd been riding at a punishing pace all morning, but she'd hardly paid any heed to their surroundings, concentrating on staying awake. Now the road ahead looked vaguely and disturbingly familiar, like a scene from some half-remembered nightmare. They were at the far edge of Etton territory, where farmland gave way to scree and boulders. The next hill marked the furthest boundary of their land, and over there…

She pulled on her reins so fiercely that the palfrey stopped with a jolt, almost throwing her head-over-heels into the dirt, but she didn't notice. All she could feel was the cold sweat on her brow and a heavy pounding like a hammer in her chest. She *knew* this place—knew every detail of the landscape, every rock and boulder, just as it had been on the day she'd ridden to her dying father's side. She hadn't ridden this way since—hadn't wanted to come back. Not ever.

Desperately she gulped for air, caught off guard by the sudden onslaught of emotion. How could she not have noticed the route they were taking? She could have prepared herself, or at least tried to. Now she felt as though she were falling apart

She took a deep breath. 'My father died there.'

'Ah...' He was silent for a moment, as if letting her words sink in. 'I'm sorry.'

'He was stabbed in a skirmish with Norman soldiers last winter.'

A muscle jumped in his jaw. 'What happened?'

'He thought he was defending his land, but he was a farmer, not a fighter. He wouldn't yield, so a Norman soldier killed him. It might have been you.'

'It wasn't.'

His tone was sharp and she felt a momentary twinge of guilt. She shouldn't have said that—not when he was being sympathetic.

'How many soldiers?' He sounded angry now.

She bit her lip, wondering how much she could tell him without giving away her real identity. Cille hadn't arrived in Etton until almost a month after their father's death, but surely there was no way he could know that.

'There were four of them.'

'Renegades, then, not a garrison. Were they wearing a crest?'

'None that I know of. Why?'

'If there were a way to identify them it might still be possible to bring them to justice.'

'The Earl would side with Saxons over Norman soldiers?'

'No. But there are other means.'

She glanced at him in surprise. He looked implacable now, every inch the warrior, fierce and forbidding, as if he might truly avenge her father. She felt a flicker of hope, quickly suppressed. Words were easy, but why would a Norman knight care about one murdered Thane? Yet something in his face told her he meant it.

'Why?' she demanded. 'Why would you avenge him?'

He looked at her askance. 'Because a man shouldn't be slain for protecting his land or his people.'

She lowered her gaze, swallowing against the lump in her throat. That pit in her stomach had opened up again, cold and empty like a wintry chasm.

'He was a good man.'

'I'm certain of it.'

'We were very close. When it happened…so soon after Hastings…after everything else… I felt like the whole world had collapsed. I'd never felt so alone. And ever since…'

She bit her tongue abruptly. Why was she telling him this? Of all people, why was she pouring her heart out to *her enemy*? No matter how carefully she phrased it, or how sympathetic he might seem, she couldn't risk confiding in him. One slip and she might give everything away. He was the last person in the world she should talk to.

She pursed her lips, trying to regain her composure. She couldn't risk Cille's safety just to ease her own pain. No matter how much it hurt, no matter how badly she needed to talk to someone, she had to bury her feelings—just as she had for the past year. Like everything else, she had to bear them alone.

Svend stole a glance at her tear-streaked face and swore inwardly. He hadn't known about her father's death. Something else the Earl hadn't told him. No wonder she hated Normans.

The rawness of her emotion had disturbed him more than he would have expected, reawakening that strange, uncharacteristic need to comfort her. Would she accept comfort from him? Would she want it? Hell's teeth, he wasn't some maid with soft words and a shoulder to cry on. What was he supposed to say?

He changed the subject instead.

'Your sister obviously knows about farming. These lands are thriving.'

That much was true. On their journey outwards lowering rainclouds had obscured much of the beauty of the landscape, but now that the weather had cleared he could see how well the fields had been managed. The rolling hills reminded him of his parents' farm, causing a pang of longing in his chest. Since leaving Danemark he'd buried his homesickness deep within himself, never expecting to find a home or hearth of his own again. Now the idea was unexpectedly appealing—as if he'd found something he hadn't known he'd been searching for. The King had promised to reward him for his services. Would he offer him land? A man could do worse than put down roots in a place like this. Strange how much his attitudes had changed since arriving in Etton…

'You know about farming?' She caught his eye, her own eyes filled with begrudging interest.

'I grew up on a farm.'

'In Normandy?'

'No.' He sighed. 'I'm not Norman, remember?'

'Oh.' She didn't apologise. 'Did you grow flax?'

'Flax?' His eyebrows shot up. If she'd asked whether he'd spun gold he couldn't have felt more surprised. 'No, our climate was too cold.'

'Aediva is thinking of growing it here next year. What do you think?'

'What do *I* think?' He hadn't thought that she cared for his opinion on anything. 'It's a tough enough crop, and the land here seems fertile. With a sunny site, it should prosper.'

She gave an enigmatic smile. 'That's what she thought.'

He looked across at her quizzically. Who was she, this woman? In the space of one morning his feelings towards her had veered from anger to exasperation to pity, and now they were talking about *farming*? He wasn't accustomed to discussing such matters with women. The ladies of

William's court were more concerned with fashion and gossip, but Lady Cille seemed genuinely interested. Not to mention that this was the first conversation they'd had that hadn't descended into insults or arguing.

'I didn't think an ealdorman's wife would take such an interest in farming.'

'It's important to know your land. Don't Norman ladies take any interest in their crops?'

'None that I know of.'

'Do their husbands, at least?'

'Some of them. The rest have stewards for the work they consider beneath them.'

She made a contemptuous sound. 'Didn't you like farming either? Is that why you became a soldier?'

'No. I liked it well enough.'

'So what are you doing here?'

He frowned. 'You're very curious. Not to mention persistent.'

'I believe I said something similar last night. Or are questions a Norman prerogative?'

'I didn't say that.'

'Well, then. You know all about me. You might as well tell me something about yourself.'

'Might as well?' He quirked an eyebrow. 'How can I refuse such a charming request?'

'Don't you think it's wise to learn as much as you can about your enemy?'

'Escort.'

'Captor. Especially if he's hiding something.'

He glanced at her suspiciously. How did she know that? Normally he rebuffed any questions about his early life, letting people assume he'd simply been born in a barracks. He'd already told her more than he'd intended—more than he had told most of his acquaintance in a year. His past was…complicated. And far too painful to reveal to a woman he'd known for little more than a day. Besides, her opinion of him was low enough already. How much lower would it sink if she knew the truth?

Why was he even still *talking* to her?

'What makes you think there's anything to hide?'

'I'm just trying to make sense of you, that's all.'

'I don't make sense?'

'Not when you turn every question around!'

Damn it, she was more observant than he'd expected. Most people didn't notice how little he told them. This was what came of letting his guard down and trying to comfort her. Typical of a woman to turn his better instincts against him! And yet for some inexplicable reason he couldn't tear himself away.

'I fell into soldiering, if you must know. And I was good at it.'

'So you're a mercenary?'

'What?' If she'd been a man he would have struck her for such a question. 'You just assume

that I'm a sword for hire? Knights don't tend to be mercenaries—even Norman ones.'

'How am I supposed to know that? I didn't mean to offend you.'

He rolled his eyes in frustration. That was probably as close to an apology as he was likely to get.

'I'm starting to think I shouldn't leave you alone with FitzOsbern. I'm afraid of what you might say.'

'Is he so easily offended?'

'He's the King's cousin—the Earl of Hereford, Gloucester, Worcestershire and Oxfordshire. What do *you* think?'

She shrugged. 'I think he sounds busy.'

'He's not a man to be trifled with.'

'Maybe not, but you still haven't answered my question. Why *did* you leave your homeland? To find somewhere warmer?'

'If I'd wanted a better climate I wouldn't have gone to Normandy, let alone come here. This must be the first dry day since we arrived.'

'Perhaps your King should have checked the climate before he invaded.'

He smiled in surprise. Was that a joke? She was being sarcastic, but for the first time there was no venom behind her words. On the contrary, her voice was soft, thoughtful, surprisingly mellifluous. Perhaps there was hope for her yet…

'I'll be sure to warn him next time.'

'So where will you go next?'

'What do you mean?'

'You seem to like travelling.'

'It hasn't always been by choice. But I might not go anywhere. A man needs to put down roots some time.'

Her body jerked suddenly. 'You mean you want to stay here?'

'Maybe. The King rewards his knights.'

'And he's going to reward *you*?'

'Yes.'

'For capturing me?'

'In part.'

'With land? *Saxon* land?'

He threw her a pointed look. 'Norman land now.'

'Somewhere like Etton?'

'Perhaps.'

She rounded on him angrily. 'So that's it? You're only admiring the land because you want to steal it!'

'Steal it?' He sighed heavily. 'Hell's teeth, I have already told you—your marriage will allow you to keep your land.'

'And I have already told *you* I don't want to marry a Norman!' Her gaze narrowed suddenly. 'Besides, what about Aediva?'

'What about her?'

'She's lived in Etton her whole life. Where's she supposed to go?'

'I'm sure arrangements can be made.'

'You don't even care!'

'Why should I? Am I supposed to care about every woman in England? *One* of you is bad enough.'

She muttered something under her breath and he ran a hand through his hair in frustration.

'For pity's sake, woman, what do you intend to do if you don't marry again? If you're thinking about joining the rebels, then don't. I've seen your sword skills.'

'I'll think of something.'

'Do that.' He clenched his jaw in exasperation. 'It's still a long way to Redbourn. I'd use the time to think, if I were you.'

Aediva turned her face away, not wanting to look at him a second longer. So *that* was why he'd been talking about farming! She'd actually thought he'd been trying to comfort her, to distract her from painful memories, but instead he'd been thinking about claiming her home for *himself*! And she'd been naive enough to feel grateful, talking to him as she might to a Saxon, as if he were someone other than her enemy!

She was still fuming as they crested the hill and started down the other side, looking out over a wide green expanse that curved all the way down to Redbourn, where William FitzOsbern was waiting for her.

The thought made her shudder.

'You're shivering.' Svend's voice was matter-of-fact now, without even a trace of sympathy. 'Renard! See if we have anything warmer for the lady to wear.'

She tossed her head, still refusing to look at him. Somehow she doubted that Renard would find anything. The Normans seemed to be wearing all of their clothing at once, wrapped up as if for the deepest of winters. All except Svend. He was wearing only a linen tunic under his gambeson, as if he were immune to the chill easterly wind.

Her mind flew back to the birthing chamber and the fur-lined cloak he'd draped so carefully around Cille's trembling shoulders. Why wasn't he wearing it now? Unless…

Her head spun back towards him. 'You gave her your cloak?'

His brow creased as his gaze slipped past her shoulder, studying the horizon as if there were something of intense interest behind her.

'She was in greater need.'

'Oh.' The word sounded ungrateful even to her own ears.

There was a long silence, broken only by the screeching of a kestrel overhead, before he drew rein abruptly.

'Hold!' He jumped down easily, striding away from the horses without bothering to help her dismount. 'We'll rest for a while.'

Aediva lowered herself to the ground, her mind at war with itself. He was a pig! Disrespectful, callous and insensitive, not to mention ungallant—and yet, much as she hated to admit it, overall his behaviour had been surprisingly honourable.

She stole a glance at his profile. He was staring into the distance, his expression stern, aloof… *Norman*. He looked like a Norman, sounded like a Norman, and yet despite his ill manners he'd behaved more like a Saxon might have done—as Edmund ought to have done. Since they'd met she'd told him she hated him, threatened to kill him, held a knife to his chest *twice*, and yet he hadn't punished her. He'd taken care of Cille and sent Henri to rescue her people. He'd noticed when she was upset, when she was cold, when she was hungry and tired. In retrospect, she'd been less than grateful.

And, as a Thane's daughter, it was her duty to acknowledge it, no matter how angry she felt.

She took a deep, faltering breath. 'What I said this morning…'

'About wanting to stab me in the heart?' He turned to face her, arms folded as if braced for a fresh verbal assault.

'Yes. I didn't mean it.'

'Really?' He sounded sceptical.

'I was angry.'

'I noticed.'

'And I'm sorry.'

His expression remained stony and she sighed inwardly. Clearly he wasn't going to make this easy. How was it possible for a Norman to make her feel like the one in the wrong? But she still had to thank him. That was what her father would expect her to do.

'I owe you my thanks. For taking care of my sister, for sending your man after our people. I should have thanked you this morning.'

'Instead of threatening to kill me, perhaps?'

She gritted her teeth. 'Instead of that, yes.'

'But…?'

'But what?'

'Speak honestly, Lady Cille. I don't like half-truths. You're sorry for this morning, and you're grateful to me, but…?'

She stared at him, taken aback by his bluntness. How did he do that? Trap her with her own words? She'd been trying to thank him. Why couldn't he just leave it at that?

'Well?' He prompted her.

'Can't you just accept my thanks? I have said I'm grateful.'

'But you're still angry.'

'Yes, I'm angry!' She felt her temper rising again. Of *course* she was angry! What else would she be?

'Because…?'

'Because you're still one of them—a Norman, or as good as. I can't help but hate you for it!'

She glared at him unrepentantly, caught up in the moment. That was the truth. Hadn't he asked for it? No matter how sorry for her behaviour or how grateful for his she might be, they were still enemies. That was obvious…wasn't it?

'So you hate all Normans?' His voice was expressionless. 'Your new husband will be pleased to hear that.'

'I can't help it.'

'Do you always hate so indiscriminately?'

'I have good cause!'

'Yes.' His expression turned sombre. 'Yes, in this case you do.'

'So?'

'So is it really that simple? Saxon good? Norman bad? Take your sister's husband, for instance. You say he abandoned her, a vulnerable woman, and their unborn baby. Do you still think well of *him* just because he's Saxon?'

She reeled backwards, staggering as if he'd just hit her. The words were so closely akin to her own thoughts that she had to turn her face away to hide her mortification. She didn't want to talk about Edmund, especially not with *him.*

'That's different.'

'Is it? I'm capable of many things, Lady Cille, but I hope not that.'

'You don't know anything about it!'

'No, I don't, but the world isn't all black and white. Hate is a very strong word.'

'Sometimes it fits very well!'

His mouth twitched, though his expression was

mirthless. 'If you're saying we can't be friends, then for once we're in agreement. As for your hatred of Normans…for your own sake I hope that you might overcome it.'

'For my own sake? Is that a threat?'

'It's a warning. You should think about it before meeting the Earl. Or your new husband, for that matter.'

She opened her mouth to retaliate and then closed it again. He had a point. She wouldn't be able to persuade FitzOsbern to do anything, let alone release her—*Cille*—from the planned marriage if she charged in arguing and threatening. She'd have to learn to hide her true feelings, her true hatred of Normans, if she were going to stand any chance of success.

As for this new husband—she fully intended to make herself as disagreeable to him as possible. After all he'd never met Cille, wouldn't know what to expect. With any luck she'd put him off Saxon women for ever.

A gust of wind caught her cloak unexpectedly, making it billow open, and Svend reacted at once, catching the edges and pulling them back together at her throat. She gasped, startled. The gesture seemed too intimate, unexpectedly tender, as if he were wrapping her tight in his arms. For a fleeting moment she felt safe and warm, as if the emptiness inside her had been banished, replaced by a warm glow that seemed to radiate outwards, along every nerve ending from the top of her head to the tip of her toes.

She looked up in alarm, saw his eyes flash with something like surprise before they both pulled away at the same moment.

He averted his gaze. 'Believe it or not, I'm trying to help.'

She cleared her throat, trying not to think about what had just happened. Even if that were true, she wasn't going to thank him for it. She hadn't asked for and certainly didn't want advice from a Norman!

'I'll think about it.'

'Well, that's progress.' He sighed. 'Now, get some rest. I want to be a third of the way to Redbourn by nightfall and I don't want you falling asleep on the ride.'

Chapter Five

Svend tightened his knuckles over his reins, the sound of soft, feminine laughter shredding the last vestiges of his temper.

He'd let her rest for over an hour, afraid that the next sound he'd hear would be a thud as she fell out of the saddle, but he hadn't expected her to wake up quite so refreshed. What was she laughing about? How could a sound be so infuriating and so intoxicating at the same time?

He cast a swift glance over his shoulder at his squire. He'd told Renard to keep watch on her, but apparently the lad had decided to entertain her as well. He didn't know which of them he was angrier with, but now he fervently wished he'd left her to fall in the dirt. She was a shrew. Even when he'd been trying to help her, after he'd thought they'd established some kind of truce, they'd somehow ended up arguing.

So why was Renard so favoured? Why was the

boy exempt from her hatred of Normans when he so clearly was not? He could almost imagine that she was doing it on purpose, to annoy him. He was not—*would not*—be jealous of his own squire!

He dug his heels into Talbot's flanks, accelerating his pace to match his anger and frustration, his attention fixed firmly on the track ahead. If she had time for jokes and laughter, then clearly he was being too easy on her.

The wind battered his skin, brisk and invigorating, as they thundered up and over the rolling hillsides. He wasn't jealous, he told himself, just irritated. Her very presence was irritating—unsettling, somehow—like a splinter under his skin that he couldn't extract or ignore. But then he wasn't accustomed to travelling with women. He was a soldier, not an escort, and the sooner they reached Redbourn and he was rid of her, the sooner he could claim his reward and the better for both of them.

'You're still one of them. I can't help but hate you for it.'

Her words came back to him now, as if carried on the wind. She'd sounded exasperated, as if he ought just to accept them. Well, *shouldn't* he? She was mourning her husband and her father, and he was her captor, returning her to Redbourn against her will. Of *course* she hated him. What else did he expect?

What else did he want?

He leaned over Talbot's mane, trying to lose himself in the pounding rhythm of hoofbeats. He shouldn't want anything. He shouldn't be thinking about her at all. He was her escort, sent by the King's cousin. Only a fool would abuse such a trust. Only a madman would consider it.

Besides, he wasn't about to be distracted from his purpose now—and definitely not by a woman. He'd spent ten years rebuilding his life, following orders and earning the King's goodwill. That was why he was here, fulfilling this one last commission. He was doing this for the reward, no other reason. Now, if he could just stop thinking about her…

The sky was darkening when he finally called a halt, setting up camp between a narrow brook and small copse of woodland. Svend slid from his horse, surprised to feel a protesting ache between his shoulder blades. He hadn't been aware of any discomfort during the ride, but clearly he'd been pushing even harder than he'd intended.

She'd probably hate him for that too.

He turned to face her, expecting anger, and was taken aback by her pale, drained appearance. She was slumped so low in the saddle that she seemed in imminent danger of falling off, her eyes so red-rimmed and swollen they seemed to take up half her face. For a stunned moment he stood motionless, stung by a fierce pang of remorse, before he strode quickly to help her dismount, surprised when she let him. She slid down without even a murmur of protest, tumbling into his arms as if she were already half asleep, her very silence a reproach. No words of anger could have been so effective.

'Lady Cille? Can you stand?'

Her legs quivered in answer and he caught her up, gathering her into his arms as she mumbled something incoherent, her eyelids closing even before her head hit his shoulder.

Guilt stabbed him anew. *He'd* done this, trying so hard not to think about her that he'd hurt her instead. He was accustomed to riding in all conditions, and for any length of time, but he should have considered the effect on someone unused to long marches—not to mention someone who'd spent the night before tending to a baby. He'd let his emotions get the better of him. Emotions he shouldn't even be having. It would serve him right if FitzOsbern punished him—and not just for his ill treatment of her.

He laid her down gently on a bed of pine needles and she curled up at once, fast asleep by the time he came back with a blanket. He tucked it around her, careful not to let his fingers linger, trying not to notice the smooth contours of her body as narrow waist curved into rounded hip.

She hadn't eaten—again—but he couldn't bring himself to wake her. She could sleep for as long as she needed, then take it more easily tomorrow. They'd travel at a slow trot all the way to Redbourn if necessary. He'd even let her insult him if it made her feel better.

He stood up and made his way around the camp, ignoring the inquisitive looks of his men and berating himself inwardly. He rarely second-guessed himself, or felt obliged to explain his motives, but something about her unsteadied him, made him feel dangerously out of control.

There was only one other woman who'd ever had such a powerful effect on him—one other woman who'd got into his head and ended up breaking his heart. But that had been a long time ago and he'd learnt a lot about women since Maren. Or thought he had. None of it had seemed to help with Lady Cille…

He volunteered for the first watch, his mind too preoccupied for sleep, settling down amidst the scattered rocks beside the water's edge as his men bedded down for the night, positioning himself with a clear view of her sleeping body. After what he'd done, he didn't want to let her out of his sight. The least he could do was make sure she wasn't disturbed. It wasn't that he wanted to look at her—not completely, at least.

He heard a crunching sound and reached instinctively for his dagger, his hand falling again as he recognised his squire.

'Ale, sir?'

Renard proffered a cup and Svend forced himself to accept. After all, the lad had only been following orders—*his* orders. Even so, he found it hard to forget their easy laughter that afternoon.

'You should get some rest.'

'I will, sir. It's just...about Lady Cille...'

'What about her?' Svend struggled to keep his expression civil. His squire's tone was mildly reproving.

'She was very tired, sir.'

'She was, but it was her own fault.'

'Yes, sir.'

'Anything else? Did I forget to curtsy as well?'

The boy shook his head self-consciously. 'No, sir. Sorry, sir. It's just... She's not what I expected.'

'You seemed to get on well enough.'

'I have five older sisters. I'm good at talking to women.'

'Indeed?' Svend smiled despite himself. 'That's quite a gift.'

'Not when they only want to mother me. Lady Cille probably doesn't think I'm old enough to be a soldier. But she and the Baron don't seem very well-suited.'

Svend froze with the ale halfway to his mouth. 'The Baron?'

'Philippe de Quincey, sir. That's who she's marrying.'

'De Quincey?' Svend lowered his cup again, unable to hide his surprise. 'How do you know?'

'The maids at Redbourn. Like I say, women talk to me. When you met with the Earl I visited the kitchens. They say he's completely besotted.'

Svend blew air from between his teeth. Philippe de Quincey was one of the richest and most powerful men in Normandy, not to mention a close friend and confidante of the King. If Renard were right it would certainly explain the urgency of his assignment, not to mention the secrecy. If the Baron wanted Lady Cille, even William FitzOsbern would make it his business to find her.

A muscle twitched in his jaw. He had no issue with the man personally. Quite the opposite. On the few occasions they'd served together he'd found him a fair and charismatic leader. Arrogant, perhaps, though that was only to be expected from a man who ruled half the coastline of Normandy. But not the kind of man to appreciate a challenge—especially not where women were concerned. No, he preferred them pliant and docile, the more submissive the better. Would this Saxon wildcat really appeal to him?

On the other hand...there was undoubtedly something captivating about her. It wasn't so far-fetched. After all, de Quincey could have his pick of heiresses. Whatever Lady Cille might bring to a marriage would be only a tiny fraction of his wealth. He must be besotted indeed to pursue such a minor alliance.

'Are you certain?'

'That's what I heard. They say it's a love match—on his side anyway.'

'And hers?'

'They didn't know. They thought she was still grieving for her husband.' Renard pitched his voice lower. 'Perhaps she found his attentions displeasing and that's why she ran away?'

Svend's expression hardened. That sounded more like her. He could easily imagine her reaction to a Norman suitor. The Baron was lucky she hadn't gelded him. But how far had his unwelcome advances gone? Was that why she'd run away? Because she was afraid of him? Damn it all, everyone knew that political alliances were necessary, but surely the woman's feelings ought to be taken into account. What kind of a man forced his attentions on a grieving widow? What kind of a man forced himself *at all*? What had the bastard done to her?

'Can I get you anything else, sir?'

'What? Oh…' He put a placatory hand on his squire's arm, regretting his earlier brusqueness. 'No, get some rest.'

His gaze followed Renard's retreating figure before drifting inexorably back towards her. From his vantage point he could just make out the pale oval of her face in the moonlight. Why hadn't she told him about de Quincey? As far as he could remember she'd never mentioned his name. Nothing she'd said even suggested the two of them had ever met. He frowned into the darkness. Not that he expected her to confide in him, but the omission bothered him somehow. What else was she hiding?

And where the hell was de Quincey? If he were really so besotted, why wasn't he here in person, saving *him* the trouble? Why make *him* complicit? He'd rather face a horde of rebels than force a woman into marriage against her will. Especially *this* woman.

From what he remembered, the Baron had been called back to his estates in Normandy in the early spring. His return was imminent, but apparently not soon enough. And so FitzOsbern had sent him instead—a warrior in place of a husband...

Snap!

The sound was faint, an almost inaudible crack in the darkness, but he froze instantly, every instinct on the alert as he scanned the undergrowth for movement, looking for telltale signs of an ambush. The noise had come from the copse behind the campsite, too loud for an animal, too quiet for a man—unless it were a man moving slowly, trying not to be heard.

Soundlessly he moved into a crouching position, poised for a counter-attack. He was only ten feet away from the camp, but it still felt too far. If they were under attack, could he reach her in time?

He peered into the darkness, but there was nothing, no one—just a heavy, unnatural stillness, as if the trees themselves were holding their breath. But there was someone out there—he knew it instinctively. Someone on the far side of the clearing, watching, waiting…for what?

Out of the corner of his eye he saw a shadow move suddenly—a man's figure, darting silently between the trees, but heading *away* from the camp, not towards it. Instantly he was on his feet and following, keeping low to the ground as he darted across the beach and into the camp, clamping a hand over Renard's mouth as he shook him awake.

'Wake the men! We're not alone.'

He started off again, quickly, and then stopped as if reconsidering something. 'Get *her* up too. I don't want her caught by surprise.'

He broke into the trees, following the direction of the shadow, treading lightly as he ducked under and around branches, trying not to make a sound. There was a rustle of leaves and a sway of branches ahead and he crept towards it, halting abruptly as the shadow stopped, every muscle immobile as an unknown gaze seemed to sweep over him. Then the figure moved again and Svend carried on, reaching the far edge of the copse just as the shadow burst into the open, the unmistakable figure of a man revealed in the moonlight.

Svend swore imaginatively. The man might be a rebel scout, or simply a lone outlaw, but he couldn't take the chance. Where there was one rebel there might be more. He wasn't going to wait around to find out.

He made his way swiftly back to the clearing, relieved to find his men grouped in a defensive circle around Lady Cille. She was standing alone in the centre, a small figure dwarfed by the burly soldiers, her pale face tense and frightened. As he stepped out of the trees her shoulders seemed to slump suddenly, her whole body slackening as if with relief. Or was it disappointment? After the ride that day she'd probably hoped she'd seen the last of him.

'Rebels, sir?'

Renard ran up to him and Svend patted the boy's shoulder reassuringly. 'Most likely. We need to leave. *Now.*'

His men didn't argue, packing up camp with quiet, practised efficiency, clearing the ground in a matter of minutes.

'Lady Cille.' He found himself drawn irresistibly towards her, his feet moving as if of their own volition. 'We need to go.'

'Why did you do that?' She straightened up as he approached, her voice high-pitched and accusatory, eyes glowing like golden orbs in the moonlight.

'Do what?' He frowned, taken aback by her vehemence. What was she angry about *this* time?

'You shouldn't have gone after him! It was dangerous.'

He stared at her, genuinely perplexed. Had she been *worried* about him? Flattering though the idea was, it seemed highly unlikely. More likely she'd been afraid for the rebels, or angry that he'd left her alone. But it wasn't as if he'd left her undefended. His men had practically built a shield wall around her.

'There's no need to be frightened. My men are more than capable of dealing with rebels.'

'Frightened?'

'You're safe with my soldiers.'

She blinked rapidly, as if she were coming out of a trance. 'Why would I be frightened of rebels? They wouldn't harm *me*.'

'No?' His temper stirred. Was she really so naive? Did she always have to provoke him? Even now when he was trying to reassure her? 'I wouldn't be so sure. They might be rebels or they might be outlaws. Either way, they're men. Are you so certain who's on your side?'

For a fleeting moment her expression seemed to waver. Then it hardened again, and her chin inched upwards in a now familiar gesture of defiance. 'If they're Saxon, they won't harm me.'

'Is that so?'

He took a step towards her, so that they stood only inches apart, the air between them seeming to crackle and strain with tension. She swayed slightly, as if she were about to retreat, then straightened again, so close that he could feel the heat of her body through her gown. She was panting slightly, her breathing shallow and erratic, her breasts rising and falling just inches away from his chest.

From the sounds around them he could tell that his men were almost ready. If he had even the tiniest shred of common sense he'd turn and walk away from her now.

She licked her lips nervously and his gaze followed the movement. Her bottom lip was full, moist, dangerously tempting. He clenched his jaw, fighting the urge he'd felt that first night, the almost overwhelming desire to pull her into his arms and kiss the defiant look off her face.

'They won't harm me,' she repeated, less convincingly.

'So you say.'

'You could leave me here.'

He frowned, thinking he must have misheard her.

'Just leave me here.' She looked hopeful suddenly. 'You could say that I ran away.'

'Just like that?'

She nodded. 'Turn around and I'll run. Then it won't be a lie.'

Svend raised his eyebrows incredulously. 'You want me to abandon you at night, in the middle of nowhere, with wolves and rebels and outlaws for company?'

'I'll take my chances.'

He studied her face intently. She meant it. She actually *wanted* him to let her run off alone. Was she brave or just reckless? Or so afraid of de Quincey that she'd actually risk her life to avoid him? His hands curled into fists at the thought.

'It's too dangerous.'

'I'm not afraid.'

'I can't let you go.'

'Please, Svend.'

He stiffened. He was used to her arguing with him, to berating him and insulting him, but pleading…? The imploring tone of her voice made his heart clench unexpectedly. The way she said his name almost finished him. For one wild moment he was tempted to do whatever she wanted—to let her go, to let her run from a marriage she didn't want.

To go with her.

He shook his head, dispelling the thought. He hadn't forgotten the last time a woman had asked him for a favour. He'd given in to Maren and look where it had got him. He'd spent the last ten years paying for it, rebuilding his life one hard step at a time. He'd learnt his lesson the hard way and he wasn't about to make the same mistake now, when his reward was almost within touching distance. Lady Cille could plead all she wanted. He wasn't going to fall for a woman's tricks again.

'We don't have time for this.' He turned his back on her stiffly. 'My men are waiting.'

'So you won't help me?'

He hardened his heart against the appeal in her voice. 'On the contrary, I'm going to keep you safe. Whether you want me to or not.'

Chapter Six

Aediva hunched down in the saddle and stared at a point between the palfrey's ears, trying not to think about the cold air biting her cheeks and numbing her fingers. Strands of hair curled out from the sides of her headdress, billowing around her face like a dark cloud, suiting her mood.

They'd ridden in silence through the night, glad of the bright moon and clear sky lighting their way. The atmosphere had been tense and defensive, lightening only as the first yellow fingers of dawn had started to splay out over the horizon.

She shifted uncomfortably in her saddle. They were travelling at a slower pace than yesterday, though after only half a night's sleep her head was still throbbing and dizzy. Not to mention her body. She was bone-weary, so leaden and saddle-sore that every mile was a slow torture. Her thighs felt as though they were covered in bruises.

It was all Svend's fault. If he hadn't set such

a punishing pace yesterday then she wouldn't be feeling so wretched today. And if he hadn't gone off alone in the night, chasing down some mysterious unknown enemy, she wouldn't be feeling so confused.

If only he'd let her go—let her run away into the night. She could have gone back to Cille, fled with her into the Fens. For a moment she'd thought she'd persuaded him, but then his expression had closed down again, like a gate swinging shut in her face. Why couldn't he understand?

Understand what?

She frowned at her own question. That she needed to get away—not just from Redbourn and the Earl, but from him too. She'd thought that she hated him, but when she'd awoken in the night and found he'd gone off alone she'd felt physically sick. And when he'd come back it had taken all her willpower not to run into his arms.

No. She shook her head. That couldn't be true. She didn't want to run into *any* man's arms. Men were rough, violent, demanding. Edmund had taught her that. She'd been relieved, that was all, as relieved as she would have been for anyone who'd charged off alone into the night. She hadn't been worried about Svend himself. He was nothing to her—worse than nothing. The man who wanted to steal her home. Her enemy.

And yet standing in that circle of Norman

soldiers she hadn't been certain whose side she was on.

'How are you feeling, my lady?'

Renard appeared at her shoulder, proffering a wineskin, and she accepted gratefully, glad of the distraction.

'There's a storm building,' he commented good-naturedly, gesturing towards the build-up of clouds overhead, massing together to form a towering grey ceiling. 'Truly, I've never known such a place for rain.'

Aediva rolled her eyes. 'What *is* it about Normans and rain? Are you so frightened of a little water?'

Renard laughed, and she found herself joining in. A few days ago she would never have imagined sharing a joke with a Norman, but the squire was so easy to tease. He was just a couple of years younger than she was, and so disarmingly friendly that she found it impossible to hold a grudge against him.

'It *has* rained a lot this summer,' she conceded, drawing rein to look out over the gently undulating hills to the south.

The vale sloped downwards here, widening out and flattening as it reached the Great Ouse River. If she followed its winding contours she could just make out the faint white outline of the sea in the distance.

'But look at the view.'

'A land worth conquering.'

Svend's deep voice made her swing round in surprise. After the events of the night, they'd been studiously avoiding each other, but now he looked different somehow, his pale hair falling carelessly across one eye, even more rugged and handsome than she remembered.

'We were just resting,' Renard hastened to explain. 'Lady Cille looked tired.'

Svend's gaze swept her features appraisingly. 'You look pale, my lady. Are you unwell?'

'No. I can keep up, if that's what you mean.'

'It's not.' He frowned at the darkening clouds. 'But we need to stop anyway—take shelter in the woods.'

'Those woods?' She glanced uneasily down the hillside towards the thicket of fir trees that rimmed the valley. They looked dark and impenetrable.

'We've no choice. There's a storm coming and we're too exposed up here.'

As if to reinforce his words there was a low rumble of thunder, followed by a fine spattering of rain. The horses shifted uneasily, unsettled by the change in atmosphere.

'Come!' He set off down the hillside at once, gesturing for his soldiers to follow.

Aediva didn't move.

It wasn't that she hadn't heard him, just that she'd heard something else as well. Against the backdrop of thunder a bittern's booming call—twice in quick succession, brief but unmistakable. She knew about the rebels' use of such signals. Was there an ambush waiting in the woods? Was she about to be rescued? Did she want to be?

The latter question brought her up short. Of *course* she wanted to be rescued! If she reached Redbourn and her deception were uncovered, who knew what the Normans might do to her? What Svend himself might do? So why did she feel this strange reluctance to be parted from him? She should grasp at any chance of escape…shouldn't she?

'Lady Cille?' Svend had stopped halfway down the slope and was looking back at her, the heavy drizzle casting a murky veil between them. 'What's the matter?'

She should move, she told herself. The drizzle was fast becoming a downpour and her hair was sticking to her face in dark tendrils. She'd only provoke his suspicions if she stayed there.

'We should try to cross the river first!' she shouted, surprising herself.

'We can't outride the storm!'

'No, but if the rain's heavy, the ford might be too high to pass later.' That made sense, even if her motives for saying so didn't.

'There isn't time!'

He started back towards her and she held his gaze with an effort, schooling her expression into innocence. Why was she hesitating? She should go with him, should lead him into the rebels' trap before he guessed something was wrong. He was her *enemy.*

'We should try the river!' she said again.

'Why?' His voice was hard, urgent, demanding an answer.

She shook her head, speechless with uncertainty. She was soaked through, but her skin felt red-hot under his penetrating stare. She couldn't lead him into a trap, but nor could she betray the rebels to him.

Suddenly she knew with utter, terrifying certainty that if it came to a fight, this man would win.

And she didn't want any more bloodshed. Not if she could prevent it.

'The river…' she whispered, her voice cracking under the strain. Who was she betraying?

A crack of thunder made the decision for them.

'Too late!'

He grabbed her reins and pulled her headlong towards the shelter of the trees, heavy pellets of rain battering their faces as if the storm itself were chasing them.

She felt as though night had suddenly fallen. Heavy branches blocked out the darkening sky, enveloping them in an eerie, overcast gloom. Svend dismounted at once, issuing orders as she peered through the trees for any sign of rebels.

But there was nothing, no one, no sign that anyone had ever been there. It must have been a coincidence after all, she thought with relief. Her imagination playing tricks on her.

No sooner had the thought entered her head than two dozen men burst from the undergrowth, swords and axes raised, their bloodcurdling cries and bearded faces immediately identifying them as Saxon rebels.

The Normans drew their weapons at once, grouping around her defensively as the palfrey snorted and whirled, spooked by its sudden entrapment.

'Cille, get down!'

She heard Svend shout, but she couldn't see him. Almost at once his voice was lost in a deafening, seething morass of metal and blood. Desperately, she sought him out, craning her neck to catch a glimpse of pale blond hair in the very midst of the fiercest fighting. He wasn't wearing armour, but it hardly seemed to matter. None of his opponents' blows even came close to touching him. He wielded his sword as if it were a mere extension of his arm, every strike measured and terrifying.

She heard a loud battle cry as one of the Saxons suddenly charged through the throng, hurling himself against the boy with the swollen eye and knocking him to the ground, swinging his axe back as if preparing to bring it down on his head.

'No!' She looked around frantically, searching for a weapon—any weapon. The boy was sprawled on the ground, looking stunned, unable to fight back even to defend himself. Norman or not, she couldn't let him be struck down in cold blood…

The Saxon's axe swung down and she froze, holding her breath, willing the boy to escape—before Svend appeared out of nowhere, barrelling into the man's side so violently that he sent them both rolling into the dirt.

A scream was torn from her lungs. Svend was already scrambling back to his feet, but so was the Saxon warrior, and this time there was no mistaking her feelings. She was frightened—no, *terrified*—of Svend being hurt. She hardly knew whose side she was on any more, but she couldn't just sit there and watch. What if he were injured? What if he were killed? She had to do something.

Impulsively she charged the palfrey into the throng, determined to cause a break in the fighting.

'Hold!'

She heard restraining cries in both Saxon and French as the palfrey wheeled about, nostrils flaring, panicking as it scented blood. In a blur, she saw men jump out of the way, then felt herself flung backwards and abruptly forwards again as the terrified beast reared on its haunches, legs kicking in mid-air, before bolting headlong into the trees.

She clung to the horse's mane for dear life, pressing her face into its neck as twigs and branches tore at her clothes and skin, ripping away her headdress and scratching her neck with long, pointed talons. She heaved at the reins but the horse resisted, dodging and weaving between the trees, running wild as it tried to escape.

At last they burst into a clearing—a small, secluded meadow in the midst of the woodland—and she lifted her head into the sleeting rain. Blasts of icy wind whistled in her ears and coils of hair whipped across her face, half blinding her. Though not enough to obscure the view of another clump of woodland looming directly ahead. And the palfrey was heading straight towards it, galloping at full speed towards trees that looked closer together and even more dangerous. If they didn't stop she'd be crushed against them for certain.

Then she heard another set of hooves—a heavy drumming that was slowly but steadily gaining on her. Heart in her mouth, she turned her head, knowing the identity of the rider even before she saw him.

'Jump!'

Svend was almost alongside, reaching an arm out to catch her as she stared at him in shock. Surely he didn't mean it? She risked a glance at the ground hurtling by and then wished that she hadn't. If she fell beneath the hooves she'd be trampled instantly. There had to be another way.

'Cille, you have to jump! Trust me!'

There were only a few seconds left. She was almost at the trees and he was her only chance. She wanted to let go, wanted to trust him, but how could she? She'd already betrayed her people. If she let him rescue her too she might as well side with the Normans completely.

'I can't!'

His destrier twisted sideways abruptly, its grey head butting fearlessly against her palfrey's flanks, knocking it off course. Bellowing in shock, her horse reared up and she found herself hurtling backwards, the reins slipping through her fingers. She closed her eyes and braced herself, knowing there was nothing between her and the rock-strewn ground.

Then an arm grabbed her waist, catching her as she tumbled through the air, and her eyes flew open with a jolt, to look up into those of the angriest-looking man she'd ever seen.

'Have you gone *mad*?' Svend's face was like thunder.

Aediva blinked at him, scarcely able to breathe. Her heart was pounding violently against her ribcage and his arm was tight around her waist, crushing her against him. He was half out of his saddle, bearing her entire weight apparently without effort, in the crook of one arm. She looked down, feeling like a tiny twig on a massive oak tree.

'You could have been killed! Can't you just trust me for once?'

Her temper flared to meet his. He was her *enemy*. How dared he ask for her trust? And why was he berating her anyway? *She* was the one who'd almost been killed!

'Let me go!' She twisted in his grip and he released her at once, letting her sprawl inelegantly on the wet ground.

'That's one less horse, then.' He glared as the back of the palfrey vanished into the trees. 'Are you intending to walk the rest of the way?'

She ignored him, shaking out her sodden dress in disgust. The rain had slowed to a drizzle, but the meadow felt like a swamp. Scowling, she pulled herself up and stalked back the way they'd come, the long grass clinging to her skirts as if trying to drag her back.

'Stop!'

He called after her but she kept moving, rubbing her neck and arms in irritation. They were covered in bumps and scratches like painful bites, where the branches had torn through her sleeves. As if losing her dignity in front of Svend weren't bad enough, she probably looked a fright too.

'I said *stop*! That's an order, Lady Cille!'

'An *order*?' She whirled around angrily, unable

to stop herself from taking the bait. 'Who are *you* to give me orders?'

He leapt down from his destrier and stalked towards her. 'You're my prisoner.'

'You're my *escort*!'

'I warned you not to try to escape.'

'Escape?' She blinked in surprise. 'I wasn't...'

'Do you have *any* idea how dangerous that was? Besides the fact that you endangered my men. I told you to get down!'

'I wasn't trying to escape!' she shouted over him impatiently. Somehow that fact felt important, as if she needed him to know.

'You weren't?' He frowned, some of his anger evaporating.

'No, I...' She stopped. What could she say? How could she explain what she hardly understood herself?

'Then what were you thinking?'

He sounded exasperated and she laughed, a bitter sound even to her own ears, throwing her arms wide as if to embrace the elements.

'Nothing! I *wasn't* thinking. But I had to *do* something. I couldn't just watch you get killed!'

She spun away from him, clamping a hand to her mouth as she realised what she'd said. She'd meant the rebels. She hadn't wanted to watch *the rebels* get killed. They were her people. They were all she cared about—all she *should* care about.

But it wasn't true.

She heard him come to stand close behind her…so close that she could feel the warmth of his breath on her neck. Her skin tingled beneath it.

'You were trying to protect me?' he murmured huskily in her ear.

She bit down hard on her lip. She *couldn't* care about him. It wasn't possible. He was her enemy. And even if he wasn't he was still a man. If she told him how she felt he might touch her, and she didn't want any man to touch her…did she?

The memory of their first meeting flashed through her mind. Of when she'd hurled herself against him in the hall, when his strong body had lain over hers, when she'd straddled his thighs… She'd resisted him then and had resisted him ever since—as she ought to resist him now. But this time she couldn't. This time she wanted him close. Closer. She felt a strange compulsion to lean back against him, to feel the curve of her body against his, to feel his strong arms around her waist.

She shook her head, her mind still protesting against her treacherous body. It was comfort that she wanted, that was all. She was still in shock after her ordeal with the palfrey. Saxon or Norman or whoever he was, she only wanted to be comforted. He could be anyone.

'Cille?'

His hand touched her shoulder but she didn't push it away. Instead she half turned her head, shivering with anticipation as his fingers slid downwards, past her elbow and along her forearm, until they circled her wrist like a manacle. As if she were his captive. Which she was.

With only the lightest of touches he tugged at her hand and she found herself turning to face him, her body just a hair's breadth from his, so close that if she swayed even slightly…

Strong fingers traced the line of her jaw, tilting her chin up and forcing her gaze to meet his. She gasped, the smouldering intensity in his eyes making her stomach quiver. They looked bigger, darker, and even more tempting—as if the ice in them had melted, leaving twin pools of irresistible cobalt blue water. Eyes she could dive into, could drown in if she weren't careful.

She swallowed nervously, seeing the reflection of her own desire. He wanted her. And she wanted him. But how could she? He was her captor, her enemy. He thought she was someone else…he thought she was a grieving widow…he thought she was…

'Cille?' He said the name like a caress.

'No…' she breathed. She wasn't Cille. She shouldn't be doing this.

'No?' he repeated faintly, bending his head so that his mouth hovered mere inches from hers, tantalisingly close, waiting for her to make the first move…

If she wanted him to stop, this was her chance.

She let her body overrule her mind, swaying

forward as if her insides had turned to water and she could simply flow into his arms. Her hand fluttered to his chest and his lips seized instantly upon hers, covering her mouth with a touch that silenced every protest.

She let her lips mould against his, caught up in a wave of pleasure that threatened to overwhelm what was left of rational thought. He was tender—more tender than she'd imagined a warrior could be—exploring her mouth with a soft but unyielding pressure as his hands gathered her against him, tracing the curve of her spine, leaving a trail of fire.

All her resistance gave way and she surrendered to the feeling, letting her body lead as she closed what was left of the space between them, reaching up on her toes as she leaned against the hard lines of his body as if she couldn't bear anything, not even air, to come between them. She felt his surprise, felt him stiffen and then respond as his arms coiled tighter around her waist, lifting her up so that her feet barely skimmed the floor, so tight that she could feel the solid muscles of his chest beneath his tunic.

A frisson of excitement raced through her body, heating her blood. All her senses seemed heightened…every nerve ending quivered. And she could feel a hot, tugging sensation deep inside, as if he were pulling her towards him by some invisible cord. It was an ache, a need, overwhelming and urgent… She ran her hands through his hair and moved her mouth against his, felt the pressure of his own lips increase, grow deeper, harder, as if they were no longer two but one body joined by a common desperate need.

They came apart finally and she arched her neck, gasping for breath as his mouth still moved hungrily over her skin, pressing kisses against her throat, her ears, into her hair. A low moan escaped her lips as for the first time in months she felt her mind start to shut down, as if her cares were floating away and there were only the two of them. If she could only hold on to this feeling, stay engulfed by his powerful arms, with the intoxicating feel of his lips on her skin, just lose herself in it and not think of the future…

'Cille…' he murmured, reclaiming her mouth.

She could feel his heartbeat, the hot pulse of his blood, but it wasn't enough. What more was there?

'Svend…?' She made his name into a question. *What next?* she wanted to ask. *What happens next?*

She'd heard gossip, of course, and Cille had told her something of what passed between a man and a woman, but this was beyond her ken, beyond words, beyond anything that she'd ever imagined.

She didn't know what her body wanted, just that it wanted, needed, *demanded* more. She'd never felt anything like this before, nothing remotely akin to this yearning. Her only experience was with Edmund.

Edmund. Her stomach plummeted.

'Cille?' Svend pulled his head back, sensing the change in her. 'What is it?'

His breathing was as ragged as hers, but his face was full of concern, as if he truly cared. If she wanted him to he'd take her in his arms and kiss her again, kiss away the bitter memory of Edmund for ever.

She caught her breath, fighting the impulse. What was she *doing*? He was a man—just like Edmund. His kisses might feel pleasurable now, but soon he'd start pushing for more, would turn pleasure into pain. She didn't want any man to touch her, let alone Svend. How much worse to let an enemy use and then betray her as Edmund had done? She shouldn't be doing this.

No matter how much she wanted to.

She pushed frantically against his chest and he relaxed his hold at once, lowering her gently to the floor.

'What's the matter?' He sounded confused.

Back on firm ground, her legs felt unsteady—as if the world beneath her had become suddenly unstable. She felt his arms tighten again and wrenched herself free, raising a hand to her swollen lips, seized by an irrational surge of anger. How *dared* he try to seduce her? Cille or not, he was supposed to be her escort—the man entrusted to take her to her new husband. What kind of a wanton did he take her for? Did he think Saxon women were so easily seduced?

'Cille?'

He reached out a hand and she clenched her fists, resisting the urge to take it. She had to go back—back to the way things had been. Better to be enemies than this.

'Do you make it a custom to seduce *all* your prisoners?'

She spat the words out as scathingly as possible, and saw something like hurt flash across his features, before it was gone—so quickly that she thought she must have imagined it. And then he was her captor again, the intimacy between them evaporating into thin air.

At the same moment she heard a commotion in the trees and a Norman soldier burst into the meadow, shouting out with relief at the sight of them.

'The rebels have fled, sir!'

She was relieved to see it was the boy with the swollen eye.

Svend raised an arm in acknowledgement, then turned back to face her stonily. For a moment he seemed on the verge of saying something, before his expression altered abruptly.

'You're soaking wet!'

She looked down, surprised to find that he was right. Her dress was sodden, clinging to her body like a second skin, leaving little to the imagination. She hadn't been aware of it until that moment, but now that he mentioned it she felt soaked to the bone. More than that, she felt cold and shivery all over.

He made a move as if to touch her, then stopped himself.

'We can't stay here. Your rebels are still close by and I can't risk any more of your heroics.'

She nodded, her teeth starting to chatter uncontrollably. 'But the horse…'

'You'll ride with me.'

'No!' She shook her head, struggling to focus. She couldn't ride with him—couldn't touch him again. She didn't know if she could trust herself.

She raised her arms as if to fend him off, then swayed dizzily. The meadow itself seemed to be tilting up towards her. Where was Svend? She spun round, then felt a pair of strong arms on her waist, scooping her up and gathering her to a broad chest that smelt of horse, leather and a musky male scent all of its own. She'd smelt it the first time he'd tackled her to the ground. She would have recognised it anywhere.

A feeling of immense tiredness swept over her. He seemed to be asking her a question, but she felt as though she were below water, straining to hear. What was the matter with her hearing? And her sight? His eyes were blurring together in front of her, coalescing into a single bright sapphire in the very midst of her vision.

'Cille? Can you hear me?'

His voice seemed to come from a long way away. He sounded concerned. He was worried about her. The thought made her smile… Maybe if she said sorry, that she hadn't meant to attack him, he would kiss her again. Now that the moment was gone she wanted it back again.

'Svend…' she murmured, enjoying the feel of his name on her tongue. 'Svend du Danemark…'

And then the fog descended and she surrendered to it.

Chapter Seven

Aediva stretched, yawned and burrowed her way deeper inside the comfort of a fur-skinned mantle, smiling as the hair tickled her cheek.

She sighed contentedly, recalling a sensation of endless motion, of something warm and strong wrapped tightly around her waist, of feeling as light as a feather and then being laid down and wrapped in something soft and luxuriant. She vaguely remembered a blurry face, filled with concern, and the gentle touch of fingers on her forehead…

But it was all hazy. She couldn't make sense of the dream and she was too drowsy and comfortable to try. She felt snug and peaceful, without a care in the world. If only Cille wouldn't come and wake her up too soon…

Cille! Her eyelids flew open as memory came flooding back. Open to the sight of a cloudless blue sky.

She sat bolt upright, clamping a hand to her head as the dull throbbing in her temples became a sudden violent hammering. She felt dizzy, as if she'd drunk too much of Eadgyth's mead, and strangely exposed…

She glanced down and gave a small shriek, clutching the blanket to her chest like a shield. She was naked!

She dropped to the ground, twisting around to see if anyone had noticed, but there was no one to see. Aside from a few bored-looking horses, the campsite was completely deserted.

Panic subsiding, she tucked the blanket under her chin and tried to gather her scattered thoughts. Judging by the position of the sun it was around midday, and as unseasonably warm as it had been cold before. How long had she been asleep?

More importantly, where was she?

The camp was strategically positioned near the top of a hill, with views that seemed to extend over the whole shire. The last she remembered they'd been north of the river, but now it stretched out behind them, a sparkling band in the distance. She had no memory of crossing the ford. Her memory seemed to stop with a kiss. One breathless and breathtaking kiss.

She inhaled sharply, caught off guard by the same giddy rush of desire, the same tingling sensation deep in the pit of her stomach. What had she *done*? She'd been swept off her feet, swept away from reason, had come dangerously close to forgetting who she was and who she was pretending to be all because of a kiss.

And it had all been *her* fault! She was the one who'd told Svend that she'd been trying to protect him. She was the one who'd leaned in for his kiss. How could she have been so weak?

But why had *he* kissed *her*? He'd done little but harangue her since they'd met. Did he think she'd make such an easy conquest? As if wanting her land wasn't bad enough! Well, he could think again. She might have succumbed once, but she'd been taken by surprise. He was her enemy and he always would be. It wouldn't happen again.

A mistake. It had all been a mistake. She'd been tired, overwrought, seeking comfort in the nearest pair of arms. And then something had happened. She'd pushed him away, felt a strange, dizzying weariness. Had she fainted? Was she ill? She pressed a hand to her forehead but it felt cool to the touch. Svend must have brought her here. Had he nursed her? Had he undressed her too? No, surely not. A knight would never do such a thing…would he?

And what was that noise?

At first she thought the pounding was in her head. Then she heard shouts and the distinctive clatter of steel upon shield and her throat turned dry. Quickly she rolled onto her stomach, looking towards the ridge of the hill where the Normans were…fighting *each other*?

She blinked, relief vying with surprise. It was no battle. They were practising their sword skills in hand-to-hand combat, though the sparring looked ferocious enough, even from a distance.

Instinctively her eyes sought Svend. He was there too, flicking a sword from hand to hand as he circled his opponent, wearing just a coat of light chainmail for protection, his windswept hair shining like burnished gold in the sunshine.

Her breathing quickened. He looked like a born warrior, with every stroke of his sword slicing the air with cool, measured precision. Sweat gleamed on his biceps, accentuating every bulging muscle as he swept the weapon up in an arc and then spun around, blocking a counterblow before knocking his opponent to the ground with a quick twist and thrust. She hadn't seen his arms uncovered before, had only felt the taut strength of them around her waist, but they looked impossibly large. Arms that could hold her close and keep her safe…

If she wanted them to.

No! She shook her head to banish the temptation. He was her enemy. She had to remember that even if he felt like the opposite. He was her enemy, no matter what else her instincts might tell her. She had too much to lose—couldn't trust another man or he'd fail her just as Edmund had done. Even if Svend's blue eyes promised differently. Even if they seemed honest and trustworthy as he watched the fighting with a smouldering intensity that seemed to make the space between them fizz with tension.

Except that he wasn't watching the fighting.

He was watching her.

She dropped down quickly, squeezing her eyes shut and pretending to be asleep. She wasn't ready to face him—not yet and definitely not naked! She had to steel herself first…build up her defences to resist him.

For a few minutes she lay perfectly still, listening. But there was nothing—not a sound besides the distant clamour of metal and her own pounding heartbeat. She exhaled, cautiously opening one eye to find herself staring at a pair of black leather boots.

'You're awake, then?'

She squeaked in surprise. She hadn't heard footsteps and yet he was crouching beside her, looking amused and wary at the same time, as if he were trying to gauge her reaction. He must have stopped to exchange his mail for a leather gambeson, but it hung open in the middle, exposing a line of pale hair that tapered down his chest like an arrow, dragging her gaze along with it.

She tore her eyes away as her cheeks flared bright red.

'Hungry?' He proffered a chunk of bread. 'Or would you prefer some water to cool down?'

She batted the bread away, furious at herself for looking and at him for noticing.

'Where are my clothes?'

He nodded towards a bundle on the ground beside her. 'There. Clean and dry, thanks to Renard.'

'Then why…?' She stopped, suddenly reluctant to bring his attention to her nakedness. 'I mean, why aren't I wearing them?'

He took a bite of bread and chewed it thoughtfully. 'They were wet.'

'So you took them off?'

'You had a fever. Wet clothes would have made it worse.'

'So you brought me here and…' she gritted her teeth '…undressed me?'

'No.' He took another bite. 'They had to come off at once. Then we came here, far enough away to be safe from your rebels, and waited for your fever to break. That was two days ago.'

She stared at him in growing horror. *Two days!* Not to mention the fact that he'd seen her naked! That idea bothered her more than the fact of her long illness.

He leaned forwards conspiratorially. 'I did my best not to look.'

She spluttered, too angry even for words, before a new, more alarming thought occurred to her. 'So what did I wear on the journey?'

He jerked his head towards one of his soldiers, a barrel-chested giant who seemed to be using his vast bulk as a battering ram. 'See Bertrand over there? His under-tunic made a passable dress.'

'You mean I've been roaming the countryside in Norman undergarments?'

White teeth flashed in a broad grin. 'So it would seem.'

She blinked, her anger suddenly forgotten. She hadn't seen him smile properly before—hadn't thought such a thing was possible—and the effect was strangely disarming. When he smiled like that she could almost forget they were enemies. A lock of white-gold hair hung over his forehead and he appeared not to have shaved in days. The layer of stubble made him look almost Saxon.

She felt her resolve weaken. Why did he have to look so heart-stoppingly attractive? More like a carefree youth than a battle-hardened commander? She didn't know which alarmed her more—the fact that he was smiling or that her heart appeared to be doing somersaults in her chest.

She remembered to breathe at last. Clearly the illness had affected her nerves. 'And where is Bertrand's dress now?'

'Ah.' Svend rubbed his hands together, brushing away crumbs. 'You were extremely feverish. After a while it simply became easier to change your blankets than your wet clothes.'

'My wet—!'

He raised a hand in mock gallantry. 'No need to be embarrassed. Even Norman ladies sweat.'

She glared at him, fuming inwardly. He thought this was *funny*! He was enjoying her humiliation. How could she ever have kissed him?

And yet someone had nursed her back to health…someone with caring blue eyes utterly unlike the ones mocking her now. But if it wasn't him, then who?

'I suppose I should thank someone for taking care of me?' she asked vaguely.

'You should—though I doubt that you will.'

She bit back a retort. 'Renard, I suppose?'

He regarded her steadily for a moment before standing up, his lips set in a tight, thin line. 'Who else? The lad was worried about you.'

She felt an unexpected twinge of disappointment. 'Well, please give him my thanks.'

'You can thank him yourself soon enough. I see your illness hasn't affected your manners.'

Svend made a stiff bow and strode away, determined to put as much distance between them as possible. She was ungrateful—as ungrateful as Maren had ever been! Even if she looked so much like a Saxon wildcat, wide-eyed and tousle-haired, lips still full and pouting from sleep, that it had taken all his self-control not to lie her back down again.

So he'd gone in on the offensive and deliberately made her angry. After what had happened between them in the meadow he'd had no choice.

He should never have kissed her—had had no right to touch her at all—but he hadn't been able to stop himself. He'd been too relieved that she was safe…his blood had still been hot and pumping from the chase. She'd infuriated him, but then she'd said that she'd been trying to protect him…

The words had caught him off guard. When was the last time anyone had cared enough to want to protect him? So long that he couldn't remember. Desire had rendered him powerless.

He stormed furiously back up the ridge. It was typical of her to wake up *now*! He'd barely left her side for days, but his men were bored and irritable, in need of some physical exertion to distract them. After her fever had broken in the night, he'd known that she was out of danger. But of course she assumed that Renard had nursed her! Did she ever miss a chance to think ill of him?

As for her clothes—surely she understood that he'd had to undress her? He'd have done the same for anyone. And he'd truly done his best not to look…even with her shift clinging so tightly to her skin as to have been almost transparent. When he'd imagined undressing her it certainly hadn't been like that. He'd been trying to save her life, dammit! He could hardly have asked one of his men to do it. Under the circumstances, it had *had* to be him.

Even if it definitely should not have been.

He snatched up a sword and charged back into

the fighting, trying to concentrate on the swing of the blade. Bertrand ran towards him and he darted quickly to the left, then switched sides again, pretending to aim for a high blow before sweeping his arm down to swipe the backs of his legs.

She was just like Maren—throwing his help back in his face!

A massive arm swung towards him and he ducked, spinning away and then quickly back again, thrusting his dagger up and under Bertrand's shield until he conceded.

Maren. He hadn't thought of her in so long that her face—that smooth oval he'd once thought so perfect—was no more than a blurred and indistinct memory. Barely a day went by that he didn't think of his lost homeland, but his reason for leaving was long buried. What had brought her to mind *now*?

He accepted a fresh challenge and circled absently around his new opponent, twirling his sword in his hand as he considered the question.

Were they alike, Cille and Maren? He racked his brains. Maren's hair had been red—a cascade of copper-coloured spirals. And her eyes…green like the sea. Beautiful and enticing, but empty and cold. Whereas Cille's… Her eyes were so deep he felt he'd barely skimmed the surface. Except when they'd kissed. Then they'd been warm and vulnerable, shining like molten gold, beautiful and beguiling and utterly impossible to resist.

She'd kissed him back—he was sure of it. He hadn't imagined her gasp of surrender or the way her hands had coiled around his neck, pulling her up towards him as if she'd wanted him as much as he had wanted her. She'd responded to his touch like an instrument, perfectly in tune, more sensual and desirable than any woman he'd ever known. Wildcat she might be, but something about her called out to him—not just to his body, but to a deeper, buried part, one he thought he'd sealed off for ever. Just thinking about her made his groin tighten and his blood heat anew.

He lunged forward, trying to banish the memory of full soft lips, battering his opponent's shield with a flurry of hard, punishing blows.

No, they weren't alike in appearance, Cille and Maren. So what was it about one that reminded him so vividly of the other? Half-buried memories tugged at the edge of his consciousness, tantalisingly close but elusive. There was something about Cille…something he couldn't quite put his finger on—a nagging intuition that something about her was…not *wrong*, exactly, but not right either. As if the real woman were hiding behind a mask. She was a phantom, in truth, impossible to pin down or decipher. Who *was* she? The woman who'd kissed him or the woman who'd pushed him away? What was she hiding?

He threw his body into one final ferocious attack, knocking his opponent to the ground with a heavy thud.

Aye, there was one clear way in which Cille resembled Maren in his mind. He'd never wanted a woman so badly.

He offered a conciliatory hand to his opponent before tossing his weapon aside and climbing alone to the crest of the hill.

If he were honest, a part of him had always known that the Maren he'd loved hadn't been real, that he'd simply been chasing an ideal, but he'd wanted her so badly that he'd ignored the warning signs. She was the first, the *only* woman he'd ever truly cared about. He'd given her his heart and she'd trampled all over it, made him into an exile…an outcast. All because she'd been fickle and selfish and deceitful.

Was Cille the same? His head resisted the idea. No, she wasn't fickle or selfish. She had stayed at Etton to care for her sister despite the risk to herself. She was loyal—a quality he wasn't accustomed to finding in a woman—and capable of love too. The kind of woman who would repay a man for loving her. Provided he wasn't part of the Conqueror's army.

Was she deceitful? He didn't want to think so, but she was hiding something from him—that was for certain. Was she lying as well? When they'd kissed he'd felt as though he were breaking through whatever mask she was wearing to reach the real woman beneath. But then her defences had gone up again, shutting him out as if he alone were responsible for the Conquest, as if she loathed him simply for being Norman.

Which he wasn't.

He ran a hand wearily over his brow. For the first time since Maren he found himself truly drawn to a woman, could imagine forging a life with her. But she wasn't for him. She wasn't his at all. And whatever mystery she was hiding wasn't his to unravel. It was de Quincey's.

His gut twisted with jealousy. He didn't want to think of her with another man, one who could touch and kiss her, lie with her. But she was on her way to marry de Quincey and he was simply the fool charged with delivering her. That was his duty. Anything more would dishonour them both.

He clenched his fists at his sides, determined to keep his mind, not to mention the rest of him, on his duty. He was finished playing with fire. If she were really like Maren then whatever he was feeling was just a passing infatuation. He was attracted to her—that was all. He couldn't be in love with a woman he'd known for less than a week, and the very last thing he needed was an emotional attachment—no matter how strongly she called to him or how badly he desired her. He wasn't about to risk his whole future for a woman again.

Besides, in another day and a half he'd be free

of her, his duty fulfilled, and enjoying whatever reward the King and FitzOsbern saw fit to bestow upon him. Whatever it was, he hoped it took him a long way from Redbourn.

He stood rooted to the spot, waiting for the thought to bring some relief.

So why did he want to turn and ride back the way they'd come?

The sun was barely skimming the horizon when they packed up the next morning. Aediva wriggled back into her clothes under cover of the blanket—not that anyone was looking. Svend's soldiers kept their eyes studiously averted, refusing to act like the Norman barbarians she took them for.

Only Renard rushed to greet her, his young face brimming with relief. 'My lady, I'm glad to see you well again!'

She returned his smile happily, taking his hands and pressing them in gratitude. 'And I have *you* to thank.'

'Me?' He looked at her blankly. 'I didn't do anything.'

'Didn't do anything? You saved my life—I'm indebted.'

'That wasn't me, my lady. I offered to help, but Sir Svend wouldn't let me. He never left you.'

'Svend nursed me?' Aediva's heart danced at

the news, though her conscience felt suddenly heavy.

She thought about Renard's words as they made their way through the lowlands. Svend had been worried about her, so worried that he'd barely left her side. Because she'd fallen ill under his protection? Because FitzOsbern would punish him for anything that happened to her? She frowned, trying to make sense of it. He might have taken care of her, but it didn't necessarily mean that he cared. Did it?

But it *did* mean she owed him another apology.

She perched silently in the saddle in front of him, forced to share his horse since her own had run wild, grasping the pommel tightly as she tried to keep their bodies apart. But it was no use. The terrain itself seemed to be conspiring against them. Every roll of the horse forced them closer together…every incline slid her further back into the curve of his chest and arms. She felt too hot, vividly aware that the base of her spine was pressed against his groin.

For the hundredth time that day she yanked herself upright, her muscles aching and sore from the effort of holding herself straight. Her back would be throbbing for days, not to mention her thighs. If she clenched them any tighter her spasming muscles might never be able to keep her upright again. Her body felt taut as a bowstring.

To distract herself, she looked around at the gently undulating flatlands. Where were they? They'd been riding all day, but she'd made the journey to Redbourn only a handful of times and her memory of the surrounding landscape was vague. How close were they? She could hardly ask without giving herself away. She was supposed to know this terrain better than anyone.

'We'll stay at Offley tonight.'

Svend's mouth was close to her ear and she jumped as his breath stirred her hair, sending alarming tingling sensations all through her body.

'Where?' The name sounded vaguely familiar, but she found it hard to concentrate.

'Offley. I'm sure the Thane will be pleased to welcome you.'

Offley! A surge of panic coursed through her. It was an outlying village of Redbourn. The Thane would have sworn allegiance to Leofric. Which meant…surely he'd have met Cille!

'Why not go on to Redbourn tonight?' She tried to keep the nervous tremor out of her voice.

'Tonight? It's still half a day's ride. Even at a gallop, I doubt we'd reach it by nightfall.'

'No, I suppose not…' She chewed her lip anxiously. If she insisted he'd only grow suspicious.

'You don't want to stop?' He sounded perplexed. 'Thane Harald was very concerned to hear that you'd left Redbourn.'

'How do you know?' She heard the shrill note

in her voice and adjusted her tone quickly. 'I mean…have you been there already?'

'We stopped on the way. They were very hospitable.'

'They're *helping* Normans?'

'They have more sense than others.'

She clenched her jaw at the insult. Now she *really* didn't want to visit Offley. On the other hand, if it had to be done it might prove a good test of her performance. If she could convince the Thane that she was Cille then she'd be less anxious about her reception at Redbourn. She only hoped that he didn't know her sister too well.

They continued in silence until the village appeared in the distance, faint tendrils of smoke coiling up from its rooftops like misty ribbons into the sky. Her heart stalled as they passed through the wooden gates, as if prison doors were already closing behind her. After all, if anyone recognised her they might as well be.

There were no signs of panic at their arrival. On the contrary, the villagers seemed completely unperturbed by the arrival of a group of armed enemy soldiers. Aediva looked around in confusion, surprised to find that Svend's men weren't the only Normans in the village. There were at least two dozen others, lounging in doorways or outside houses as if they'd already taken up residence. The only flurry of commotion came as they approached the Thane's hall, where a tall, gaunt figure accompanied by two women bustled out through the doorway, adopting expressions of dutiful acquiescence.

'Sir Svend!' The man bent almost double as Svend swung out of the saddle before him. 'I'm glad to see you again.'

'Thane Harald.' Svend bowed respectfully, before gesturing towards her. 'As you can see, we've been successful in our search. Your guess was correct. Lady Cille had returned to her home village of Etton. I'll be sure to tell the King of your help in finding her.'

The Thane's face lit up avariciously, though his tone remained humble. 'It was an honour to serve our new King. You remember my wife Merewyn and my daughter Joannka?'

Svend nodded politely, a faint look of surprise crossing his features before he turned to present her again—more emphatically this time. 'And this is Lady Cille, of course.'

'My lady.' The Thane turned towards her at last, his voice coldly polite. 'I'm glad to see you safe and well.'

Aediva bent her head in acknowledgement, hiding her eyes as well as her expression, seized by a feeling of instant dislike. Svend had never explained how he'd discovered Cille's whereabouts, but apparently Thane Harald was the man to blame. She wondered how close a friend he'd been to Leofric and how quickly he'd betrayed him.

Surreptitiously, she glanced at the two women. They were both strikingly attractive—two versions of the same flaxen-haired, doe-eyed model—and they both appeared to share the Thane's interest in Svend, gazing at him as if he were the King himself. It was an impression that he was doing nothing to dispel, bowing gallantly to kiss each of their hands in turn. She fought an unexpected pang of jealousy. He hadn't kissed *her* hand when they'd met—though under the circumstances she supposed that would have been difficult. Still, there was no need for him to be quite so charming now. Did he think to seduce *every* Saxon woman he came across?

'Danemark!'

She looked around as another man emerged from the hall, bellowing a greeting as if he intended the whole village to hear. From his appearance he was Norman, almost as tall as Svend but twice as wide, with dark, close-cropped hair and a sneering expression that made her immediately distrustful.

'You're back, then?' He gave Svend a look that implied he was less than thrilled by the fact.

'Armand.' Svend's face was equally unenthusiastic. 'I see you've made yourself at home. I thought you were ordered to Wales?'

'So I was.' The other man smirked and slid an

arm around Joannka's waist. 'But the Thane and his family have been *so* welcoming. I thought I'd stay a while and enjoy the scenery.'

'Scenery?'

'Whatever you call it.' He leered unpleasantly. 'You needn't look so outraged, Danemark. There's plenty to go round. I see you've found your own trophy.'

Aediva bristled angrily. How dared he talk about Saxon women like that? If she were Joannka she'd have slapped him at least. Not that the Thane's daughter seemed to mind. On the contrary, she appeared to be enjoying the attention, sliding herself up against Armand even as she made eyes at Svend.

This new man was a brute—a vulgar, ill-bred swine, and the very epitome of everything she'd imagined about Normans. If *he'd* come to Etton… She frowned, dreading to think what might have happened. What would *he* have done if she'd held a knife to *his* throat? Would *he* have forgiven her? Somehow she doubted it. Perhaps she'd been lucky that Svend had come after all.

'This is the Lady Cille.' Svend sounded terse.

'De Quincey's bride?' Armand regarded her with fresh interest. 'Not what I expected, but not bad either.' He grinned suddenly. 'Pity for you, though. De Quincey doesn't like sharing. You'll be lonely tonight.'

She saw Svend's fists tighten and she slid off

the saddle abruptly, hardly knowing what she intended, but needing to break the tension somehow. Clearly there was no love lost between Svend and Armand, but his men outnumbered them two to one. Besides, this was a Saxon village. If there was going to be bloodshed she didn't want innocent bystanders to get hurt.

'Ow!' She yelped as her strained back and legs jarred painfully on the hard ground. She'd forgotten exactly how long she'd been sitting, but now she felt as though she'd aged ten years in one afternoon.

'Lady Cille?' Svend was beside her at once, taking hold of her elbow to steady her.

She licked her lips, tasting blood. 'I'm all right...'

'Perhaps you'd like to rest?' Thane Harald looked at her sourly. 'If you'll honour us by accepting our hospitality tonight, Sir Svend?'

'If it pleases Lady Cille, we'd be only too glad to accept.'

Aediva blinked in surprise. Beneath his courtier's tone, Svend's words were a clear reproof. The Thane and his family were looking at her now with varying expressions of outrage.

'I'd be delighted.' She gave her brightest, most insincere smile and saw Svend's lips twitch upwards. 'Normans have such excellent manners—don't you agree, Thane Harald?'

She didn't wait for a response, sweeping into

the hall with her shoulders back and her head held high.

Revenge left a bittersweet aftertaste. She had a feeling it was going to be a long night.

Chapter Eight

Aediva drained her third cup of mead and stared moodily into the hearth, watching as tendrils of smoke twisted up to the rafters and out through the chimney.

She needn't have worried about being recognised. The Thane and his family had eyes only for Svend. She might have been invisible for all the notice they were taking of her. If she hadn't felt so relieved, she might have been offended for Cille. Clearly the Thane had no problem with Normans. On the contrary, from the way his gaze was sliding speculatively back and forth between the two knights and Joannka it seemed he was already planning his own Saxon-Norman alliance.

Against her will, she found her gaze drifting back towards them. Thane Harald was leaning so close to Svend it was a wonder he didn't simply climb into his lap, while Joannka seemed to have abandoned Armand and was batting her eyelashes at Svend so furiously she seemed in danger of blinding herself. Not that Svend was doing anything to repel her. Whatever she was simpering about was clearly engrossing. He was even *smiling*!

She stood up, unable to watch any longer as Joannka tossed her head provocatively, draping a blonde tendril over Svend's arm.

'Forgive me, Thane Harald, but I have a headache.' Somehow she doubted he cared. 'I'd like some air.'

'Of course.' The Thane threw her a cursory glance.

'I won't be long.'

She stepped outside with relief, tipping her head back to inhale the fresh evening air. The sky was darkening fast, revealing a spattering of stars on a backdrop of blue-grey. She stared up at them thoughtfully. They were the same stars she could see from Etton, and yet everything else in her world seemed to have been turned upside down. She hardly knew who she was any more. She felt…*lost*. Protecting Cille was the only thing left to hold on to—the one thing that still made sense.

'May I join you?'

She didn't need to look to know it was Svend. No one else could have approached her so soundlessly. No one else could have made her skin tingle just by standing beside her.

She started to turn and then stiffened, remembering the way he'd smiled at Joannka.

'There's no need to accompany me.'

'FitzOsbern might think otherwise.'

He offered an arm and she glanced at it dubiously. She'd spent all day trying to avoid physical contact with him, and had the aching limbs to prove it. She didn't want to fail now.

'I won't try to escape.'

'I'm glad to hear it.'

'I'm perfectly capable of taking a walk by myself.'

'Even after three cups of mead?'

She looked up sharply, but his expression was guarded. How did he know she'd had three cupfuls? She hadn't thought he'd been paying her any attention at all.

'I wouldn't want you to fall, my lady.'

She gave a snort of derision. 'I doubt Thane Harald would care.'

'Perhaps not. He's not as clever as he thinks.'

'What do you mean?'

'Antagonising the soon-to-be wife of his future liege lord... He has a lot to learn about diplomacy. But it's still my duty to protect you.'

She gave a wry smile, the three cupfuls of mead starting to take effect. 'I thought you were my captor?'

'That too.'

'And what makes you think I need protecting?

Just because I charged into a skirmish, let my horse bolt and caught a fever?'

He was silent for a moment, as if weighing his words with care. 'There is that. And also because you remind me of someone.'

'Oh?' She felt taken aback. 'Who?'

'Someone I knew a long time ago.'

'A woman?'

'Yes.'

A woman you cared for? The question sprang to her mind unbidden but she pushed it away. She couldn't ask him *that*.

'A good woman?'

'No.'

'No?' Her face fell abruptly, the effects of the mead evaporating in an instant.

He shrugged, though his shoulders were tense. 'Her name was Maren. She was a girl from my village in Danemark. I thought I loved her, but… Suffice to say she didn't love me.'

Aediva stared at him, speechless. He was comparing her to a woman he'd loved! Her heart soared and then plummeted again. No, he'd only thought that he loved her. What did *that* mean? As bad as it sounded, she had to know.

'What happened?'

He hesitated for so long that she thought he wasn't going to answer. Then he sighed, meeting her eyes with a look of grim intensity.

'She liked pretty things…stole a necklace from the local manor. When the theft was discovered she came to me, begging for help.'

'You took the blame?'

'Yes.' He looked faintly surprised. 'She said that she loved me, that she'd be true to me if I took her punishment. I was young and naive enough to believe her. She found someone else instead.'

'She betrayed you?'

He nodded. 'I was outlawed, sent into exile—away from my home, my family, everything I loved. Eventually I found myself in Normandy.'

'So you're an outlaw?' She hardly dared say it aloud. The very word was a terrible one, conjuring up images of wild, lawless men. And he was one of them. If it hadn't come from his own mouth she would never have believed it. The admission made him seem stronger somehow, even more honourable. 'Does the King know?'

'*Only* the King knows. And you.'

'Oh.' She felt a stab of conscience. 'So…she broke your heart?'

'I thought so at first, but the woman I loved wasn't real. I thought I could trust her, but she was only pretending to be someone she wasn't.'

'And I remind you of her?'

There was a long silence, broken only by the frantic pounding of her heartbeat. *She was only pretending to be someone she wasn't.* The words struck like a blow to her heart. He'd lost everything because a woman had deceived him. And *she* reminded him of her! Was he trying to tell her something? That he knew she was deceiving him too, pretending to be someone else? Could he see the guilt in her face? No, it was worse—far worse. He was confiding in her, taking her into his trust. A trust that she didn't deserve.

Suddenly she wished there were a pit she could jump into.

'Cille.' He spoke at last, his expression softening. 'You remind me of her…but not like that.'

'How, then?' Her voice was the faintest hint of a whisper.

'Some women are…dangerous.'

'I'm *dangerous*?' She stared at him, uncomprehending, as he took a step closer towards her.

'To me.'

Aediva caught her breath, elation vying with despair. She was dangerous to him. Dangerous because he wanted her. His stern features were glowing with emotion in the moonlight, with desire, tenderness, with something like love. Something that surely couldn't be love but that made her heart soar.

But she was as bad as Maren. She'd been deceiving him from the start, pretending to be someone she wasn't. And if he ever found out he'd never look at her in the same way again.

'You shouldn't be here.' She averted her face quickly. 'You should go back to your friends.'

'Friends?' He sounded bemused. 'How bad must my *enemies* be?'

'You seemed to be enjoying their company.'

'It doesn't pay to alienate anyone.' His lips curled upwards. 'Interesting that they're Saxon, though—Armand excepted.'

'What do you mean?'

'It's just interesting that they're Saxon and you don't like them. I thought that all Saxons were on your side?'

She narrowed her eyes suspiciously. Was that why he'd been so gallant and attentive? To prove a point?

He smiled. 'Sadly, they overestimate my influence at court. I suspect their friendship might cool when they find out.'

'Surely a knight has *some* influence?'

'A small shred, maybe, but no lands and no money—not yet.'

'Poor Joannka.'

'Joannka?' He looked at her askance. '*That* kind of woman can't be happy unless every man in the room is looking at her. Don't tell me you're jealous?'

'Don't flatter yourself. I just thought Saxon women had better taste.'

'Then perhaps she's ill too.'

Aediva felt her heart skip a beat. Since she'd

woken up from her fever neither of them had made any mention of their kiss. She'd almost come to think it had been part of her illness, that she'd simply imagined it. But what else could his words mean?

'Now, shall we walk more than five paces from the door?' Svend leaned towards her, his voice deepening huskily. 'Before my *friends* decide to follow us? Or is my company really so onerous?'

She hesitated, looking around as if searching for an excuse in the darkness, guilt and excitement blending together in a heady combination. If their kiss had happened, *really* happened, then the last thing she should do was take a moonlit stroll with him. After everything he'd just told her she ought to turn and run. But suddenly she felt as though nothing on earth could make her.

Instead she placed a hand on his forearm, trying and failing to feel only the cloth and not the muscles beneath as they meandered slowly towards the edge of the village.

Desperately she tried to arrange her thoughts into some kind of order, but now she had space to think and darkness to cloak her emotions she found herself utterly incapable of doing so. His presence beside her made it impossible to think about anything clearly. All her being seemed focussed on the warm, solid pressure of his arm against hers.

She cleared her throat, trying to distract herself. 'Renard said it was you who nursed me through the fever.'

'Did he?'

'Why didn't you tell me?'

He ignored the question. 'And how do you feel, after all my hard work?'

'What do you mean?' She glanced at him warily. He'd sounded faintly amused.

'I mean how do you feel after the ride today? I've never seen anyone look more uncomfortable on a horse.'

She scowled, glad of the darkness concealing her crimson cheeks. How did he know how she felt? Did he notice *everything*?

'I told you, I'm just a little stiff.'

They came to a halt at the top of the village, looking down over the thatched roofs to the moonlit valley below. To the east she could see the boggy morass of the Fens, to the north the hills they'd just crossed. She peered into the distance towards Etton, far over the horizon now. It was a long and more dangerous road than she'd given it credit for—a road that Cille had travelled alone just five months before.

Until now she hadn't truly appreciated the risks her sister had taken. Cille had known she was carrying a baby, so why had she made such an arduous journey alone? She'd said that she'd wanted to come home, but that answer seemed inadequate now, the danger too great. For the first time Aediva wished that she'd asked more questions, been more persistent in getting answers. But Cille had been reluctant to talk about anything, retreating inside herself, silently mourning the loss of their father, of Leofric…

A memory stirred at the back of her mind. Cille *had* wanted to tell her something. Just before she left. Something about the baby…

'It'll take her a while to recover.' Svend's gaze followed hers, and his voice was low and reassuring. 'The babe's strong and healthy. And Henri won't leave until he's sure they're both out of danger.'

'He knows about babies?' She looked up dubiously, an image of the battle-scarred soldier popping into her mind.

'I doubt that.' Svend's teeth flashed white in the darkness. 'But he'll take care of them. Don't worry.'

'I know.' She paused for the space of a heartbeat. 'I trust you.'

'Trust a *Norman*?'

'You're not Norman.'

'Ah.' He nodded thoughtfully. 'That must be it.'

For a moment neither of them spoke, as if the atmosphere were already too heavy for words. Why had she said that? The mead was clearly affecting her senses, pushing Cille and Maren and all the reasons why she shouldn't be alone with him to the back of her mind. She shifted uncomfortably, wincing as a taut muscle spasmed in her back.

'Just a little stiff…?'

She set her teeth against the pain. 'I'm fine.'

He sighed and pulled her towards him suddenly, one hand grasping her waist while the other slid up and down her spine, teasing the sore muscles.

She made a strangled sound in the back of her throat, the shock of his touch coursing through her body like lightning through her veins. What was he doing?

'Relax.'

It was a command, not a request. Strong fingers stroked the curve of her back, tracing circular patterns around the knotted muscles, kneading them in a firm, smooth rhythm. She bit her tongue, holding back a groan of pleasure as she swayed towards him, lulled into submission. This was madness. Wrong—definitely wrong. But it felt too good to stop…too good to do anything but surrender.

'Better?' His fingers pressed deeper and harder, forcing the tension out of her body.

'A…a little.' She sighed, tipping her head back so that her spine arched beneath his touch.

'Just a little?' His voice was gently teasing.

She was almost panting now, and her head was

screaming a warning so loudly she couldn't hear herself think. Not that she wanted to. Not when his touch was sending toe-curling sensations all through her body, making every fibre of her being ache and shudder with longing.

Slowly his hands slid up and around to cup her breasts, his fingers spreading out to stroke the nipples. They hardened at once, stiffening beneath the fabric of her tunic as if they were straining to reach him.

'And this?' His lips skimmed the side of her throat.

'Much...better...'

She sagged against him, engulfed by the feeling of his strong body moulded to hers. How could two hands—hands that had held her imprisoned, hands that she'd pushed away in anger—now be controlling her so effortlessly? Her whole body throbbed with pleasure.

He pulled her round gently, his lips drifting across the line of her jaw towards the neck of her gown, his teeth grasping the lacings and pulling them loose until she gasped aloud, feeling the whisper of air on her skin.

She murmured his name, unable to bear the tension any longer, feeling a stirring sensation deep in her stomach. It was a warm glow and a yearning at the same time...an intense pleasure and a tantalising pain all mixed into one. If she didn't kiss him now she would scream. She grasped his head and pulled it down to hers, lips seeking his hungrily.

This kiss was different—not slow or tender, but hungry and forceful…a kiss meant to last. His tongue traced the line of her lips and she opened them eagerly, letting him inside and entwining her own tongue with his, searching, questing, losing herself in the touch and taste of him.

They came apart at last and she clung to his shoulders, dazed. Her heart was beating so fast she felt dizzy. She'd never imagined that a kiss could be so all-consuming. If the Thane and his family had stood watching she doubted she would have noticed. How long had it been? Time seemed to have stopped. It felt like hours and yet not long enough.

'I've wanted to do that from the first moment I saw you.' Svend's breathing was as unsteady as hers.

She started to smile and then stopped. 'You kissed me after the ambush! Had you forgotten that?'

'How could I forget? But that was different. You caught me off guard.'

'I caught *you* off guard?'

He grinned. 'I knew I wanted to kiss you, I just didn't realise how much. This time I was better prepared.'

She smiled, appeased, swaying back into his arms as his lips brushed her neck.

'I never knew it could be like this.'

'What's that?' His teeth tugged gently at her earlobe.

'Like this.' She stretched her body like a cat, wanting to feel every inch of him. 'I never imagined it could feel so wonderful.'

His lips stilled against her ear, his grip on her waist tightening imperceptibly. 'Not even with your husband?'

She froze in his arms, brought down to earth with a jolt. In that moment she'd forgotten that she was supposed to be Cille—forgotten everything but him and the feelings he aroused in her.

'Cille?'

'It wasn't… That is… It's different.'

Desperately she tried to remember what she'd said. Had she revealed too much? Did he suspect her?

'You didn't feel the same way?'

'No.' She tried to pull away, but his arms held her tight.

'And now?'

His voice was insistent, demanding, as if her answer were important to him.

How *did* she feel? She didn't know what to say. He didn't suspect her. He really wanted to know—as if he truly cared about her answer, as if he wanted her to care too. She felt a wholly inappropriate desire to laugh. She felt like a traitor and a slave at the same time…as if she were standing on the very brink of a precipice, peering over the edge, unable to take a step backwards and save herself.

She opened her mouth, the words on the very tip of her tongue. She wanted to tell him the truth. That she'd never felt this way about anyone, had never imagined such a feeling was even possible, that she wanted him—a Norman—more than any Saxon she'd ever known! But how could she tell him any of it without admitting who she really was? Without failing Cille?

She couldn't.

'Let me go!'

She wrenched herself out of his arms, stumbling away into the darkness. How could her feelings for him have altered so much in a few days? Less than a week ago she'd tried to stab him, and now… Now she was afraid of hurting him as Maren had. Was this love? Did she *love* her enemy? What kind of Saxon did that make her? What kind of sister and daughter? All she knew was that she had to get away from him—away from the temptation of his arms. The longer she stayed, the more likely it was that she'd give herself away.

'Cille…' He sounded contrite. 'I shouldn't have asked. Your husband and your past are none of my business.'

She stared at him helplessly. If she went back to him now she'd be lost. She rocked on her heels, fighting the urge to run into his arms and tell him everything.

'We should go back. They'll be wondering where we are.'

'Cille…' He held out a hand to her.

'No!' Her voice was harsher than she'd intended and his hand fell at once.

'As you wish.'

She walked silently ahead of him, her emotions in disarray, desperate to get away and yet dreading the moment of parting. She couldn't tell him who she really was, but she didn't want it to end like this.

They reached the hall at last and she turned to face him.

'When we reach Redbourn will I see you again?'

His face was impassive. 'That depends on FitzOsbern. He may have another commission for me.'

'Oh.'

Her heart felt like a stone in her chest. Even if she saw Svend again, this was probably the last time they'd be alone together.

'Then this is goodbye, Svend du Danemark. I won't forget you.'

He nodded sternly. 'Goodbye, Lady Cille.'

She turned away, but his voice arrested her.

'Cille, if there were another way…'

She attempted a smile but failed, moving away

before she could change her mind. If there were another way, she thought miserably, one of them would already have found it.

Chapter Nine

'I'm sorry you can't stay any longer.' Thane Harald laid a restraining hand on Talbot's bridle. 'You'll be sure to tell the King of my service?'

Svend nodded tersely. The Thane's obsequious manner had ceased to be entertaining and was starting to grate heavily on his nerves. If the man didn't let go of his horse in a moment he'd wrench his whole damn arm off.

'We're grateful for your hospitality, Thane.'

He pulled sharply on the bridle, hardly bothering to hide his contempt. The old hypocrite had made endless declarations of loyalty to the King, though he'd failed even to offer the loan of a horse.

As a result, he and Cille were still sharing a mount—her small body was still perched in front of him as they rode out of Offley and into open countryside. It was slow torture, being so close and yet unable to touch her the way he'd touched her last night, the way he wanted to again…

Silently, he studied the base of her neck. It was smooth and swanlike, with her long hair swept carelessly over one shoulder in a loose braid. Every time the horse swayed he found himself tempted to reach down and bury his face there. And if she pressed any further back against him she'd know how badly he wanted to.

Neither of them had spoken a word to the other all morning. What could they say? Nothing that would ease the tension between them. Nothing that would take back what had happened.

He should have known better—*had* known better—but he hadn't been able to resist following her out into the night. Clearly she wasn't the only one who'd drunk too much mead. That and the moonlight had made him reckless, made him say and do things he should never even have thought about.

He'd told her about his past. Why? Because she reminded him of Maren? No, it was more than that. He was as powerfully attracted to her as he'd been to Maren, but the feelings *she* aroused in him were completely different.

Over the past few days he'd found himself thinking of his lost home more and more, her presence evoking half-forgotten feelings of warmth, affection, loyalty…belonging. Since he'd met her he'd started looking at the land in a new light too, wishing it were possible to start again, to build a new home, to belong somewhere, with someone. *With her.*

For the first time in ten years he'd wanted to tell someone about his past, wanted to share something of himself and not just his sword arm. He'd told her the truth, the whole truth, and her reaction had taken him completely by surprise. In his experience most people despised outlaws, whether they were guilty of their crimes or not, but she hadn't condemned him—hadn't questioned his innocence even for a moment. She'd actually seemed angry *for* him, not towards him, and there had been something else too—some emotion he couldn't quite put his finger on… something like guilt.

But what did she have to feel guilty about? More likely she'd been offended that he'd compared her to Maren, making it sound as if he didn't trust her either.

Did he trust her?

The thought gave him pause. She was still hiding something from him. Somehow he'd hoped that by telling her about Maren she might return the favour, but if anything she'd pulled even further away. She'd surrendered to his kisses eagerly enough, but when he'd asked about her husband she'd actually looked frightened, recoiling as if his very touch had scalded. Clearly she still thought of him as her enemy, still retreated into silence when he demanded answers.

That had been a mistake. He shouldn't have pushed her to answer. But when she'd said she hadn't felt the same way with her husband he hadn't been able to stop himself—had hoped for one brief, thrilling moment that there was more than just physical attraction between them, that she might care for him too.

But it was hopeless.

If there were another way…

There wasn't. He'd lain awake most of the night, faced with a choice that was none at all. If he cared for her, he had to let her go. As a low-born knight he couldn't challenge the Baron, but he could hardly run away with her either. He was a landless warrior, reliant upon the King's good-will, with nothing of value beside a skilled sword arm. Nothing to offer any woman—especially one used to a fine hall and a wealthy husband—and he wouldn't wish the life of an exile on anyone, wouldn't expose her to that kind of danger. She'd be better off with de Quincey.

At least he had the comfort of knowing she'd be well treated. The Baron was an honourable man, and would take good care of her. Though if he ever found out what had happened between them he'd have his guts on a spike. Svend shrugged the thought aside. Whatever punishment the Baron might devise paled beside the thought of her marrying him. That was punishment enough.

Talbot shied slightly and he reached forward, adjusting the bridle. For a heart-stopping moment his hand brushed her wrist and he found himself wanting to grasp it, to hold tight and never let go. But he had to let go. In a few hours he had to bid her goodbye.

When had she stopped being his prisoner? he wondered. And when had he become hers?

They joined the approach road to Redbourn around noon. Aediva recognised their surroundings now—had ridden this way in the past with Cille. They were on the last leg of their journey… would be there that afternoon. Soon Svend would leave her behind, riding out of her life possibly for ever.

The thought of parting from him made her feel sick to her stomach, undermining all her resolve of the previous night. In the cold light of day the last thing she wanted was to let him go. Not now—not when she'd only just realised how much she cared.

She half turned her head, trying to fix an image of him in her mind. It wasn't so much to ask, surely? Just a few more hours in his company? Time to treasure and savour once they were parted? It wouldn't hurt Cille. If anything, it would gain her more time. Where was the harm?

She racked her brains, trying to think of a means of stalling. She couldn't ask him outright. If he refused she'd feel humiliated. Could she pretend to be ill again? No, she had the feeling he'd see through any pretence. How else could she persuade him?

Renard cantered alongside and she could have kissed him in gratitude.

'The men want to know if they can remove their chainmail in this heat, sir. 'Tis not far now to Redbourn.'

Svend scanned the vale, as if scouring every tree and shrub for a trap. 'We're close enough, I suppose. I doubt there'll be rebels this far south.'

'Perhaps your men would like to bathe?' She asked the question casually, testing his reaction.

'Bathe? I don't see a river.'

'See those two streams?' She pointed up the valley triumphantly. 'They run into that wood. There's an old dam where the water pools into a lake. It's stony, but safe.'

Svend hesitated for a moment, before shaking his head. 'We can't keep FitzOsbern waiting any longer. He'll be impatient enough.'

'But this way you'll arrive fresh.' She batted her eyelashes, mimicking Joannka.

'Do we smell so bad?'

His lips twitched and she felt a frisson of excitement. She'd never been able to flirt with Edmund, but somehow it felt natural with Svend—enjoyable, even. He didn't make her feel tense and uncomfortable. He made her feel as no man ever had before…as if her body finally made sense.

She cupped a hand to her mouth, testing the limits of her power as she stretched up to whisper in his ear, gesturing towards Renard. 'Don't tell him how bad he smells!'

Svend heaved on his reins, changing direction so abruptly that she had to grab the sleeve of his tunic to steady herself.

'One hour.' His voice sounded husky.

She nodded happily, still grasping his sleeve as they entered the wood.

His soldiers were charging towards the lake in a stampede of hooves and catcalls, stripping off their armour and tunics barely before they'd leapt from their horses, splashing into the glassy water like a herd of thirsty cattle.

Aediva averted her face, blushing furiously. The prospect of quite so many naked Normans had never occurred to her. She'd been thinking of only one.

'I don't want anyone getting cramp!' Svend shouted above the clamour. 'Renard, keep an eye on them! Bertrand, take lookout!'

He dismounted and took hold of the destrier's reins, leading him away from the uproar to the furthest end of the lake, where the trees were thickest, blocking out the sounds of shouts and splashing.

The pool here formed an almost perfect oval, its water clear and inviting.

'You'll have to excuse my men,' he commented drily, reaching up to help her dismount. 'They're not accustomed to travelling with ladies.'

'I noticed.'

She slid into his arms, her cheeks still red with embarrassment. His gambeson gaped open at the neck and her gaze fell upon a jagged scar between his chest and his shoulder. She hadn't noticed it before, but the collarbone protruded outwards beneath, as if it had been broken and reset badly. She stared at it distractedly. He seemed vulnerable suddenly, less like a Norman and more like any other man.

'What's this?' Without thinking, she pushed the leather aside, tracing the line of the scar with her fingertips.

'An old injury.'

'What happened?' Her fingers stroked the length of the bone. She was surprised by the soft texture of his skin. She would have expected a warrior to be rough and callused, but he felt silky smooth.

'I fell out of a hayloft when I was ten.'

'That's not very heroic. You should say it's a battle scar at least.'

His hands were still clasping her waist, but she didn't pull away. No one could see them. They were surrounded by trees, and his destrier made a surprisingly effective screen. Slowly her fingers traced their way back to the point of the bone. It must have hurt when it had happened. Somehow she wanted to make it better. Instinctively she leaned forward, pressing her lips against the scar.

'Cille...'

He groaned and she jerked her head back guiltily.

'Did I hurt you?'

His eyes fell on hers with a look that was part desire, part amusement. His eyes were so clearly, blindingly blue that they seemed to mirror the lake beside them. Her stomach lurched, filled with a thousand fluttering butterflies. No, she hadn't *hurt* him. She was close enough to feel the effect of her kiss pressing forcefully between them.

Svend cleared his throat and moved away, looking towards the lake as if nothing had happened. 'Do you want to swim?'

'I...yes...perhaps.' She forced herself to sound light-hearted, as if she *hadn't* just noticed the evidence of his desire pushing between her legs. 'There's a small pool below. No one will see.'

She walked away quickly, following the path that led to the dam, peeking back over her shoulder just in time to see Svend's feet vanish beneath the surface of the water. She stared at the ripples, then saw him emerge ten feet further out, swimming away from her with long, practised strokes.

Could she tell him the truth?

She pushed the thought away, concentrating instead on her footing as she climbed down the side of the dam. The water levels were high where the edge dropped away suddenly, pouring over the rock in a smooth cascade into the smaller pool below.

She clambered down carefully, sighing with relief as she dropped out of sight of the others. It felt good to be alone, to be herself again however briefly. She felt as if she'd been holding her breath for days.

Could she tell him who she really was?

No! She kicked off her shoes and stepped into the shallow water. It tickled her feet, luxuriously cool and so crystal-clear she could see the sandy floor beneath. Hoisting her dress around her knees, she wandered further in, letting the water lap around her thighs. After the heat of the day the ripples felt like gentle caresses.

With a quick glance around, she pulled her dress over her shoulders, letting her body slide under the water. Then she lay back, listening to the bubble of water in her ears, trying to shut out her thoughts along with her senses. A willow was draped over the edge of the pool, its wispy tendrils swaying gently in the current, and a robin hopped along one of the branches, bobbing its head as if studying her. She smiled. Saxon or Norman, some things didn't change. If only she could be as free.

Could she tell him the truth?

She kicked her feet in frustration. Had the fever addled her brain? Even if she *could* trust him, how could she tell him now, after what he'd said about Maren?

On the other hand, how could she not? He wasn't Edmund. After everything he'd done for her, didn't she owe him the truth? He'd shown he could be trusted. If she kept on deceiving him then she *was* truly no better than Maren. And at least if she told him the truth herself there was a chance he might forgive her. Whereas if he found out on his own…

There was a flicker of movement behind her and she dipped quickly back under the water, clasping her arms over her breasts as she spun around.

Then she saw him. He'd finished swimming and was already half-dressed, walking barefoot in just a pair of hose along the top of the waterfall, his broad shoulders tapering into a well-defined waist, still streaming with water. The muscles of his toned chest rippled as he walked, so solid that they seemed to be sculpted from wood.

She stared, speechless. She'd seen men without shirts before, villagers working in the fields, but none who had looked like this. She doubted that one man in a thousand could look so effortlessly intimidating, so powerful, and yet in such complete control of his body.

He hadn't seen her. He seemed to be examining the structure of the dam. If she didn't move he would pass her by completely.

If she didn't move.

She swept her arms wide, letting the ripples spiral outwards, drawing his gaze towards her like a siren.

Could she tell him the truth? Would he forgive her? Would he help her?

Either way, and no matter what he might think of her afterwards, she owed him the truth.

His gaze locked with hers and her whole body clenched. What was he thinking? He wasn't walking away, but he wasn't moving either. Instead his expression seemed to be at war with itself—hungry eyes vying with a stubborn-set jaw. Had she shocked him? The temptation to do so again was overwhelming.

She lay back, kicking her legs up as she dived in a loop, emerging just below him like a mermaid tempting him into the water. Then she stood up, slowly and deliberately, keeping her arms at her sides until she stood naked, waist-deep in the pool, the water lapping just below her belly.

It wasn't too late. If he came to her now then she'd tell him everything. And he'd help her—she was sure of it. He would find a way to protect Cille if anyone could. Maybe he could think of a better plan too—one that didn't involve deceiving FitzOsbern. Maybe they could go back to Etton and work it out together.

She held her breath. If he came to her now she'd hand herself over to a Norman.

Svend stood on the side of the dam, keeping every part of himself immobile through sheer force of will.

What the hell had he been thinking, bringing her here? Had he lost his mind? They should be at Redbourn by now. He should be leaving her with her new husband—not thinking about jumping into the water beside her. It was a matter of honour. He was honour-bound to deliver her safely to FitzOsbern, and he wasn't in the habit of seducing other men's brides. No matter how badly he wanted to. No matter that she'd kissed him first…

What had she said? *'No one will see.'*

When she'd left, he'd torn off his clothes and hurled himself into the water, letting the cold restore his sense of clarity, his temperature still soaring from the memory of her touch on his skin. When she'd pressed her lips to his scar he'd wanted to throw her to the ground and take her right then. Strange how sometimes she seemed more like an innocent maid than a grieving widow. Surely a woman who'd been married five years would know the effect her touch might have on a man? But she'd seemed genuinely shocked by his arousal.

He'd still been grappling with the contradiction when he'd seen her just now. Now he kept his gaze fixed firmly on hers, trying to concentrate on what his mind was telling him and not other parts of his body.

Damn it all—how much self-control was a man supposed to have?

The thunder of hooves took them both by surprise.

Svend spun around instantly, searching for his sword on the lakeside, mentally calculating the time it would take him to reach it. *Too long.*

He muttered a volley of colourful oaths. Normally he prided himself on never being caught unprepared or off guard—but then he'd never normally have brought his men here, never let his warrior instincts become sluggish and distracted.

There was nothing *normal* about the effect she had on him. He was still burning with desire for her, and he didn't know whether he felt more frustrated by that fact or the timing of this attack.

He crouched down, muscles coiling. If he could reach the trees without being seen he would be able to grab his sword and come up behind them—whoever they were. They might have the advantage, but he wouldn't make the fight easy.

Just as soon as he knew she was safe.

'What's happening?'

Her voice was close to his ear and he started, surprised to find her peering over the top of the dam beside him. Somehow she'd found a foothold and clambered up. Instinctively, he glanced downwards, but her long tresses were shielding her body from view.

'Do you know the way to Redbourn from here?'

'Yes, but…'

'Stay hidden. If I don't come back, wait until dark and then go.'

He started towards the shore and then stopped abruptly, bursting into relieved laughter. A Norman patrol was pushing its way through the rim of trees, their white tunics and pointed helms shining with light reflected off the water.

'Svend? What is it?'

She was staring at him as if he'd suddenly sprouted two heads, and he fought the temptation to jump down and gather her in his arms. How long before somebody found them? Not long enough for what he wanted to do.

'Nothing to fear.' He raised a hand, waving a greeting to the knight in front. 'Just a friend.'

He looked down again, but she'd already slid off the rock and ducked back under the water. Tendrils of hair spread around her like an ink stain. As he watched the ripples gradually stilled, revealing the shimmery outline of her body beneath.

He dragged his gaze away. 'We should go.'

'I'll follow.' She looked shy suddenly. Even her shoulders seemed to be blushing.

'There might be more soldiers on the way.'

'I won't be long. Besides, if they're Norman I should be safe, shouldn't I?'

Her tone challenged him to deny it and he nodded reluctantly, pulling his tunic over his head as he collected Talbot and made his way back around the edge of the lake, walking fast to quell his desire.

At least Hugh was a friend—one of the few knights who judged a man on ability rather than birth—and he knew how to keep a secret. Under the circumstances, it might have been a lot worse. If de Quincey had found them, for instance…

'Hugh!' He hailed a man with cropped chestnut hair and a broad, friendly face.

'Danemark? You're the last person I expected to find here! Are you lost?'

Svend gave a disarming smile before jabbing the other man in the ribs, dropping him heavily to the ground.

'You have either the best or the worst timing, my friend.'

'That's the thanks I get for finding you?' Hugh clutched his stomach, winded. 'You know Fitz-Osbern doesn't like waiting. Where have you been?'

Svend proffered a hand. 'There were…obstacles. Finding Etton was more of a challenge than we anticipated.'

'But you found it?'

'Eventually.'

'And...?' Hugh's face lit up inquisitively. 'What's she like, de Quincey's new bride?'

'She's not an ogre.'

'Dark or fair?'

'Dark.'

Brown hair kissed by the sun. Eyes like the purest honey.

Hugh smirked. 'He likes them dark. Is she pretty?'

More than words can describe.

'Pretty enough.'

'Is that it? I'll never understand you, my friend. You talk more about horses than women.'

'She's a woman—the same as any other.'

Hugh heaved a sigh. 'Truly, I wouldn't be as cynical as you for the world! My heart is open to all. Whoever broke yours has a lot to answer for.'

Svend looked up sharply and Hugh practically whooped with delight. 'I'm right, aren't I? Somebody *did* break your heart! I knew it! What was her name? Beatrice, Mathilde, Alice—?'

'Maren.' Svend cut him off sharply. 'And if you ever mention her again I'll personally cut your tongue out.'

'Maren...' Hugh blew air from between his teeth. 'And I thought your defences were unassailable. I'd like to meet the woman who could get past them. Wait!' He gave a low whistle. 'Is *that* de Quincey's bride?'

Svend turned his head, feeling his chest tighten

at the sight of a small figure on the shoreline, the long coils of her damp hair swinging around her hips as she seemed to float rather than walk towards them.

It was no easy thing to march through a garrison of enemy soldiers but she did it, as brave as any warrior he'd ever known. Amidst the soldiers she looked even more tiny, even more beautiful—a Saxon wildcat with sheathed claws. How could he ever bear to let her go?

'"Pretty enough"?' Hugh's tone was sceptical. 'Are you *blind*?'

Aediva followed the curve of the lake, doing her best to look like the virtuous, albeit slightly bedraggled widow of an ealdorman.

Heads swivelled as she passed by. The new Norman soldiers were regarding her with undisguised curiosity. She ignored them, searching for Svend in the sea of new faces, half eager, half afraid to find him. After what had just happened at the waterfall she needed to see him again, needed to judge his reaction. What did he think of her? What did she think of herself?

Everything had happened so suddenly, so unexpectedly, that already it seemed unreal—like a dream. Had she really bared herself to him? Had he made a movement towards her or had she simply imagined it? She tried to remember, but the sudden jolt of reality had scattered her thoughts.

The Norman patrol had arrived and the moment had gone, leaving her more breathless and confused than ever.

She found his face at last and raised her eyes nervously, her step faltering as she saw the raw desire in his. He was watching her hungrily, as if he wanted to carry her back to the waterfall right there and then. It made her stomach flip and her breathing quicken all over again.

Quickly she turned her attention to his companion. His gaze was openly appraising, though his curiosity was quickly concealed behind a courtly flourish. If he felt any surprise at her dishevelled appearance he gave no sign of it, bowing low as she finally stopped in front of them.

'You must be Lady Cille. It's an honour to meet you at last. I am Sir Hugh Rolande.'

He spoke slowly, as if he didn't expect her to speak French, and she dipped into an elaborate curtsy, responding fluently. 'The honour is all mine, Sir Hugh.'

His eyebrows shot up, though his answering smile appeared genuine. 'I'm truly delighted to meet you. And I can see why it's taken my friend here so long to share you with the rest of us. For the pleasure of your company, I'm sure.'

Aediva kept her face calm with an effort. What was *that* supposed to mean?

She forced a smile, emulating his tone. 'On the

contrary, Sir Svend has been nothing but honourable. Unfortunately I fell ill on the journey.'

Hugh feigned alarm. 'I'm sorry to hear it. Fortunately you couldn't have been in better hands.'

'No, indeed. He has been consideration itself.'

'And you are recovered now, I trust?'

'Quite recovered, thank you.'

'Are we at court already?' Svend folded his arms over his chest with a look of exasperation. 'Or can we speak plainly?'

Hugh laughed and pressed a kiss to her fingertips. 'Forgive my friend—he doesn't care for court manners. But might I add that Saxon women never cease to amaze me?'

Aediva's brows snapped together. Sir Hugh was as charming as Svend was most definitely *not*, but something about his manner grated. She didn't want charm—not from a Norman. She wanted a man who would speak plainly. Unconsciously her gaze slid towards Svend.

'Then you must be easily surprised. Did you think we were a nation of savages?'

Hugh's mouth fell open. 'Forgive me…' He smiled sheepishly. 'I meant no offence. Perhaps we might start again? My name is Hugh.'

Aediva gave a conciliatory smile, hoping it would suffice. She couldn't call herself Cille any more—not with Svend standing so close—couldn't lie so brazenly in front of him.

'But what are you doing *here*?' He turned back towards Svend.

'Taking a rest. My men have earned it.'

'FitzOsbern expected you a week ago.'

'Then a few more hours shouldn't matter.'

Aediva shifted uncomfortably. Svend's terse manner was doing nothing to dispel the tension between them. If anything, he was making it worse. Surely Hugh could sense it too? She didn't want him guessing the reason as well.

'It's my fault,' she said smoothly. 'I suggested a swim. I wanted time to gather my thoughts before meeting the Earl.'

'Of course.' Hugh's gaze darted speculatively between them. 'But we ought to be going now. If he finds out that you've been *swimming*, of all things…'

'Not yet.' Svend pushed him aside deliberately. 'There's something I need to discuss with Lady Cille first.'

'Can't we talk and ride?'

'No.'

'What is it?' Aediva felt a rush of panic. The seriousness of his expression alarmed her.

A muscle tensed in his jaw. 'You need to prepare yourself, my lady. Redbourn has changed a great deal since you left. The fortifications needed improving. It's not the home you left…' He paused meaningfully. 'It would be best if you tried to accept it.'

She caught her breath as his eyes bored into hers. He was trying to warn her, to prepare her for her meeting with FitzOsbern, but all she could hear was the note of finality in his voice. He was saying goodbye.

She took refuge in anger. 'And you're only telling me this *now*?'

'There was no point before. I didn't want to alarm you.'

She dug her nails into her hands, fighting back tears. She didn't care about the changes to Redbourn. Her memories of Cille's home were hazy, at best. At least now she wouldn't arouse suspicion because of it. But it was better to be angry than to admit that she cared about him—about the fact that he'd been hiding things from her just when she thought she could trust him.

Just as she was hiding everything from him.

Her shoulders slumped in defeat. Who was she to accuse him? She'd been deceiving him all along. And it was too late to admit it.

If Hugh was right, and the Earl was really so impatient, it was too late to turn back. She had to go ahead with her deception, no matter what. If she told Svend the truth now he'd be forced to choose between exposing her and lying to the Earl. And if he took her side and something went wrong he'd be a traitor...an outlaw all over again. She couldn't do that to him—not like Maren. It wasn't just Cille and her nephew she was protecting any more. It was him too.

She took a step towards the horses, suddenly desperate to get the journey over with.

'My lady.'

He followed to help her mount and she stopped short, stiffening as his fingers touched her arm. They felt warm and strong. They were *all* she could feel. At that moment they seemed to be the only thing holding her up.

She mumbled something incoherent and clambered up quickly, hoping he couldn't see the effect that even such a slight touch had on her body. He mounted behind and she shifted forward self-consciously, keeping her back as straight as a spear, determined this time to keep their bodies apart. She couldn't let him touch her again—not when she needed a clear head.

'Cille?'

His lips skimmed her ear when Hugh's back was turned, his voice low and intimate, but she shook her head, refusing to answer. If she spoke to him now she might fall back into his arms and never let go.

And for Cille's sake—for all their sakes—she had to let him go. Whatever awaited her in Redbourn, she had to face it alone.

Chapter Ten

Svend stormed into the gatehouse, pounding his fist into the wall so hard that fragments of stone dust erupted in a small cloud.

'It went well, then?' Hugh had followed him inside, closing the door carefully behind them.

Svend scowled and flung himself into a chair. It was over. She was gone. He'd left her on the steps of the hall—had handed her over to the Earl's steward as if she were any other prisoner, as if his heart hadn't been ripped from his chest, acutely aware of Hugh's eyes following them both.

'You're a terrible actor, my friend. I saw the way you were looking at her.' Hugh picked up a flagon and poured two cupfuls of ale. 'The way she was looking at you too, for that matter. But you ought to be careful. De Quincey's a dangerous man to have as an enemy.'

'So am I.' And if de Quincey harmed so much

as a hair on her head he'd find out exactly how dangerous…

'True, but he's been like a bear with a sore head for the past week.'

'He's back from Normandy?'

'A week ago, and so impatient he almost went after you.'

Svend took the cup and drained the contents in one draught, relieved that he'd chosen not to escort her inside the tower after all. The last thing he wanted was to watch her reunion with de Quincey. Hugh was right—he was no actor. If he saw them together he'd want to smash the other man's head into a wall. He might still do it, too, given half the chance…

'I suppose the rumours weren't true, then?' said Hugh.

He ran a hand over his face wearily. 'What rumours?'

'That she was p—'

Hugh stopped mid-sentence as the door burst open suddenly and Renard dived headlong into the room.

Svend leapt up at once, grabbing his squire's arm before he fell. 'What's the matter?'

'I've been looking…everywhere…' Renard was bent over, gasping for breath. 'I went…to the kitchens…'

'And they refused to feed you?' Hugh guffawed

loudly. 'Or have they poisoned you with Saxon food, lad?'

Renard shook his head, straightening himself up with an effort. 'I spoke to Hawisa—one of the maids. I didn't see her last time, but she said something about Lady Cille…'

'What?' Svend tried to suppress a feeling of dread.

'She said the reason Lady Cille left was…she was with child.'

'What?'

For a few seconds he couldn't move. She'd been *pregnant*? He felt a visceral blow as shock coursed through his veins like poison. Of *course* she'd been pregnant! Every nagging suspicion, every question he'd been asking himself for the past week, all the pieces of the puzzle fitted together suddenly like stones in a wall. Lady Cille had been pregnant. Which meant…

'It's not her husband's child either!' Renard's voice followed him outside. 'It's de Quincey's!'

Svend charged through the bailey, blood roaring in his ears as he shoved and fought his way through the throng of soldiers. *The wrong sister!* He'd brought the wrong sister! How could he have been so blind?

His mind raced back to that first day in Etton. The two women had been almost identical. *Almost.* Damn it all, he'd had his suspicions. Why hadn't he followed them through?

Because he'd been distracted—that was why. Distracted by a pair of bewitching golden eyes in an impostor's face, just as she'd intended he would be.

He felt a surge of white-hot anger. He'd been tricked by a woman again—another duplicitous, treacherous woman! Every moment he'd spent with her, every time he'd kissed her, she'd been lying to him. She was no better than Maren—letting him believe that she cared, using him for her own selfish purpose.

But for *what* purpose? What did she hope to achieve by taking her sister's place? Was she simply stalling for time or did she think she could lie to the Earl with impunity? Surely she knew she wouldn't get away with it? She'd be exposed as a liar the moment de Quincey laid eyes on her.

Unless…

Was it possible that she didn't *know*?

He searched his memory for a word, a hint—for any indication that she knew about de Quincey and her sister. He'd assumed that she'd been avoiding the subject, but now the reason seemed far less complicated. And if she *really* didn't know, if for some reason her sister *hadn't* told her, did she think that the babe was Leofric's? Quickly he counted the months since Hastings. It was just about possible…especially if she wanted to believe it.

He dodged around a cluster of carts, every footstep a furlong too far. What about de Quincey? Did *he* know about the baby? By all accounts Lady Cille had fled Redbourn just after he'd left—five months before. A pregnancy might not have been obvious. And if de Quincey had known of an heir surely he wouldn't have gone back to Normandy.

No, de Quincey *couldn't* know. But if the rumours were true he'd certainly know the difference between the two sisters.

A rush of panic overtook his rage. He'd left her to face FitzOsbern alone—a man who was implacable towards enemies and traitors. If—*when*—he found out she was lying, she'd be lucky ever to see daylight again. And he'd be lucky to see *her*.

He charged up the steps of the hall, trying to hold his panic in check. How was it possible to feel so angry and so afraid at the same time? Was she crazy or just reckless? He'd asked himself that question before, but he was no closer to knowing the answer. Either way, he had to reach her before anyone else did. He didn't want the Earl to punish her. That was *his* job.

Aediva paced up and down the antechamber, fighting the urge to turn tail and run. Back in Etton the idea of taking Cille's place had seemed so simple and straightforward, but now she was here it felt like madness. She'd been so distracted by Svend that she'd hardly thought about what to do next. Somehow she had to stop the marriage and convince FitzOsbern to let her go, but as to how…

A thousand fears crowded her head. What if she gave herself away? What if the Earl asked something only Cille could know? What if she couldn't persuade him? What had she got herself into?

She tried to distract herself, looking around the cavernous antechamber with a mixture of amazement and dread. Svend's description of Redbourn as having changed was the worst kind of understatement. She'd never seen a place like it. New stone ramparts loomed twice as high as the old wooden palisade, encircling a bailey she scarcely recognised—a maze of wooden buildings, tents and one giant tower.

The old Saxon town had been remodelled as a new Norman fortress. And fluttering over it all was the King's banner—two golden lions on a red background—its presence serving as both a declaration and warning.

There wasn't the faintest hope of escape. She was trapped in a tower filled with Norman knights, in the very heart of a bailey packed with Norman soldiers, surrounded by a massive Norman-built stone wall. If she'd been trying she couldn't have imprisoned herself more effectively.

If she couldn't find a way to stop the marriage she might be trapped here for ever.

The door to the great hall swung open and her legs trembled unsteadily. Was it time? Had the Earl summoned her already?

But it was just a lone knight, emerging from the throng inside, striding past her as if she were invisible, leaving the door slightly ajar.

She crept towards it and put her eye to the gap. If she could just take a peek at least she would know what to expect, try to prepare herself for the ordeal ahead…

Like the tower, the hall was built in a new design she'd never seen before. Long and high-ceilinged, its walls were decorated with teardrop-shaped Norman shields instead of round Saxon ones, ornate tapestries instead of antlers and horns. And at the far end, on a dais, stood a man with red cropped hair…

She clutched a hand to her mouth as bile rose in her throat. There was no doubting the man's identity. His lean body was wrapped in a black bear fur, thick and luxuriant enough to stop the point of a blade, and his fingers were draped in more jewels than she'd ever imagined. This was William FitzOsbern, the Conqueror's cousin, one of the men who'd brought the whole Saxon world to its knees…whose soldiers had murdered her father.

But he was also the man she had to persuade to call off the marriage and let Cille go. And if she were going to persuade him to do that—going to persuade him of anything—she'd have to swallow her anger, hide her true feelings as well as her identity.

She didn't know if she could.

'Lady Cille?' A steward opened the door. 'The Earl's ready for you, my lady.'

She cleared her throat, willing her mind to stay calm and her feet to start moving. She had to do this for Cille—to protect her and the baby. That was why she'd come, why she'd deceived Svend. If she failed now it would all have been for nothing. And she couldn't—*wouldn't*—deceive him for nothing.

Svend. He'd bade her a formal goodbye on the steps of the hall, riding away from her without so much as a backwards glance. But it was for the best. If anything went wrong with her plan she didn't want him there to witness it—didn't want to see his face when he found out that she'd lied. If he was going to hate her she'd rather he did it from a distance.

The steward prompted her and she stepped up to the door. One foot was hovering over the threshold when a hand grabbed her elbow, pulling her roughly back again.

'What—?'

She yelped, startled, spinning around and colliding with a man's chest.

'Svend!'

She felt a momentary rush of happiness, quickly dispelled by the thunderous look on his face.

'Danemark?' The steward looked confused. 'She has an audience with the Earl.'

'She's not ready!'

Strong fingers clamped over her arm, hauling her away as the steward's panicked voice followed after them.

'But she's been summoned! He's waiting!'

'She's indisposed!'

'Svend, what are you doing?' She tried to pull away, but he swung her into an alcove out of sight of the hall.

'What am *I* doing?' he growled. 'What the hell do you think *you're* playing at?'

Desperately she searched his face, looking for any trace of warmth or affection, but there was none. There was no empathy now, only raw, unrestrained anger. He was a conquering warrior again, every bit the Norseman and just as frightening—nothing at all like the knight at the waterfall. He looked dangerous, angrier than she'd ever seen him.

As angry as a man who'd just found out he'd been lied to.

No, she reassured herself quickly, he couldn't

have. It wasn't possible. She'd barely seen anyone since their arrival, and the only person she'd spoken to was the steward. Who could have recognised her? Who could have told him so quickly? Her heart started to race frantically. How could he possibly know?

'Let me go!' She tried to twist away, but his grip on her arm was unyielding. 'Svend, I've been summoned! I have to go!'

'Do you?' His voice was a snarl laced with quiet menace. 'Are you sure it's *you* who's been summoned?'

She stiffened, willing her face to remain calm, trying to brazen it out. 'I don't know what you mean.'

'No?'

He dropped her arm abruptly and she staggered away from him, stomach churning, trying to give herself space to think. Still he pursued her, intent and relentless, giving no quarter as her back hit the wall with a thud.

She stared up at him mutely. Something in his face warned her not to lie. Besides, what could she say? If he already knew, if he'd somehow discovered the truth, then there was nothing she *could* say.

If…

She waited, letting the silence between them lengthen. Every moment was deeper and more dangerous as he came ever closer, stopping with barely a sliver of air between them.

'Tell me your name.'

For a moment the room seemed to spin as she pressed her palms into the wall, gripping the stone to hold herself up. Certainty overtook fear.

He knew.

He knew everything.

She felt a thud in her chest, as though her heart had stopped beating and then started again. He knew who she was, knew that she'd lied, and from the fearsome look on his face it seemed as though he'd come to punish her himself. For a moment she was tempted to take her chances with the Earl.

'No!'

She tried to push past him but he blocked her way, trapping her between his body and the wall. She wasn't sure which was the more unyielding.

'Tell me who you are.' He placed a hand on either side of her, obstructing any chance of escape, his pale eyes as cold and cutting as shards of ice. 'Who you *really* are.'

She lifted her chin. It was too late to argue or to explain, or even to defend herself. That moment had passed at the waterfall. But she wouldn't show fear—not to him or any other Norman. No matter what he intended to do with her she'd face it like a Saxon, like the Thane's daughter that she was.

'My name is Aediva.'

'The sister.' He didn't sound surprised.

'Yes. What are you going to do with me?'

Svend stared at her furiously, letting the woman he'd thought of as Cille turn slowly into Aediva.

She'd deceived him. For more than a week she'd let him believe she was someone she wasn't. She'd made a fool of him—would have made a greater fool of him in front of the Earl. He'd told her about his past and she'd betrayed his trust.

And now she was looking straight at him, defiant and undaunted, asking what he intended to do with her.

He knew what he ought to do. He ought to march her in front of the Earl and expose her before the whole court. He had the opportunity and more than enough motive. If he had any sense he'd be in there already. But all he could think about was getting her as far away from the tower as possible.

He muttered an oath, his heart at war with his head. Was he mad? He'd lost everything for a woman once before. Was he truly prepared to lose it again? If he helped her he'd be an accomplice, but if he did nothing…if he let her go ahead with her plan…he might as well hand her over to the Earl's guards himself.

'How did you find out?' She asked the question warily.

'Does it matter?'

'It depends who else knows. If it's only you—'

'It's not,' he interrupted brusquely. 'Renard heard a rumour. The kitchen maids here know more than the Earl.'

'But if you're the only Normans who know…' She looked up at him imploringly. 'You could still let me go. Let me tell them I'm Cille. No one else will know the difference.'

'Believe me, if you go into that hall someone will know.'

'Who?'

'Trust me.'

'But—'

'Enough!'

He slammed the flat of his hand against the wall. They were wasting time. She hadn't the slightest idea of how much danger she was in. He had to get her out of there. *Now.*

Quickly he glanced around the antechamber. Save for a couple of guards, it was empty. There was no time to think or reconsider. If he was going to save her, it had to be now. And there was only one place he could think of to take her.

He must truly be mad.

'Come on!' He grabbed her wrist and pulled her out of the antechamber, down the tower steps and towards a cluster of tents on the far side of the bailey.

'Svend, what are you doing?' She tugged at his arm, almost running to keep up.

It was a good question. As far as he could see

there were only two choices. Escape and become fugitives, or throw themselves on the mercy of the Earl. Neither option seemed likely to end well.

'First I'm going to get you out of here. Then I want to know what the hell you think you're doing.'

They reached the tents and he threw a swift glance over his shoulder, checking for any sign of pursuit. There was none. They had that in their favour at least. Now, if they could just reach his tent without being seen he could keep her hidden while he worked out what to do next.

He found it at last and whipped back the flap with relief, pushing her roughly inside.

'Ow!' She stumbled into the tent, bumping against the side of a low pallet bed.

He ignored her, searching his narrow quarters for any sign of occupancy, but everything was as he'd left it a few weeks before, his small sack of belongings untouched. *Good.* At least no one had thought to take advantage of his absence. No one would interrupt them. He didn't want to be disturbed—not until he had some answers.

He folded his arms in the doorway, trying to ignore the fact that she was sprawled on his bed. 'You told me you were Cille!'

She sat up, rubbing the backs of her legs. 'No, I didn't. You assumed.'

He ignored the distinction. 'Why did you lie?'

'I had to!'

'Why?' He was getting impatient. 'Tell me quickly. We don't have much time.'

'Before what?'

'Before the Earl wonders why you're ignoring his summons!'

'I'm not!' She leapt to her feet accusingly. '*You're* the one stopping me!'

His anger exploded. 'I just saved your life! Do you have *any* idea what would have happened if I hadn't stopped you? Bloody hell, woman, you were about to lie to the *King's cousin*!'

'Not lie exactly…pretend…'

'What's the difference? It's still treason!'

'It's only treason if he's *my* King—which he's not!'

He closed the space between them in two footsteps. 'Say that again and you'll get us *both* killed!'

She blanched at once. 'What do you mean?'

He didn't answer, distracted by the lock of honey-coloured hair tumbling across one golden eye, tempting him to brush it aside. He swallowed the impulse, resenting his own weakness. How could she still have such a distracting effect on him? He ought not to be able to stand the sight of her and yet, standing so close to her, it was all he could do not to pull her into his arms. If they were going to be caught, he wanted to feel her lips again first…

'If you're not Cille—' he spoke through clenched teeth '—then what are you doing here?'

'I thought if I could speak to the Earl…convince him that I was Cille… I could ask him to stop the marriage.'

'Just like that?'

He could hardly believe his own ears. Was she *really* so naive? Did she think it would be so easy to change the Earl's mind?

'I had to do *something*! You saw Cille—she'd just had a baby. I couldn't let you take her.'

He scowled at the implication. 'I would never have brought her before she was ready.'

'And how long would that have been? A few days? A few weeks? What if she had never been ready?'

Svend clenched his jaw. Their voices were raised now. If they weren't careful they'd bring the Earl's soldiers right to them.

'So you just decided to take her place?'

'Why not? Cille left Redbourn before the Normans arrived. None of them would have known the difference.'

His brows snapped together. 'Who told you that?'

'Cille did.' She frowned, her defiance faltering momentarily. 'At least she never mentioned any Normans…'

'She never mentioned de Quincey?'

'Who?'

He swore violently, ignoring her shocked intake of breath. This was maddening. She had no idea about *any* of it—about de Quincey and Cille or the real identity of the baby's father. There wasn't the faintest inkling of suspicion on her face. She couldn't see the truth even when it was right in front of her.

On the other hand he couldn't fault her motives. Part of him even admired them. She'd lied for a reason. She wasn't simply duplicitous, deceiving him for her own selfish ends like Maren. She'd been trying to protect her sister and her nephew, acting out of love after all. Just not for him.

But why had the real Cille let her go through with such a dangerous pretence? Even if she hadn't wanted to tell her about de Quincey, why hadn't she stopped her?

He thought back to the morning of their departure from Etton, when he'd threatened to carry her out of the hall. She'd said that her sister was still asleep. Was it possible that they'd never had a chance to speak? That the real Cille had never even known her intentions?

He struggled to keep a lid on his temper. It wasn't just possible—in all likelihood she'd taken her sister's place without even telling her because she had simply assumed that everyone hated Normans as much as she did. The idea of her sister having a relationship, let alone a child with a Norman had likely never occurred to her.

Of course it hadn't. He'd been deluded to think she might even consider the possibility. She hated all Normans—had told him that from the start—and had probably hated him all along. He'd been fool enough to think she might care, but she'd only been playing a part—stringing him along so he wouldn't get suspicious, as good an actress as Maren had ever been.

He could feel the heat of his anger abating, to be replaced by something colder and harder. Well, he'd wondered who the real woman was and now he knew. She wasn't the woman who had kissed him…she was the one who had pulled away. Every look, every touch, every kiss… None of it had meant anything to her.

And now that the red fog had lifted he felt almost as angry with himself as he was with her. He'd known better than to trust a woman again. He'd even known that she was hiding something. He was almost as much to blame as she was.

'Svend?' She looked up at him guilelessly. 'Who's de Quincey?'

He fought the urge to laugh. If only she'd asked that question a fortnight ago! For a moment he was tempted to take his revenge—to tell her the truth bluntly and see the scales fall from her eyes. But, as much as he wanted to punish her, he couldn't bring himself to hurt her, couldn't be that cruel.

'Aediva.' He tested her name on his tongue, tried not to like it. 'Your sister hasn't told you everything.'

'What do you mean?' She went very still suddenly.

'De Quincey is the Baron she's supposed to marry. You said she left Redbourn in the spring?'

'Yes, she wanted to come home.'

'The King's soldiers arrived in Redbourn only a few weeks after Hastings—in the autumn, when she was still here. De Quincey was with them.'

'No.' She shook her head in bewilderment. 'You must be mistaken. If Cille was here when the Normans arrived, why didn't she tell me about them?'

She looked so confused that for a moment he almost felt sorry for her. He had to stamp the feeling down quickly.

'How long do you think it takes to build a fortress?' He paused significantly, but her expression didn't alter. 'Even the King's masons couldn't have done all this in five months. They've had to work night and day to do it in nine.'

'But…'

'Think of the baby.'

'Leofric's baby…?' Her voice wavered slightly.

'No.' Did he really have to spell it out? 'Leofric wasn't here nine months ago. De Quincey was.'

Her lips parted. The truth was dawning at last. 'But the babe was late!'

'By two months?'

'No!' She backed away from him as if she might run from his words. 'It's not true!'

'Why not? Because he's *Norman*?' His voice hardened again. 'Aediva, whether you want to believe it or not, de Quincey didn't just *meet* your sister, he conceived a child with her too. *That's* why I was sent to find her—because he wants to marry her.'

'You said it was for FitzOsbern!' She glowered at him accusingly.

'He rules half of Normandy! He doesn't need one English fortress!'

'But…but what about Leofric?'

'I don't know.' He shook his head. 'Things happen in war…people act differently. You'll need to ask your sister. But she has a child with de Quincey. Isn't it possible that she cares for him too?'

'No!'

'You think it impossible to love a Norman?' He couldn't keep the bitterness out of his voice.

'He must have *forced* her!'

Svend clenched his jaw. Apparently her opinion of Normans was even lower than he'd thought. 'I wouldn't throw such accusations around lightly.'

She ignored the warning. 'She must have been afraid of him! Why else would she have run away?'

'Aediva…'

'Why would she have come back to Etton if she

was in love with a *Norman*?' She spat the word like an insult. 'Why call the babe Leofric if not after his father?'

'Maybe because she knew you wouldn't understand. You've said that you hate Normans often enough. Maybe she thought you'd hate your nephew too!'

'No!' She looked stricken. 'I would *never...!*'

'Wouldn't you? If I'm right then he's half-Norman.'

'She could have told me!'

She tried to turn away, but he followed after her remorselessly, grabbing her shoulders and wrenching her back round to face him.

'Maybe she tried.'

For a moment he thought she was going to argue. Then her gaze misted over, as if she were struggling to remember something.

'She did… Just before I left… I said that the baby's hair was dark, not like hers or Leofric's… She was upset, said there was something she wanted to tell me… I should have listened.'

Svend exhaled slowly. He wasn't going to argue with that. If she'd only listened and not been so blinkered in her hatred of Normans then neither of them would be in this position.

'I didn't know…' Her expression was distraught. 'Svend, truly, I didn't know.'

His grip on her shoulders slackened, though he still didn't release her. No, she hadn't known—

hadn't even guessed at the truth. *That* was the problem.

'And de Quincey's here. With the Earl. And if I'd gone into the hall he would have known...' She took a deep, tremulous breath. 'You saved me.'

He watched her steadily, saw her look of gratitude turn suddenly into one of panic.

'But you told the steward I was Cille! They're expecting her!' She jerked in his arms. 'Svend, I have to go to the Earl or they'll think that you lied. I'll tell him the truth before anyone else does—that I'm an impostor, that I deceived you.'

'It's too late for that.'

'It *can't* be!'

'The steward saw us leave together.'

'But this is all my doing! Take me back to the tower—say that you only just discovered the truth.' She held out her wrists, pressing them together. 'I'll be your prisoner again.'

'No.'

'Svend!' She stamped her foot. 'You shouldn't have rescued me. This was my plan, not yours. I won't let you be punished for it!'

He raised his eyebrows, surprised by her vehemence. She might have deceived him like Maren, but she wasn't asking him to take the blame. On the contrary, she seemed determined to take whatever punishment the Earl might mete out on her own. Was it possible that she cared for him after all? At least enough to want to protect him? Or was she simply reluctant to share the blame with a Norman?

He let his gaze drift over her face, over her bow-shaped lips and smooth, round cheekbones. She wasn't who he'd thought she was, but she was still the same wildcat who'd attacked him that first day in Etton—the woman who'd said she hated all Normans, who'd lied to his face.

'Svend, I never thought I'd put you in danger. I thought the risk was all mine.'

He gave a bitter laugh. Danger he was used to. He cared less about that than the fact that she'd lied to him. That deceit outweighed all the rest. She seemed sorry, but how could he know for certain? She was Maren all over again, just as desirable and even more dangerous. He couldn't trust her—couldn't trust anything she might say or do ever again.

But it was too late to save himself. He'd known that the moment he'd pulled her back from the threshold of the hall.

At least this time he'd walked into the trap with his eyes open.

'We're in this together now, Aediva.'

'No! You have to let me go.'

'Not on your own. We'll go to the Earl together.' He tightened his grip on her shoulders again. 'We'll just have to hope he's in a forgiving mood.'

'Forgiving?'

The tent flap flew open suddenly, revealing the

figure of a man standing framed in the entrance, his dark eyes blazing like hot coals as his expression veered from disbelief to murderous fury.

'The Earl might forgive you. *I* won't.'

Chapter Eleven

'Let. Her. Go.'

The new arrival stalked menacingly towards them, sliding his sword from its scabbard in one slow, deliberately drawn out movement.

'De Quincey!' Svend stepped in front of her at once, using his body as a shield.

De Quincey? Aediva stared at him in amazement. This was *him*? The man her sister was supposed to marry? The man she already had a child with? In her mind she'd envisaged a monster, but this stranger was unquestionably one of the handsomest men she'd ever seen, with hooded grey eyes, a granite square jaw, almost impossibly symmetrical features and a shock of dark hair.

Hair that was jet-black, just like that of Cille's baby…

Cille… Her head was still whirling from everything Svend had told her—everything she hadn't known about her own sister. And she cared less about any of it than she did about his behaviour. She'd tried to explain why she'd deceived him but he was still furious with her. Somehow she'd thought that he'd understand, but he seemed too angry to try. Couldn't he see that she'd only been trying to protect Cille? Or was his pride hurt too badly?

Well, if he couldn't understand why she'd lied then there was nothing else to say. He wasn't the man she'd thought he was and she wasn't going to beg for forgiveness.

'It's not what you think, de Quincey.' Svend drew his own sword defensively, shifting his weight forward as he tensed for combat.

'And what *do* I think?' De Quincey's voice was a sinister monotone. 'Enlighten me.'

'She's not Cille.'

The Baron gave a disbelieving laugh. 'Is that the best you can do?'

Aediva looked fearfully between the two men. De Quincey's footsteps were curving ever closer towards Svend, and the tension in the room was so heavy she doubted even their weapons would be able to slice through it. Physically they were evenly matched, but she didn't want to find out who would emerge the victor. In such a small space there would be hardly any room to swing a blade. The fight would be up close and personal, bloody and brutal. And the Baron seemed driven by an emotion more powerful than anger—something more akin to jealousy.

She felt a flicker of triumph. Apparently she made a more convincing Cille than Svend had realised. In the dim light of the tent de Quincey had truly mistaken her for her own sister.

But if she didn't convince him otherwise there'd be bloodshed for certain.

'Wait!' She darted around Svend, evading his outstretched hand. She wasn't going to risk him getting killed because of her—not when he'd just saved her life. At least this way they'd be even.

'Get back!' Svend's voice was tense with fury.

She ignored him, staring down the length of de Quincey's blade as she willed him to see the truth. 'Look at me. I'm not Cille.'

'What?' The Baron stared at her for a long moment before dropping his sword to the floor, his face paling as if he'd just seen a ghost. 'Your eyes… Who are you?'

She let out a breath of relief. 'My name's Aediva. Cille is my sister.'

He kept on staring at her, seemingly unable to drag his eyes from her face, though his words were addressed to Svend. 'You told the steward… You were touching her… I thought the two of you…' He rubbed a hand over his face suddenly. 'Sweet mercy, I could have killed you.'

'You could have tried.' Svend lowered his weapon at last, throwing her a look that was part anger, part relief. 'There's been a misunderstanding. Lady Aediva is here on her sister's behalf.'

'But you found Cille? Is she all right?'

'Yes.' He hesitated briefly. 'We left her a week ago.'

'Then why isn't she here?'

'She's well, but not fit enough to travel. Her sister came as a gesture of goodwill.'

'Goodwill?' De Quincey's brows drew together in a thick black line. 'What does *that* mean?'

'Just that she intends to return to Redbourn as soon as she's able.'

Aediva spun towards Svend indignantly. How could he promise that? They still didn't know why Cille had run away—at least not for certain. What if she didn't want to come back and marry de Quincey? How dared he simply assume?

She caught the Baron looking at her and adjusted her expression quickly. A gesture of goodwill ought not to be glaring, no matter how indignant she might feel. But he seemed distracted, his face haunted by some overpowering emotion.

'I don't understand what happened…' He dropped down onto the bed suddenly. 'Everything seemed all right when I left. I thought the problems between us were over. When they told me she'd run away I felt desperate. But I was too far away…the message had been delayed for weeks. I sent word to FitzOsbern as soon as I could.'

Despite herself, Aediva felt a surge of pity. There was no doubting the look of anguish on his face, nor the depth of his emotion. He looked tormented, as if he truly cared for Cille. He even spoke as if she cared for him too. No, this man was no monster. But he was still Norman…

She waited for the customary sense of outrage, but it didn't come. A week ago—a day ago, even—she would have hated him, would never have believed that her sister could care for a Norman. Now the idea didn't seem so outlandish. The idea of loving her enemy seemed almost…natural.

'Did she say why she left?' He sounded desperate. 'What did she tell you?'

Nothing. Aediva's stomach plummeted. Cille hadn't told her anything.

She turned away, shamefaced. She'd learned so much in the past hour—not just about her sister, but about herself too. Cille had come home for help and then hadn't dared to confide in her because she'd been so intractable, so full of hatred, never questioning her own prejudices against Normans. Cille hadn't retreated inside herself—*she'd* pushed her away. And when Svend had arrived she'd been too impulsive, taking Cille's place without even asking, charging recklessly ahead and endangering everyone around her—him included.

So why had he rescued her? She stole a glance towards him, confused. If she'd known about de

Quincey she would never have let him help her, let him endanger himself by dragging her away. Besides, she didn't want his protection—not like this! He looked as stern as granite, a different man from the one who'd kissed her so tenderly the night before.

He wouldn't kiss her again. That much was certain. So why was he still trying to protect her? Lying to the Baron to hide *her* deceit? Clearly he was as stubbornly honourable as she was impulsive. That made her feel doubly guilty. He wouldn't let her take the blame even when she asked for it. Now she wished he'd left her at the tower. If he was so angry, why had he even bothered to rescue her?

'Aediva?'

His stern voice prompted her now. Apparently he expected *her* to tell de Quincey about the baby. Well, she wasn't going to soften the blow—not for a Norman. She hadn't changed her mind so completely.

'She was with child.'

The Baron's face turned even paler. 'She was carrying my child?'

'A boy.' Svend shot her a glance of warning. 'Born a week ago. He's healthy and strong.'

'You didn't leave them alone?'

'No. Henri's with her, and ten of my men. They're safe.'

'Then I'm indebted.' He stood up shakily,

clasping Svend's shoulder for support. 'I have to go to her.'

'I'll give you directions. You can be there in three days.'

'Good. I'll go to the Earl now. I want to leave immediately. Tonight.'

He made for the flap and then stopped, as if suddenly remembering why he'd come. 'You ought to come with me. You'll still have to explain why she ignored the Earl's summons.'

Aediva tensed, but the Baron's expression was thoughtful.

'Perhaps it was my fault… Perhaps I came across her and couldn't wait for news of Cille… Perhaps all this time she's been assuring me of her sister's good health…'

'Perhaps.' Svend's expression was guarded.

'As for what you told the steward…a slip of the tongue after such a long journey would be understandable. Or perhaps he simply misheard?'

Aediva's mouth fell open. This Norman—this man she'd assumed was a monster—was offering them a lifeline. She clenched her jaw, trying and failing to hold on to her resentment.

'And perhaps…' De Quincey looked faintly amused. 'She might want to change her clothes before meeting the King's cousin.'

Mortified, she looked down at her tattered dress. He was right. She looked as though she'd been dragged through a hedgerow backwards.

Twice. No decent Saxon lady would ever have appeared in such a state. Certainly Cille would never have done. Had she looked so ragged all week? What must Svend think of her? He had seemed to find her attractive despite her dishevelment, but now his averted gaze spoke volumes. He didn't even want to *look* at her.

'Wait here.' The Baron smiled gallantly, as if to take the sting from his words. 'I'll have someone escort you to Cille's old chamber. Her clothes are still there. You can choose a new gown.'

'I...' She hardly knew what to say.

'In the meantime—' he turned back towards Svend '—we need to speak with the Earl.'

'But shouldn't I come with you?'

The two men exchanged glances and she stiffened. Did they think they could just leave her behind while they spoke to the Earl? As if she ought to stay put while Normans decided her future? She should have a say at least. If she were going to be condemned by FitzOsbern she wanted a chance to confront him first.

'Stay here.' Svend's tone was peremptory, brooking no argument. 'You'll be safe.'

'But *I'm* the one who was summoned!'

'It's best if we speak to him alone.'

'You said we'd go together!'

'That was before.'

'So why can't I come now?'

'Because we didn't stand a chance before.'

'But—'

'I don't trust you!'

She took an involuntary step backwards, too shocked to respond. The look on his face was even worse than before—worse than any look she could have imagined. When he'd spoken of Maren his eyes had glittered with anger and bitterness, but now they were blazing with something else—some fierce emotion she didn't recognise. Did he hate her so much, then?

'You'll see the Earl tonight.' De Quincey broke the silence at last. 'Trust me, Lady Aediva, you'll be perfectly safe with my men, but we have to go. We need to speak to FitzOsbern before he sends someone to arrest the pair of you.'

'Promise of *goodwill*?' De Quincey gave him a sceptical look as they crossed the bailey.

'It was the best I could do at short notice.'

'It might have worked too, if she hadn't looked so angry.'

Svend grimaced. That was true. For a woman who'd managed to deceive him so completely, she'd been remarkably poor at hiding her feelings around de Quincey.

'Do you think the Earl will believe it?'

'I'm not sure. There's been a spate of Saxon raids recently. He's not in a temper to forgive rebels—even suspected ones.'

'She's not a rebel.'

'Are you sure?'

No. He wasn't sure about anything to do with her. After a week in which she'd done little but lie to him he was a long way from sure. He certainly wasn't going to risk taking her with them to FitzOsbern—couldn't trust her not to say or do something to get them arrested.

All his warrior's instincts told him the same thing. He couldn't trust her. But he still couldn't give her up.

'What's going on?' De Quincey looked at him meaningfully. 'You didn't really give Cille's name by mistake.'

'No, I only discovered the truth half an hour before you did. She was trying to protect her sister.' Against his will, he found himself defending her. 'She thought if she pretended to be Cille she could stop the marriage. She didn't know anything about you.'

'Cille never told her about me?' De Quincey halted mid-stride, his brows knitting together thoughtfully. 'Then again, she never told *me* about the baby. She could have sent me a message. I've never claimed to understand women, but this…'

His voice trailed away and Svend stayed silent. Whatever had happened between the Baron and Lady Cille was none of his business. His only concern was the younger sister, and getting her as far away from Redbourn as possible. The sooner she was gone, the sooner he could stop thinking about her and start trying to forget.

'Do you care for her?' The Baron's eyes narrowed inquisitively.

'She lied to me.'

'That's not an answer.'

'Isn't it?'

He glowered ferociously. *Did* he still care for her? He didn't know what he felt. Only one emotion made sense.

'I'm angry.' He turned the question around. 'Aren't you?'

'With her—a little. With Cille—extremely. It doesn't mean I don't love her.' De Quincey shook his head, as if amazed by his own admission. 'I couldn't stop even if I wanted to.'

Then that was the difference between them, Svend thought bitterly. *He* wanted to.

'But you want to protect her?' De Quincey persisted.

'Yes.' This time he didn't hesitate.

'Very well. But you know that it's risky. If Fitz-Osbern suspects the truth…that she intended to lie to him…it will be dangerous for you both. A sensible man might balk.'

'I've never been accused of too much good sense.' Svend smiled grimly. 'I know it's a risk. I don't ask you to share it.'

'What would I tell Cille, then?' De Quincey clapped a hand on his shoulder. 'We'll do this together, but let *me* explain to FitzOsbern. You look like you're marching into battle. I'll do the talking. You take over if we need to fight our way out of there.'

They mounted the steps two at a time, and the Earl's guards fell back as they recognised the Baron. Svend strode at his side, struggling to arrange his features into a calm, neutral expression—an endeavour that was ruined every time he thought about her. He swallowed an oath. This wasn't going to be easy.

'Danemark!' The Earl's voice boomed out to greet them as they entered the hall. 'One minute they tell me you've brought de Quincey's new bride, the next that you've run off with her. Are you two here to fight a duel?'

'Quite the opposite, I assure you.' De Quincey's voice was full of good humour, revealing none of his earlier distress. 'But if we might have a word in private?'

'A *word*?' The Earl waved a hand to dismiss his retainers, his gaze sharpening at once. 'I thought to meet your new bride. Under the circumstances, I think I've been patient enough.'

'So you have, but sadly my wedding will have to wait. There's been a slight misunderstanding regarding the lady's identity.'

Svend stood immobile, listening in amazement as de Quincey launched into a heavily embellished version of events, so artfully expressed that he almost believed it himself. Somehow he managed to keep the surprise off his face. The Baron must love Cille indeed to risk straining the truth so dangerously.

Then again, hadn't *he* been prepared to do the same? What did that say about *him*?

He pushed the thought aside as de Quincey drew to a close and the Earl beckoned for wine, staring thoughtfully into his cup.

'So this woman, Aediva, brought you news of her sister?'

'Yes, and about the child—my son.'

'Did she say why Lady Cille ran away?'

For the first time de Quincey looked unsure of himself. 'No, but I intend to find out. With your permission, I'd like to leave for Etton at once.'

'No.' The Earl looked up sharply. 'This business has taken too long already. I need to head towards Ely, attack the core of the rebellion, and I need a man here I can trust. There have been too many incursions already. The woman will have to wait.'

'But my son—!'

'The rebels shouldn't pose too great a threat, my lord.' Svend intervened hastily as de Quincey's composure started to crack. 'The ones we encountered were badly organised and easily scattered. The Baron could travel to Etton and deal with any threat he found on the way.'

'Indeed?' FitzOsbern peered at him speculatively. 'And, in your opinion, how many men would it take to bring the rebels completely to heel?'

'To clear the shire? Thirty should suffice.'

'You have twenty under your command?'

'Twenty-two.' A suspicion flitted across Svend's mind, but it was so outlandish that he dismissed it at once.

'I could spare some of mine.' De Quincey sounded calmer again. 'And you said you wanted a man you could trust. Why not Danemark?'

The Earl's fingers toyed with the stem of his cup. 'It's not a bad idea. I could almost suspect that you've agreed to it already.'

'It works for all of us.' De Quincey's tone was smoothly persuasive. 'I've no desire to come back here. This was Cille's home with her first husband. Once I find her, with the King's permission, we'll go back to Normandy and make a fresh start.'

FitzOsbern nodded slowly, his gaze fixed on Svend. 'The King promised to reward you, did he not?'

'Yes my lord, but…' Svend was speechless, his surprise giving way to incredulity. He was the son of a farmer, an outlaw. He could never aim so high…

'You haven't failed the King yet. Though we'll have to do something about the woman.'

'My lord…?' His brow furrowed at once.

'As the Warden of Redbourn you will need a

Saxon bride. And since Lady Cille is already spoken for the sister will have to suffice. Unless you have any objection?'

Svend hesitated. The Earl was offering him a reward greater than any he'd ever imagined. Land, a castle, a home of his own…

A home with a woman who'd deceived him, a woman he'd almost, *almost* loved. That morning he would have agreed in a heartbeat, but now… How could he live side by side with a woman he didn't trust?

'So reluctant?' The Earl looked bemused. 'Most men would have bitten my hand off by now. I'm offering you a castle and half of the shire to boot. Surely the prize is worth tolerating one Saxon maid?'

'Yes, my lord…' He faltered, fumbling for an explanation.

Tolerating her wasn't the problem—at least not in the way the Earl meant. He wanted to do a lot more than just tolerate her. The very idea was dangerously tempting. But desire could be conquered, overcome. It *had* to be. He couldn't bed a woman he couldn't trust. They would lead separate lives. She could go back to Etton if she wanted. That would probably be best for both of them.

'You think she's untrustworthy?'

FitzOsbern looked suspicious and he shook his head hastily.

'It's not that, my lord, I'll vouch for her. But she might not want me.'

'I hadn't intended to give her a choice.'

'I never thought to marry at all.'

'Then this is your chance.' The Earl's gaze narrowed perceptibly. 'You should take it, Danemark. I won't offer twice.'

Svend felt a muscle twitch in his jaw. He was being foolish—ought to grab the prize with both hands before FitzOsbern retracted his offer. This was the reward he'd worked so hard for, the reward he'd thought that he'd lost—everything he wanted with just one proviso. *Her.* Somehow they'd become bound together, woman and reward, and if he couldn't take one without the other he'd have to take both.

He made up his mind. He wasn't going to let a woman take everything from him again.

'You honour me, my lord. I won't fail you.'

'Good.' The Earl raised his cup in salute. 'Then it's decided. You can tell her the news. These things always sound better from a lover.'

He smiled, as if the description were incongruous, and Svend gritted his teeth. The very word brought to mind things he didn't want to imagine. As her husband he'd be free to touch her, to hold her, to explore her body and all its hidden spaces…all the things he had to resist.

Of course that was *if* she agreed to the marriage. Somehow he doubted she'd take the proposal calmly. She'd be as thrilled by the idea as he was. On the other hand there was a kind of poetic justice to their predicament. He couldn't think of a more fitting punishment for her deceit. She was the one who'd pretended to care for him. Now she'd have to live with the consequences.

And so would he.

He made a formal bow and strode out of the hall, already bracing himself for the interview ahead. He'd tell her the Earl's decision, but he wasn't going to ask her to marry him. Castle or not, he wasn't going to ask her for anything. If the idea were abhorrent to her she could tell the Earl so and deal with the fallout herself. He was finished with protecting her. From now on she could take care of herself.

And if she said no…would he still get Redbourn? He frowned, wondering what the Earl would do if she refused. What would happen to his reward then?

For the first time in as long as he could remember he didn't care.

Chapter Twelve

Aediva flung herself onto Cille's bed and stared hopelessly up at the rafters, watching as a spider wove its intricate web above her head.

De Quincey had been as good as his word, sending a man to escort her to Cille's chamber in the old Saxon hall, which was still standing side by side with the new Norman tower. She felt as though she were in some uncanny, half-known version of reality, taking comfort in the familiar surroundings despite the army outside.

Her situation was far worse than she could ever have imagined. She'd set out to save her sister, only to find that she'd failed from the start. She'd deceived Svend for nothing, miring herself ever deeper in a lie because she couldn't bear to admit her own burgeoning feelings for him. A lie he'd uncovered for himself and for which he apparently couldn't forgive her. He'd been prepared to face the consequences of her deception alongside her, but he'd done so out of honour—not love. And now she was alone, waiting for whatever verdict the Norman Earl might pass on her.

She'd made a mess of everything.

She pulled her knees up to her stomach and groaned. She shouldn't have let Svend go to the Earl without her…should have insisted on accompanying him. Anything would have been better than this waiting. The suspense was bad enough, but being alone with her thoughts was even worse. The look on his face when he'd left the tent still haunted her. He hadn't wanted her to go with them, hadn't trusted her not to make their situation even worse.

Well, after everything she'd done she supposed she couldn't blame him, but at least there was one way she could prove him wrong.

She heaved herself up off the bed, her spirit reasserting itself. She'd got them into this mess and now she could help get them out of it. For Cille's sake she'd go along with whatever version of events Svend and de Quincey invented. What had they said? That she was there as a gesture of goodwill, that she'd come to bring word of Cille's good health…

She repeated the lines inwardly. When she went to the Earl she'd be the very model of restrained behaviour, would show them all how well a Saxon lady could behave.

If she went to the Earl…

The fact that Svend still hadn't come back was worrying in itself. It must have been an hour since he'd left with de Quincey. If anything had happened to him because of her she'd never forgive herself.

She wrestled her fears back under control. If she were going to be any help at all she had to start by following de Quincey's advice. He was right—she couldn't attend the Earl in her tattered gown. She was a Thane's daughter and it was high time she started to dress and behave like one.

Carefully, she opened the lid of one of Cille's old coffers, running her fingers over an impressive array of velvet gowns and intricately embroidered headdresses, tasselled belts and linen girdles. She'd never felt more like an impostor. Cille had always been naturally poised and elegant, rarely allowing so much as a hair out of place, while *she* on the other hand…

What was she supposed to *do* with so many clasps and ribbons?

There was only one way to find out.

Slowly she untied the laces on the front of her gown and let it slide over her hips to the floor. Then she slipped off her shoes, standing barefoot in her shift as she started to unravel her braid. Her hair had still been damp when she'd retied it after her swim, so that now it tumbled down her back in a riot of waves, swirling around her body like a cloak.

There. She gave a nod of satisfaction. Stripped down to basics, she could start again. She might have arrived in Redbourn looking like some kind of wild creature, but she would leave—*if* she could leave—like a lady.

She delved back into the coffer, selecting an ivy-green gown trimmed with dark velvet and embroidered with an intricate pattern of gold thread. The neck was cut in a square, the bodice tighter than she was used to, and the sleeves were so long she'd likely trip over them if she wasn't careful, but at least she and Cille were the same size. It would fit—if she dared to wear it.

If... She draped the fabric against her body and then dropped it again, distracted by a commotion outside—the sound of muffled voices and heavy footfalls, the squeal of axles and the thud of hoofbeats. Was it something to do with Svend? Quickly she ran to the wall, looking for a gap in the timbers, a hole big enough to see through, finally finding one up near the rafters.

With an effort she dragged the coffer underneath and clambered on top, peering out at a scene of organised chaos. No, this had nothing to do with Svend. Everywhere she looked was a hive of activity, as if the army itself were preparing to move. Was it possible? She felt a flicker of hope. Were the Normans leaving?

A man cleared his throat behind her and she spun around in alarm, wrapping her arms around her body as if she could somehow hide the fact that she was wearing only short undergarments.

'Svend?'

For a moment she didn't recognise him. He looked the same, and yet different somehow, as if the features she remembered had been deliberately wiped clean. His tunic was gleaming white, a striking contrast to his usual dark-clad appearance, and his blond hair was swept back off his face, making his chiselled features look even more defined, even more dangerous, somehow, as if they were carved from stone.

He was a stranger, this Svend who didn't trust her, as strong, formidable and remote as an ice-topped mountain. Everything about him looked stern and forbidding. Everything except his eyes. They were blazing at her in a way that made her tremble all over.

She gasped, suddenly aware of her precarious position, standing on a coffer, bare-legged and covered in only the thinnest of shifts. Quickly she jumped down and snatched up a blanket, wrapping it tightly around her shoulders.

'Apologies.' Svend cleared his throat again, more huskily this time. 'I called out, but there was no answer.'

'I didn't hear.' She tried her best to sound casual. 'I was trying to see what was happening outside.'

'Ah.' His gaze flickered down to her bare legs and then up again, as if reluctant to linger. 'The Earl wants to leave Redbourn tomorrow. The army is preparing… But perhaps I should leave you to dress before we talk?'

She felt her blush deepen from pink to burgundy. Last night he'd wanted to undress her and now he was telling her to cover up! She couldn't have felt any more mortified.

'There's no need.' She straightened her shoulders, speaking abrasively. 'I'm sure whatever you have to say won't take long.'

'It won't.' His gaze frosted again, cold and hard as sharpened steel, utterly devoid of emotion. 'I've been sent by the Earl.'

'Oh?' She felt her pulse start to race. Was that why he looked so forbidding? Because the Earl hadn't believed their story? Was he here to arrest her?

'De Quincey told him you'd brought news of your sister. He seemed to believe it.'

'So it's going to be all right?' Her shoulders sagged with relief.

'In a manner of speaking. He's appointed me Warden of Redbourn.'

'*You?* What about de Quincey?'

'He wants to take your sister to Normandy after

they're married. He thinks Redbourn might contain too many memories.'

'Normandy? But this is her *home*!'

'The home she ran away from. Perhaps she won't mind.'

'So you... He...'

She spluttered at him, surprise giving way to anger. She'd spent the last hour torturing herself, worrying about the danger he might be in, when apparently she needn't have bothered! He'd been rewarded—not punished. He'd been given a *castle*! She'd been stupidly naive, thinking that he'd gone in to protect her when all he cared about was getting his hands on Saxon land! And she'd let it all be decided without her! De Quincey was to claim Cille and Svend was to get Redbourn. It had all worked out perfectly. *For them.*

'So the Earl just *gave* you Redbourn?' She eyed him suspiciously.

'Not exactly. There are conditions.'

'How inconvenient.' She didn't bother to hide her sarcasm. 'But at least you still get your reward.'

'I've earned it.'

'Yes, you must have been *very* convincing.'

His eyelids flickered dangerously, though his stern expression didn't waver. 'The credit belongs to De Quincey. He truly loves your sister.'

She gave him a withering glare. Even if that

were true, it didn't necessarily mean that Cille loved *him.* And she wouldn't know that until she returned to Etton and asked her. At least now she could leave with de Quincey.

'So if you're the Warden, am I free to go?'

'No.' He held her gaze steadily. 'Not yet.'

'You said the Earl believed you.'

'He did. He wants us to marry.'

Marry? She mouthed the word, though it didn't come out. Instead she stared at him soundlessly, thinking she must have misheard. He'd said it so matter-of-factly, without so much as a flicker of emotion, that surely she *must* have misheard. If he'd said that the Earl himself wanted to marry her she couldn't have felt more surprised.

'He wants the Warden to marry a Saxon.'

'But…' She licked her lips, trying to loosen them. 'Why me? I don't have anything to do with Redbourn.'

'It was the Earl's choice.'

She flinched as if he'd just struck her. It was the Earl's choice—by implication not *his.* Well, what else had she expected? To be told that he'd asked for her, loved her, actually *wanted* to marry her? He looked distant and withdrawn, as if marriage to her was the very last thing he wanted. All he wanted was Redbourn.

'So I'm a…*condition*?'

'One of them.'

She bristled. So the Earl thought he could simply dispose of both her and Cille in one fell swoop, shaping their lives to his own advantage! Or had he guessed her deception after all? Was this some kind of twisted revenge? Forcing her to marry a man who clearly didn't want her?

'And when does the Earl want an answer?'

'He wishes it to be settled before he leaves.'

'But you said he was leaving *tomorrow*!'

'He is. Arrangements are already in place for de Quincey's wedding to your sister. If you're agreeable, we'll have our wedding feast tonight.'

'Tonight?'

'As I said, if you're agreeable.'

She staggered away from him, her mind whirling. Agreeable? How could she be *agreeable*? The very idea of marriage was abhorrent to her. She hadn't wanted to marry anyone since the first time Edmund had touched her.

As for marriage to *Svend*? The thought didn't repel her in quite the same way, but how could she possibly marry him now? At least when he'd been angry with her he'd *felt* something. Now his glacial expression made her feel cold all over. Whatever feelings he'd had for her were clearly long gone. If he'd only show some sign of emotion… melt just a little. Otherwise their marriage would be doomed from the start. How could she…? How could they…?

She swallowed nervously. Would it be a marriage in truth? Would he want to lie with her?

He seemed to guess the direction of her thoughts. 'You've nothing to fear from me. You can return to Etton in a few weeks, if you wish. Your sister inherited the land so it forms part of the Redbourn estate. You can look after the village as before. Our marriage will be a formal arrangement, that's all.'

'Oh.' She felt an unexpected twinge of disappointment. 'And if I refuse?'

'Make your objections known to the Earl, by all means.' He gave a dismissive shrug and then frowned, as if admitting something against his will. 'But I doubt he'll let you return to Etton if you refuse. He doesn't like to be thwarted.'

She froze, horrified, hardly knowing whether to laugh or cry at the irony. She'd started off pretending to be Cille and now she was becoming her in truth! If she married Svend she'd be mistress of Redbourn—become the very Saxon bride she'd come to rescue. But if she didn't who would take care of Etton? If this was the only way to protect her people what choice did she have?

'Unless…' Svend's frown deepened, as if a new thought had just occurred to him. 'Unless there's another reason you can't marry me?'

She looked at him askance. Did he mean besides the fact that he didn't love her? Or was love so unimportant to Normans?

'What do you mean?'

'You're of an age for marriage.' He looked suspicious. 'Who's Edmund?'

'What?' Her stomach twisted painfully. 'Why?'

'In Etton you said that was the name of your sister's husband. Who is he really? Yours?'

'No!'

'No…?'

He took a step closer and she clasped the blanket to her throat defensively. She hadn't thought that he could look any colder, but now his whole demeanour was positively chilling.

'When you asked about Cille's husband his was the first name I thought of.'

'So who is he?' His voice sounded clipped, as if he were keeping a tight rein on his emotions.

'If you must know, he is the son of a neighbouring Thane. My father wanted me to marry him.'

His face darkened and she felt a momentary surprise. He looked the same way de Quincey had done in the tent—as if he were jealous. But he couldn't be. He was probably just afraid of anything that might thwart his ambitions for Redbourn.

'And…?'

'And I didn't care for him—not like that.'

His expression shifted slightly. 'So you're not married?'

'Do you think I would have kissed you if I'd been married?'

'You seemed prepared to go to any lengths to protect your sister.'

'I wouldn't do *that*.'

He shrugged callously. 'You were pretending to be someone else. How do I know what else you were pretending?'

Aediva clenched her hands into fists, tempted to pick up the nearest blunt instrument and hit him with it. So that was what he thought of her? That she was the kind of woman who would use her body to get her own way? Every intimate moment between them felt tainted. Bad enough that he didn't trust her, but now he'd insulted her too! How dared he insult her and ask for her hand in marriage at the same time?

'How could you think such a thing?'

He took another step towards her, that icy demeanour slipping. 'How could you lie to me for so long?'

'I couldn't tell you the truth!'

'Not even last night?'

She faltered, the memory of their moonlit kiss arresting her anger. 'I thought I was doing what was best.'

'You didn't trust me.'

'I couldn't take the chance!'

'After I saved you from a bolting horse and nursed you through a fever? After everything I told you about Maren? You *still* didn't trust me?'

'What could you have done?' She squared up

to him combatively. 'If I'd told you the truth then you'd have had to arrest me. Otherwise you'd have been a traitor, an…'

She stopped and he raised an eyebrow, his lips curling sardonically as he finished the sentence for her. 'An outlaw?'

'Yes.' She jutted her chin up. 'Would you have thanked me for that?'

'No. But did you *really* think I'd arrest you?'

She caught her breath. Had she truly thought that? No, somehow she'd known from the first that he wouldn't do anything to hurt her. She'd been afraid of him discovering the truth, but not because of that. She'd feared something else entirely—had feared him hating her the way he hated her now.

She shook her head hopelessly. 'I was going to tell you this morning at the waterfall. I wanted to tell you. But then Sir Hugh arrived and it was too late.'

For an instant his expression seemed to waver. Then it hardened again, smoothing out into a hard, cynical mask. 'It *is* too late. For that and for this. The Earl's waiting. If you want to decline his proposal you can do it in person.'

'Now?'

How could she decide right now? There was too much to think about—for herself and for Etton too! How could she possibly make such a momentous decision so quickly?

He nodded icily. 'Marry me or don't. It's up to you. But decide quickly. I'll wait outside.'

Svend let the oxhide fall shut behind him, tempted to wrench it off with his hands. Keeping his emotions under control had been far harder than he'd expected. An enemy he could face down and fight, but who was *she*? Friend or foe? He was used to clarity, used to knowing who his enemy was. Damn it, where was a rebel raid when he needed one?

He rested his head against the timbered wall, letting his breathing return to normal. He shouldn't have gone in unannounced, but when she hadn't responded to his call he'd been afraid that she'd done something reckless and run away.

And when he'd seen her… His breathing had quickened again. Incredibly, she'd looked even more desirable than she had at the waterfall. The memory of her naked beauty was seared into his memory, but her loose-fitting shift and tumbling curls had been almost a provocation too far. Standing on the coffer, her small breasts on a level with his face, she'd looked so wantonly desirable it had been all he could do not to haul her into his arms and consummate their marriage right then.

He forced his body back under control. Bedding her would only make his life more complicated, and he needed clarity where she was concerned. Whatever his heart felt, his head was still in command—at least for now.

She hadn't given him a definite answer about the marriage, but he'd been surprised at how calmly she'd taken the Earl's command. She'd actually seemed more shocked than angry, had hardly ranted about Normans at all.

The thought of Edmund had occurred to him only belatedly, sending a surge of jealousy coursing through his veins. Until that moment he'd thought that he wanted a way out of the marriage, but when the possibility had arisen he'd found himself wanting to fight for her instead. He'd insulted her by asking, but he'd needed to be sure. Was she married or not? And if she wasn't…if her heart and body were still untouched…if she'd kissed him because she wanted to and not simply because she was deceiving him… The thought was more than a little enticing.

That was *if* she agreed to marry him.

The look on her face when he'd told her about Etton made him wonder. He hadn't wanted to mention it at all—hadn't wanted to sway her answer—but she needed to know the truth. If she refused the Earl's command he wasn't likely to let her go home.

For the first time he found himself wishing she *were* more selfish, like Maren. If she only thought of herself then at least he'd know what she wanted. He knew she felt a strong sense of duty towards her people. It would be typical of her to agree to the marriage just to protect them. It certainly wouldn't prove anything about her feelings for *him*.

Well, their marriage would be based on duty—not love. Hers to her people, his to the King. He wasn't about to succumb to temptation and let her make a fool of him again. He'd marry her for Redbourn, nothing more.

The oxhide swung open again and he tried his hardest not to react. She was dressed in an emerald-green gown, cinched at the waist with a tasselled belt, showing the curve of her hip to tantalising perfection. Her dark hair was covered with a veil, held in place with a copper headband that made her eyes seem even bigger and brighter, flickering like jewels in the candlelight.

'Is this better?'

She ran her hands over the fabric self-consciously and he felt his blood surge with desire. *Better?* He'd found her alluring enough when she'd been dirt-stained and tattered, so this was almost more than he could bear. She looked stunning—more beautiful than any woman he'd ever laid eyes on. He felt himself harden just looking at her. If it weren't for the Earl expecting them they'd get no further than this hall…

'Better.'

He offered an arm gruffly and she took it, resting a hand on his bicep as they crossed the bailey in strained silence.

The hall itself was a riotous assault on the senses, crowded with knights and a scattering of ladies, and all eyes swivelled like magnets as they entered. Svend clenched his jaw fiercely. Every man in the room was looking at her with undisguised admiration, most of them hardly bothering to hide what they were thinking. He raised his spare hand to cover hers on his arm, saw her glance at him in surprise.

'Lady Aediva—at last!' FitzOsbern's gaze swept over her approvingly as they approached the dais. 'There seems to have been some confusion regarding your identity, my lady.'

Svend felt her hand tremble slightly on his arm, though her face showed no trace of fear as she dipped into a low, graceful curtsy.

'Apologies, my lord. The fault was all mine.'

'Then I hope you're here to make reparation? I trust you've been informed of my wishes?'

For a moment she didn't answer, and Svend felt himself tense. If she were going to refuse the marriage then it would be now. And suddenly he wanted very badly for her to agree.

'I understand that you wish for us to marry?'

His heart sank. Her voice was loud and clear, carrying to all four corners of the hall, too bold, too defiant, as if she were preparing to refuse the Earl after all.

'Indeed.' FitzOsbern stood up expectantly. 'So, Lady Aediva, we're here for a wedding. Are you willing?'

'If it pleases you, my lord, I am.'

Chapter Thirteen

Aediva sat miserably at the high table, trapped between the Earl and her new husband, keeping a rictus smile on her face. If she smiled any harder she thought her face would crack. Or she would.

She winced as a seemingly endless array of dishes were paraded past her trencher: duck drenched in honey, chicken stuffed with egg yolk, kidney and liver, woodcock and wild boar—more food than she usually saw in a month. She wondered where it had all come from. The Conqueror's army had plundered the land, leaving the Saxons starving, but here at the Earl's court there was no sign of shortage. The contrast would have turned her stomach even if his presence had not.

Absently, she twisted the copper band on her finger. How had it happened? She was *married*. To her enemy. Not by force, not against her wishes, but willingly, without so much as a murmur of protest, and in the presence of the Earl himself. What would her father have thought of her now?

But she was protecting Etton, she reminded herself. That was the reason she'd done it—the only reason that made any sense. She didn't care for Svend…not after every insult and accusation he'd heaped on her. She was protecting her people, acting the part of Saxon lady and willing bride. That was her duty. Even if it meant life with a man who despised her.

She cast a sidelong glance towards her new husband, but his whole attention seemed riveted on the entertainment before them—a brightly coloured collection of jugglers, dancers and musicians. He'd been politely attentive all through the meal, loading her trencher with an array of delicacies, though he'd barely spoken a word, the smile on his lips never reaching his eyes.

Well, it wasn't as if *she* wanted to be there either. She felt more alone in this crowded hall than she ever had at Etton. At least there she'd been amongst her own people, but now she could see nothing but strangers. Who were they? Who was *she*? Was she still Saxon or was she now Norman by marriage? Or Danish? Whoever she was, she felt surplus to requirements. This feast had been planned for de Quincey and Cille. Her marriage to Svend was just an excuse. If she slipped away she doubted anyone would notice. Probably not even her husband.

She chewed her lip resentfully. She wasn't exactly sure what she ought to be doing on her wedding night, but she was quite certain that she shouldn't be doing it on her own.

'Did you know your husband plays the lyre?' FitzOsbern's voice broke through her reverie.

Svend's head snapped round at once. 'Not well.'

'Passably well.' The Earl's smile was teasing. 'When he came to Court he knew nothing of music or culture. I told him a knight had to do more with his hands than just fight. Come, Svend, honour us with a tune. A song for your new bride.'

'As you wish.' Svend inclined his head and stepped down from the dais, borrowing a lyre from one of the musicians. 'I'll play, but I don't sing.'

Aediva knotted her hands in her lap as he strode to the centre of the hall. If he were playing for her, then silence would be more appropriate. It certainly wouldn't be a love song.

He looked at her thoughtfully for a moment, then started to run his fingers lightly over the strings, skilful as a weaver at his spindle. Aediva listened, spellbound. She'd never imagined him caring for pursuits such as music. It seemed so unexpected and incongruous, his warrior hands too big for such a small instrument, but he looked perfectly at ease. It was a ballad of some kind—a tune she didn't recognise—bittersweet and soulful.

'He's a fine musician.' FitzOsbern leaned conspiratorially on the arm of her chair, too close for comfort. 'You're lucky to have such a champion. I only hope that you're worth it.'

Worth it? She stared at the Earl, perplexed. Worth *what*? The words implied that Svend had lost something by marrying her, but that didn't make sense. He had the reward he'd always wanted and more. That was the reason he'd married her. *She* was the one who'd been threatened with the loss of her home. As far as she could see he hadn't sacrificed anything.

'Of course,' FitzOsbern continued, 'I have to wonder why you left your sister so soon after her birthing.'

She started, caught off guard by the abrupt change of subject. The Earl's tone was pleasant, but his words made her scalp tingle.

'My message was urgent.'

'And yet Svend could have delivered it himself.'

'There were things my sister wanted me to explain in person.'

'Such as why she left?' He raised his eyebrows, his expression shifting menacingly. 'Strange...de Quincey seems no wiser about that. But keep trying, Lady Aediva, you might still convince me.'

'Convince you?' She struggled to keep her voice calm.

Green eyes narrowed like daggers, pinning her to the spot. 'Normally I don't tolerate my men hiding things from me, but then some men are more useful than others. I won't ask what you're *really* doing here, but Svend has a job to do. If he fails me I'll know who to blame.'

Aediva inhaled sharply. There was no mistaking the threat behind his words. Apparently Svend and de Quincey hadn't been as convincing as they'd thought. FitzOsbern suspected her of something, even if he didn't know what.

A round of applause interrupted them and she turned to find Svend watching her. His song had drawn to a close without her noticing, and his gaze was moving suspiciously between her and the Earl. She had the distinct impression that he hadn't missed so much as a glance of their exchange.

'Excellent!' The Earl cheered. 'Now for the bride's turn! I've heard a great deal about Saxon music. Perhaps you would oblige me, Lady Aediva?'

She felt her stomach lurch. How could he expect her to sing with his threat still roaring in her ears? *What* could she possibly sing? Bad enough to be made a spectacle for so many Normans—now she was expected to entertain them as well? Her throat had never felt so dry. Every eye in the room was on her and she couldn't remember so much as a child's rhyme.

Slowly she descended from the dais, stalling for time as she searched her memory for a song, a melody—anything to end the torturous silence. Svend brushed past her and for a fleeting moment she felt his hand grasp hers reassuringly. Then he was gone and her mind was an ever greater blank, coherent thought banished by the unexpected thrill of his touch.

What did *that* mean?

'It seems Saxon music is overrated,' the Earl murmured, sending a ripple of laughter around the tables.

Desperately she looked towards Svend, but he wasn't laughing. He was looking straight at her, his gaze sharp and intent, as if he were willing her on, trying to send her words.

She opened her mouth and let an old Saxon love song pour through her lips, the words emerging even before she knew what she was singing—words she hadn't known she remembered—the notes soaring and dropping in a tale of unrequited love and heartache. It was a song she'd never truly thought about, never understood until now.

She closed her eyes, fighting the bitter sting of tears. The last time she'd heard the song had been at Cille's wedding, long before the Conquest, when the Saxon world had seemed so strong and unchangeable. Now everything was so different she almost wished that she hadn't remembered it. The words, the memory—they all meant too much.

She let the last note linger, opening her eyes

at last to a hall held still and silent, as if gripped by some enchantment. Svend's gaze was still on her, his eyes glowing with something more than appreciation, as if he felt and understood the song too. As if he understood her.

'A sad song for a bride,' the Earl commented drily, and the spell was broken.

'Dancing!' someone called, and she found herself swallowed up in a sea of couples, Svend's face vanishing behind them.

Quickly she wiped her tears on her sleeve and made for the door. The urge to escape the hall was becoming unbearable. She needed some air… just a few minutes alone to recover. Surely no one would notice if she stepped outside for a moment?

'Care to dance?'

Sir Hugh bowed unsteadily before her, his brown eyes sparkling with wine, and she shook her head, wishing she could simply push past him. If she didn't get out of there soon she would scream!

'Not tonight, Hugh.'

Svend's voice at her shoulder sent a tingling sensation down her spine, making her relieved and apprehensive at the same time.

'The lady's already spoken for.'

'Thank you.' She looked up at him nervously as Hugh staggered away, surprised that he had been able to reach her so quickly.

'You looked in need of rescuing.' He took her

arm and tucked it inside his. 'Where were you going?'

'Just outside.' She flexed her fingers on the hard muscles of his bicep. 'I don't know any Norman dances.'

'And I have two left feet. We'd make a pretty pair on the dance floor. Are you ready to escape?'

'Escape?' She felt irrationally offended. This was their wedding feast! He could at least *pretend* to be happy. 'You mean you aren't enjoying yourself?'

'About as much as you are.'

'And who says I'm not?'

'Your face is quite expressive, my lady. But if you want to stay…'

'No!' She tightened her grip on his arm hastily. 'You win. But don't we *have* to stay? Won't anyone mind?'

He gave her a wry look. 'I think we've done our duty. Besides, most of them have more wine in their veins now than blood. They wouldn't notice if we flew out of here.'

She bit her lip, suppressing a smile. She couldn't argue with that. It wasn't so much a dance going on around them as a stumble.

'We just need to ask permission from the Earl first. Come on.' He swung around, pulling her after him before she could protest. 'Let's get this over with.'

Get this over with?

She stumbled after him, torn between resentment and alarm. Was he *determined* to offend her? That had to be the least romantic thing she'd ever heard. Besides which, this was their wedding night! He wasn't just escorting her out of the hall. He was going to go with her. And the last thing she wanted was to be alone with him. He'd said that she had nothing to fear, but he was still her husband.

Suddenly she wished she'd accepted Hugh's offer to dance.

'Ready to leave so soon?' The Earl's face broke into a lascivious grin as they approached the high table. 'Are you so eager, Danemark? Or is it the lady who desires your company?'

'A man can dream.' Svend put a hand on his heart with mock gallantry. 'Sad to say, my new wife is tired. With your permission, I'll show her to bed.'

'And tend to her in it, no doubt.' The Earl smirked. 'You may leave us.'

He waved a hand to dismiss them and she spun around instantly, wanting to get the hall, the banquet, the whole evening behind her. Her husband too, if she could. How could he joke about her so publicly? It would serve him right if—

For a moment she didn't know what was happening. She staggered slightly, then felt a sharp tug on her arm, followed by a jolt as her knees buckled and she stumbled over her sleeves, falling headlong into a pair of familiar strong arms.

'It seems she can't wait for your embrace, Svend!' The Earl was bent over, laughing. 'Perhaps you ought to carry her?'

She felt a flash of panic, swiftly followed by outrage as Svend's hands swooped around the back of her legs, lifting her into his arms.

'Put me down!' She kicked her feet indignantly. 'Everyone's looking!'

'I'm not surprised.'

'Let me down!'

'Not in *that* dress. You'll break a limb if you're not careful.'

She glared at him. So much for her attempt to act like a lady. Just when she'd thought things couldn't get any worse, it seemed he didn't like her dress either.

They reached the antechamber and he turned away from the main door, heading towards a narrow staircase in the corner.

'Aren't we going to Cille's chamber?' She twisted her head in surprise.

'No.' His step didn't falter. 'The Earl's given us use of the main chamber a day early. He thought we might be more comfortable there.'

'Oh.'

She kept her face averted as they entered the room and he kicked the door shut behind them. A fire was blazing in the hearth and the floor was strewn with fresh rushes, making it look new and homely, bigger and more luxurious than any bedchamber she'd ever been in before. If she'd been on her own she might have found it inviting. In Svend's arms she found her eyes drawn inexorably to the large, intricately carved wooden bed in the centre.

She'd barely had a chance to look before he dropped her unceremoniously on top of it, tipping her in a tangle of skirts and sleeves onto the softest, most comfortable mattress she'd ever imagined. For a moment she was tempted to stay put, before scrambling up again hurriedly as he started to undress.

'What are you doing?'

'Isn't it obvious?' Svend unfastened his belt, letting it coil in a heap on a floor. 'It's been a long day. I'm going to bed.'

'But you said that you… That we wouldn't…'

'We're not.' He pulled his tunic over his head and tossed it aside. 'I told you—you're safe with me. This is a marriage of convenience. I want it as much as you do.'

'I don't want it at *all*!'

She swung her legs off the side of the bed, affronted. No groom could have looked less pleased to be alone with his bride. How dared he talk as if he were the injured party when she'd practically been blackmailed into marriage?

'I'll sleep on the floor.'

He kicked his boots into a corner with a sigh. 'Aediva, unless you want this marriage annulled then we have to at least pretend to share a bed.'

At least? She looked up in alarm. The words suggested the possibility of more.

'Who's going to know where I sleep? We're sharing a room, aren't we?'

'We are.'

His hands dropped to the ties of his hose and she averted her eyes quickly, though not before she saw the flash of humour in his.

'So long as you explain what you're doing to the Earl's men.'

'What?' Out of the corner of her eye she saw his hose fall to the floor.

'Let's just say they like to make sure the marriage contract is sealed. But if you can think of a reason why you're down there and I'm up here… Perhaps you can say you rolled off?'

'But surely they won't come in *here*?'

'Not if they value their limbs.' He laid himself out on the bed with an exaggerated groan. 'Unless the Earl orders it. Then they'd have no choice.'

'But…'

'We'll have to wait and see.' He gave a sardonic laugh. 'Then at least we'll have *some* excitement tonight.'

She shot him a dark look. What kind of barbaric Norman custom was that? She had a feeling he was trying to scare her, but it sounded plausible enough to be true. Well, he wasn't going to rattle her so easily. She'd stay awake and guard the door all night if she had to. She wasn't going to climb into bed with him voluntarily.

'I'll move if I hear them coming. I doubt they'll be able to approach quietly.'

'As you wish.' He sounded half asleep already.

She undressed quickly, scooping up a blanket to drape over the rushes before settling down to unravel her braid, letting the tresses splay out over her shoulders.

'I like it loose.'

She glanced up in surprise. She'd thought that he was already asleep, but he was propped up on one elbow, watching the progress of her fingers through her hair admiringly.

'I can never decide if it's dark gold or light brown…' He seemed to be genuinely considering the question.

'It's hair.' She dropped her hands at once, tempted to find the nearest shears and give herself a cropped Norman haircut just to spite him.

'Obviously.' Pale brows arched upwards. 'How's the floor? Comfortable?'

'Perfectly.'

'Good.' He settled down again. 'I'd hate to inconvenience you on our wedding night.'

Before long his breathing altered and she glowered into the darkness. She hadn't heard him snore at all during their journey to Redbourn, and now she was almost certain he was doing it on purpose. Worse still, the wooden floor felt as hard as rock. She wasn't accustomed to luxury, only a straw-filled mattress, but no matter how she twisted or turned she couldn't get comfortable. At this rate she wouldn't get a wink of sleep.

She sighed, inwardly conceding that she ought to have shared the bed. He was her husband, after all. There was nothing wrong in it. And, no matter how angry he was, she trusted him not to do anything she didn't want.

It *was* what she wanted—that was the problem. Despite everything, the thought of sharing a bed with him wasn't nearly as repellent as it ought to be. Far from it. And she definitely didn't want him to find out about that.

She curled up into a ball, trying to make a cocoon of body heat. The fire was fading and she felt too cold to sleep now—probably due to the icy presence of her husband. Surely a knight ought to give up his bed for a lady? Or did those rules not apply to Saxon wives?

And then he was beside her, lifting her up before she knew what was happening.

She squealed, looking towards the door in panic. 'Are the Earl's men here?'

'No, but we'll neither of us get any sleep if you're going to writhe about all night. Get in!'

He laid her down on the bed, gently this time, drawing the blankets in around her before striding to the door and dragging a wooden coffer across it.

'Is that better?'

She nodded, answering a different question, enjoying the feathery comfort of the mattress, not to mention the warm space left by his body. This was what she'd been afraid of, and yet the very last thing she wanted was to go back to the floor.

'Good.' He walked to the other side of the bed and climbed in. 'Like it or not, Aediva, we're stuck in this together. We might as well try to make the best of it. Now, get some sleep. Trust me, I'll break the arm of any man who comes in here.'

Chapter Fourteen

Somehow they'd come together in sleep. Svend opened his eyes to find their bodies entwined, her cheek nestling against his chest as his arm curved protectively around her waist, holding her to him as if he couldn't bear to let go.

So much for punishing her. He hadn't even been able to leave her on the floor.

Instinctively he started to pull away, but she made a faint murmur of protest and he stopped, wondering how to extricate himself without waking her. Not that he particularly wanted to. She felt soft and warm, and her hair smelt of honeysuckle and daisies, heady and intoxicating. He took a deep breath, inhaling the now familiar scent, fighting the urge to pull her even closer.

He'd slept surprisingly well beside her, so deeply that he had no idea which of them had initiated the embrace, but their bodies fitted together perfectly, like two parts of a whole. There was no other way to describe it. Her being there felt *right*.

He felt a stirring in his loins and shifted his lower body quickly. The last thing he needed was for her to wake up and find him like this. He'd come this far through the night in bed with her—he wasn't about to lose control now. They might be married, but nothing else between them had changed. She'd still deceived him and he still couldn't trust her.

Even if, lying beside her, he could hardly trust *himself*.

He pulled away—determinedly this time. But she rolled after him, eyes still closed, arms outstretched, as if she wanted to hold him still. A surge of desire coursed through him and he stamped it down quickly. Judging from the sound of horses and marching feet outside, not to mention the slivers of light pouring in through gaps under the rafters, he'd already stayed too long abed. He had duties to attend to—the Earl's departure, for one.

He dressed quickly, pulling the coffer away from the door as quietly as he could before descending the tower steps and stepping outside. The sun was even higher than he'd expected, the bailey already half empty as the Earl's army marched out through the castle gates.

'The Warden emerges at last!' The Earl swung

his destrier round in greeting. 'We'd almost given up hope of seeing you this morning.'

'My lord.' Svend inclined his head. 'I couldn't let you leave without saying goodbye and expressing my thanks once again.'

'For Redbourn or for your wife? I've never known you to be late for anything before.'

'For both, of course.'

'Then I'm glad you're enjoying them.' FitzOsbern's smile widened as his mount stamped at the ground impatiently. 'Redbourn's a fine castle. You've earned it—now take care of it.'

'Yes, my lord.'

'And remember I'm counting on you. Don't let me down, Danemark.'

Svend nodded sombrely, watching as the Earl and his knights thundered out through the gates, most of them looking distinctly the worse for wear. In the bright light of day even Hugh's good-natured face looked unusually strained, his brown eyes bloodshot and bleary as he waved farewell.

At last they were gone and he glanced back up at the tower, his thoughts returning to the woman in his bed, before forcing his attention back to the bailey.

FitzOsbern was right. Redbourn was a fine castle. It was a formidable example of Norman engineering, and it was *his*. He could still scarcely believe it. The building work was nearing completion—the masons' hammers echoed loudly in the morning air—but now that the army had gone he could see Saxon structures too: wooden dwellings, stables and barns scattered in amidst the new Norman stone buildings.

He felt a twinge of unease looking at the two different worlds, Saxon and Norman, side by side and yet distinctly apart, as if the differences between them were too great to merge into one.

That was a sign, if ever he'd seen one.

He frowned. What the hell was wrong with him? He ought to be happy. He had everything he'd ever wanted and more. So why couldn't he stop thinking about one woman?

He shook his head impatiently, gazing out over the battlements. The day was cold but bright, with thin wisps of cloud scudding across a pale blue sky—perfect for a ride to clear his head. Rays of sunshine were kissing the tops of the hills in the distance, as if challenging him to catch them, and he felt a shiver of anticipation.

But sunshine wasn't all he had to catch. The Earl had been explicit in his instructions, giving him a month to clear the county of rebel incursions and establish Norman control. As far as the first days of his marriage went, hunting down his wife's countrymen made for an ominous start, but those were his orders. Otherwise he might find himself out of a castle as quickly as he'd found himself *in* one.

He set his jaw determinedly and made for the stables, summoning his men as he passed. The sooner they got started the better. Idle soldiers made for ill discipline and worse behaviour. He'd set a bad enough example this morning, by tarrying in bed. It was time to get back to work. That was what they were there for.

And this time there wouldn't be a woman to distract him.

Aediva felt it the moment Svend moved away, heard herself murmuring in response. Unconsciously, she reached out towards him and then froze, hardly daring to breathe as he dressed and left the room without her.

Then she opened her eyes and let out a sigh of relief. That was that. The door had stayed closed and somehow she'd got through her wedding night untouched and unscathed. As far as anyone else was concerned the marriage contract was sealed and she was Svend's wife.

She stretched her arms, rolling into the warm space left by his body. She didn't know how their bodies had ended up together, but she hadn't wanted him to move. She hadn't felt repulsed or horrified or even reluctant. She'd felt safe in his arms, safer than she'd felt in a long time, as if she somehow belonged there.

But it wasn't real. He'd made it clear enough how he felt about her. And she didn't want a man who didn't trust her, no matter how safe she felt in his arms.

She heard voices outside and strained to listen, but the words were muffled, followed by ribald laughter. They were probably laughing about *her*. She wanted to bury her head under the covers and stay there, but what jokes would they make about her then? Besides, she wasn't going to hide as if she had done anything to feel ashamed or guilty about. She'd done what was necessary to protect her people. Just as Svend had done what was necessary for his reward. That was their arrangement.

The fact that he'd carried her to bed and she'd woken up in his arms meant nothing.

In any case, she had her own business to attend to. Now that the Earl was leaving, she ought to try and find out what had *really* happened between Cille and de Quincey. If what Svend had told her was true, then somebody in Redbourn had to know something.

'Lady Aediva?' A maid poked her head around the door. 'The Warden thought you might be hungry. I've brought you some porridge.'

'Oh…thank you.' She felt a moment's surprise. Apparently Svend had been thinking about her even as he'd left.

The maid handed her a bowl and Aediva looked at her thoughtfully. There was something familiar about her round face and strawberry blonde curls.

'Were you one of my sister's maids? I think I've seen you before.'

'Yes, my lady, I was with Lady Cille when she was in Redbourn.'

'Judith!' She sprang forward impulsively, grasping the other woman's hands. 'You're Judith!'

The maid nodded shyly. 'I didn't think you'd remember me.'

'Well, I do.' She pulled back, smiling. Somehow just being with someone who knew her sister made her feel closer to Cille. Besides, it felt good to speak Saxon again. She'd been surrounded by Normans for so long she'd almost forgotten how.

'How *is* my lady?' Judith sounded anxious. 'They say de Quincey's gone after her.'

'He still wants to marry her. Did she tell you what happened between them?'

'No.' Judith shook her head. 'She wasn't happy with Leofric, but she was always loyal to him. She mourned his death after Hastings. Then when de Quincey arrived she seemed different…agitated, somehow…but I never knew why. Everyone could see he was smitten, but she never said anything—not to me or the other maids.'

'She was unhappy with Leofric?' Aediva felt a jolt of surprise. 'She never told me that. What was the matter?'

Judith looked hesitant. 'It's not my place to say, my lady.'

'Did she spend much time with de Quincey?'

'They dined together, and they spoke about the building work, but she never showed him any special favour. It wasn't until after he was gone that she seemed…' Judith frowned, as if searching for the right word. 'Frightened…'

'Frightened?'

'But I never thought she'd run away like she did. Not in her condition.'

'So you knew she was pregnant?'

'I suspected. She was sick in the mornings. And there were rumours.'

'But you don't *know* that de Quincey's the father?'

'No, but…who else?'

Aediva chewed her lip thoughtfully. At least she wasn't the only one who'd been surprised by Cille's behaviour, but she still didn't have the answers she was looking for. And if Judith didn't know…

She clambered off the bed. She wasn't going to be defeated so easily. She'd ask every man, woman and child in Redbourn if she had to.

Just as soon as she got dressed.

She stopped short in the middle of the floor, struck by a new dilemma. 'My clothes! They took them for washing and Cille's gowns are in the other hall.'

'Don't worry, the Warden thought of that too.

He's having one of Lady Cille's coffers sent up. Your old gown isn't fit to be seen.'

'He's sending the clothes *here*?' Aediva's eyes widened in surprise. If he were having clothes sent to the bedchamber did that mean he expected her to sleep there permanently? He'd said that they would lead separate lives, and she'd assumed that this would be his room, not hers. Or did he intend for them to share it?

'He's very handsome.' Judith gave her a sly look.

'He's Norman. Sort of.' She took refuge in the old argument.

'That doesn't make him less pleasing to look at. There's plenty here that would have him, but he seems to have eyes only for you.'

'He does *not*!' She felt a telltale blush spread up and over her cheeks. 'Not like that anyway. Maybe once, but not now.'

Judith smiled serenely. 'If you say so, my lady. But I saw his face this morning. It was the same as de Quincey's when he met Lady Cille last year. And look what happened there…'

It was twilight by the time the scouting party returned, the clouds turning to misty drizzle as they rode back through the gates, sodden and saddle-sore.

Svend let his men disperse quickly. They'd ridden across half the county that day, finding signs of rebel activity although no rebels themselves. But it was a promising start. The trail was warm—could be picked up again tomorrow. They'd find them soon enough…he was sure of it.

He ate a brief dinner and then made his way to the bedchamber, pausing with his hand on the door. Would Aediva be inside? There'd been no sign of her in the hall, but that was hardly surprising. She'd probably gone back to her sister's old room. But there was still a chance…

He opened the door and felt an unexpected pang of disappointment. So much for his wife. He'd been the one to leave her that morning, and yet somehow he'd hoped that she'd still be there. Even after such a long day—*especially* after such a long day—he'd wanted to see her. After a week in her company he'd grown accustomed to seeing her, had felt a vague sense of unease at their being apart.

Damn it all, he'd *missed* her.

He strode to the table and plunged his hands into a bowl of fresh water, rubbing them vigorously over his face. How was it possible? Except for his mother and sisters, he'd never missed a woman in his life. He certainly hadn't missed Maren after she'd betrayed him. So how could he miss his wife—a woman he hardly knew and barely trusted? It was ridiculous, irrational. He was tired and wet and not thinking straight. Her absence was the best thing for both of them. He definitely didn't want another argument tonight.

'Svend?'

He turned around in surprise. Of all the places he'd thought to look for her, the bed itself had never occurred to him. But there she was, facing towards him, a tiny bump beneath a pile of blankets. No wonder he hadn't noticed her.

His heart seemed to skip a beat.

'You've been gone all day.' Her voice was quietly accusing.

'Yes.' He felt a twinge of conscience. He probably should have left some kind of message, to say where he was going, but the thought had never occurred to him. He wasn't used to explaining himself—especially to a woman. But a husband ought to have done so.

'Where have you been?'

Hunting Saxons. He grimaced, wishing he could give a different answer. 'The Earl ordered me to clear the county of rebels. We've been searching for them.'

'And?'

'We've taken no prisoners today.'

'Oh.'

She sounded relieved and he took a tentative step towards her.

'Did I wake you?'

'No. I wasn't asleep, just…thinking.'

'Have you been in bed all day?' A wicked smile

tugged at the corners of his mouth. 'People will wonder what I've done to you.'

'Of course not!' Her cheeks flooded with colour. 'I've been trying to find out about Cille and de Quincey.'

'Ah. And what have you learned?'

'Nothing.' She gave a plaintive sigh. 'No one seems to know anything.'

He took another step towards the bed. 'And that bothers you?'

She nodded, pulling herself upright. 'We never used to have secrets from each other. She was always more than a sister. Our mother died when I was born, and Cille took care of me. She was only a child herself, but she knew what to do. When she came back to Etton last spring I wanted to look after *her*, to protect her the way she'd protected me.'

'You did.'

'No, I let her down. That's why she didn't tell me about de Quincey.' She shook her head, her eyes glittering with unshed tears. 'Now it's like I don't know her at all.'

Svend folded his arms, resisting the urge to comfort her. Sitting up in bed, with her arms wrapped around her knees, she looked smaller and more vulnerable than he'd ever seen her.

'What about her first husband? Leofric? Did she ever talk about him?'

'No.' She sniffed unhappily. 'People say the

marriage wasn't happy, but she never told *me* that either.'

'So it wasn't a love match?'

'No, it was a peace-weaver. Their marriage sealed a union between the north and south of the shire. There had been raiding between villages, not to mention from the marshes. It got so bad that an alliance became necessary. So Cille was sent to Redbourn.'

'But there were no children? In five years?'

'No, she was afraid she couldn't have them.'

'Until she met de Quincey?'

'Until she met de Quincey,' she repeated softly. 'I never thought she might be unhappy with Leofric. Everyone said it was a good match. But it must have been terrible for her, married to a man she didn't…'

She bit her lip and Svend gave a twisted smile. 'Didn't love? Quite. But she might still find happiness with de Quincey.'

'I hope so.'

She saw his sceptical expression and drew herself up indignantly.

'I do!'

'Even though he's Norman?'

'Yes, if she loves him. I want her to be happy.'

He moved away from her into the shadows, feeling a surge of some powerful emotion in his chest, as though the knot of resentment there were slowly uncoiling. She seemed genuine, but how could he be sure? It didn't sound like her, but then she'd already changed so much in one week… Was it possible that she didn't hate Normans quite so vehemently any more? If she could let her own sister be happy, what did that mean for *them*?

'It sounds like you need to talk to her.'

'You said de Quincey was taking her to Normandy…' Her voice was faint, strangled with emotion. 'When will I ever see her again?'

He swore under his breath. Had she been upset about that? He could have saved her that anguish at least.

'You'll see her soon enough. I have asked him to bring her here before they leave.'

'You asked him that?' Her face was transformed suddenly. 'Svend, I don't know what to say. Thank you.'

He gave a grunt of acknowledgement. She looked beautiful, positively radiating happiness, but he didn't want her gratitude. He wanted… He dug his heels into the rushes, resisting the temptation to move back towards the bed. He wasn't sure *what* he wanted, but he didn't want her to feel that she owed him anything.

'When do you think they'll be here?'

'A couple of weeks, maybe. You can get your answers then—though you might have your own explaining to do.'

'What do you mean?'

'She might be curious about us.'

'Us…?' Her voice wavered slightly.

'The last she knew, you were threatening to kill me. Now we're married. And you say *she's* mysterious?'

'This is different. There's nothing mysterious about us. You married me for Redbourn.'

'As you married me for Etton.'

'Exactly. Cille and de Quincey are in love. Probably.' Her brow furrowed slightly. 'We're not.'

'And that seems better to you?' He gave a bitter laugh.

'I didn't say that!' She threw herself down on the bed, turning her back on him. 'It's just how it is.'

Svend muttered an oath, hurling his clothes across the room as he started to undress. She hadn't changed at all! She was the same argumentative, intractable shrew he'd met a week ago. If there was no mystery, it was only because he'd already uncovered her deceit! And if they weren't in love, it was because *she'd* lied to him! He hadn't *asked* to marry her, he'd simply been stuck with her. None of this was his fault.

He climbed into the bed, still fuming. 'I didn't think you'd be here.'

'What do you mean?'

He saw her shoulders tense and gave a curt smile. 'I thought you'd be back in your sister's old room.'

'You had my clothes sent here.'

'I assumed you'd need some this morning. I didn't think you'd stay.'

'Oh.' She was silent for a moment. 'I thought you said we had to pretend?'

'For the Earl.' He stretched out, enjoying the obvious embarrassment in her voice. 'But he's gone.'

She sprang up at once, swinging her legs off the bed as if she'd just felt a mouse in the mattress. 'Then I'll go.'

'Don't be ridiculous.' He threw an arm behind his head. 'If I send my wife out in the rain the whole castle will hear of it.'

'Fine.' She eyed him warily over her shoulder. 'I'll stay—but just for tonight.'

He shrugged and she climbed slowly back under the blanket, curling up on the edge of the bed as far away from him as she could get. He felt a twinge of guilt, already regretting his words. He'd been cruel, venting his anger by making her feel she wasn't welcome when in fact the very opposite was true. He didn't want her to go. He wanted to stretch out beside her and pull her face close to his…

Damn it, this was intolerable! How could he possibly share a bed with his wife and not touch her?

'Aediva…' He stretched a hand out and then thought better of it, shifting his body sideways instead. 'Move over. I won't bite. I had your things sent here so that you'd have a choice of clothing. You can move them back whenever you're ready.'

'They're not *my* things.' Her voice sounded muffled.

'I doubt your sister will mind you borrowing them.'

'Won't she?' She rolled over to face him again. 'What if she doesn't understand? What if she doesn't forgive me?'

'For borrowing her clothes?'

'For the rest of it! You're right—I *do* have some explaining to do. She came home for help and I failed her. I left her alone. I was supposed to take care of her, but I came here instead and married you. This is *her* land, *her* castle! I didn't mean to, but somehow I stole it! What if she doesn't forgive me?'

'You were trying to protect her—she'll understand that. And, as I recall, you didn't just leave her alone. I almost had to drag you away. Tell her the truth and she'll forgive you.'

'*You* won't.'

'What?'

She regarded him sombrely. 'You said that you understood, but you still won't forgive me.'

He exhaled slowly. 'I can forgive you, Aediva. I just can't forget.'

'Because I lied? Like Maren?'

'I don't trust easily.'

'So that's it?' She pulled herself up angrily.

'I make one mistake and you hold it against me for ever?'

'One mistake? I could have lost everything!'

'But you didn't! You got your reward.'

'Do you think that's all that matters to me?'

'Isn't it…?' Her voice faltered. 'I thought it was all you wanted.'

'Not *all*.' He felt his resolve weaken. 'Aediva, why do you think I lied to the Earl?'

'Because you were being honourable.'

'Honourable?' He stared at her in disbelief. 'I'm an outlaw, remember?'

'You *were* an outlaw—now you're a knight. And you're more honourable than you think. You've been nothing but honourable since we met. I just didn't appreciate it at first.'

'That's not why I lied to the Earl.'

Her eyes widened. 'Then why?'

'Because I didn't want to see you get hurt. Is that so hard to believe?'

'No. It's what an honourable man would do.'

'Oh, for pity's sake! Forget it, Aediva, it doesn't change anything.'

'It changes *everything*!' She put a hand on his chest tentatively. 'Svend, I know that you saved me, and I know what you risked. I wouldn't lie to you again—not after that. You can trust me.' Black eyelashes fluttered closed and then open again. 'If you want to.'

'*Want* to?' He felt every part of himself stiffen

at once. He had a feeling they weren't just talking about trust any more. 'Do *you* want to?'

She nodded silently and his voice turned to a growl.

'Be careful what you wish for.'

Aediva held her breath. His voice was low and dangerous and achingly familiar. It made her body feel tight, as if all her nerve endings had sprung to life at once. He'd said that he wanted to protect her. He'd said that he could forgive her. Could he learn to forget as well? And if he could…if he *didn't* only care about his reward…was there still a chance for them?

Did he still want her? Did she still want him?

Yes.

A thrill of anticipation coursed through her, impossible to resist. She knew the answer with every fibre of her being. And if his voice could arouse her so easily, what could the rest of him do?

He cupped a hand around the back of her neck, scrutinising her face as if he were searching for something. 'I need to trust you, Aediva.'

'You can.' She trailed her fingers down the length of his jaw. It felt strong and solid and unmistakably male. She ached to explore the rest of him.

'No more lies.' His own fingers tightened convulsively, as if he were struggling to hold himself back.

'No more.'

Emboldened, she slid her hands over the hard contours of his chest, scarcely able to believe her own daring. He gave a sharp intake of breath and she froze, waiting for him to push her away, but he didn't move. Did he still want her? She had to find out.

Slowly she let her fingers drift lower, over his taut stomach and then down, and found the answer ready and waiting, throbbing against her fingers, harder and stronger with every pulsating heartbeat.

She gasped and then his lips seized hers, his tongue pushing its way inside her mouth as if he wanted to punish and possess her at the same time. She responded at once, her lips meeting his with equal ardour, a low moan of desire giving way to one of pure, unrestrained pleasure.

Strong hands gripped her shift, half pulling, half tearing it over her head. Then for a tantalising moment he held himself still, his blue eyes black with desire as they raked over her body.

He groaned and she smiled in answer, pushing herself up towards him as he gathered her into his arms. Instinctively she wrapped her arms and legs around him, revelling in the touch of his skin and the weight of his body, stunned by the depth of her desire. His lips and hands seemed to be everywhere—trailing kisses over her breasts and stomach, along her thighs, up the insides of her legs…

She moaned. She felt as though he were tightening something inside her, winding it tighter and tighter until she thought she might snap. Now that she lay naked and vulnerable beneath him she wanted urgency, but he seemed to be taking his time, torturing her with pleasure. She wasn't sure what she wanted, but she wanted it *now.*

'Hurry…' She moaned in frustration and he gave a low answering laugh, circling a nipple with his tongue and gently licking the tip. 'Svend…' She dragged her nails over his back in retaliation and he shifted upwards at once.

'I don't want to hurt you.' His breathing was ragged.

'You won't.' She arched her body beneath him, felt the heat of him straining between her legs.

'Cille…'

Cille! She froze abruptly, feeling as if a bucket of ice had just been hurled over the bed.

His mouth stilled at her throat and she stared helplessly up at the rafters, panting and breathless. It had been a slip of the tongue, she told herself. A mistake. Understandable under the circumstances. No reason to feel hurt or humiliated, even if she did wish the ground would open up and swallow her.

But it had brought her lie back between them.

'Aediva,' he said flatly, rolling away from her onto his back. 'That will take some getting used to.'

She threw an arm over her face and took a deep breath, willing her heartbeat to return to normal. There was so much for them to get used to. Her name was only the start of it.

He touched her arm but she shook her head, refusing to pull it away. She couldn't look at him—not now. It was hopeless. There was no chance of him ever trusting her again. He couldn't forget what she'd done. He couldn't even remember her name.

She heard him sigh and move away, but she kept herself rigid, willing sleep to descend. If she could only sleep then perhaps they could put this catastrophe of a night behind them, pretend it had never happened…

If she could only sleep…

Every nerve and sinew was still alive and throbbing, every part of her still straining towards him.

If she could only sleep…

Somehow she doubted that would happen for a very long time.

Chapter Fifteen

Svend counted the prisoners, trying and failing to keep his mind on the task. They'd captured more than a dozen rebels that morning, and each one of them was now glaring at him with the same expression of blatant barefaced hostility, but he hardly noticed. All he could see was the distraught look on his wife's face when he'd called her the wrong name.

If he'd wanted to punish her, it appeared he'd succeeded.

That had been almost a fortnight ago. She'd moved back to her sister's old chamber the next morning and he hadn't objected—hadn't known what to say. He'd barely seen her since, most of his time having been spent away from Redbourn. The little he'd glimpsed of her, she'd been busy with her new duties as chatelaine, and with organising the harvest with practised efficiency. Even from afar he'd admired her hard work and commitment. She hardly needed his help to settle in at Redbourn—quite the opposite, in fact. She was a favourite with both Saxon and Norman alike.

He frowned. For the first time in ten years he had a home. When would he be able to live in it? If it hadn't been for the Earl's orders he would have relished taking up the role of farmer again, but he couldn't exchange his sword for a spade just yet. He had a soldier's business to finish first. And the sooner he got it over with, the better.

'The prisoners are ready, sir.' Renard approached him. 'Are we going back to Redbourn tonight?'

Svend shook his head. There were still a few hours of daylight left and he didn't want to waste them. If Henri had been there he might have delegated more of the tracking, but there was no one else with sufficient experience for the task.

'Take half a dozen guards and lead the prisoners back to Redbourn. You can be there by nightfall. The rest of us will camp overnight.'

'What about Lady Aediva?'

'What about her?' Svend shot him a savage look and Renard took an involuntary step backwards.

'It's the first new moon of the month, sir. Her birth date.'

'How do you know?'

'Her maid Judith told me.' Renard looked abashed. 'I'm sorry, sir, I thought you knew.'

Svend felt a twinge of bitterness. No, he hadn't known—had barely spoken to his wife for two weeks. He'd wanted time apart from her, hoping that distance would bring some clarity to his emotions, but it hadn't worked. He still couldn't get her out of his head. Every time he closed his eyes he could see her face, hear her voice asking him to trust her.

Could he?

He still didn't know.

But it was her birth date. He ought to see her at least. He even had the perfect gift—the one thing he knew that she wanted…

The ghost of a smile crossed his lips. Perhaps it wasn't too late to repair the damage between them. For a few brief and intoxicating moments that last night he'd thought that a new start was possible. Perhaps it still was.

He grimaced. If he could just remember to get her name right…

Aediva stood in the doorway of the Saxon hall, staring up at the darkening sky anxiously. Dusk was falling and there was still no sign of Svend. It seemed increasingly unlikely that he'd be returning that evening and she couldn't help but worry about him, camping out in the open, vulnerable to rebels and outlaws alike. Despite everything that had happened between them she found it impossible to sleep until she heard the thud of returning hoofbeats.

She'd hardly slept at all for weeks.

'Lady Aediva?'

Judith appeared at her elbow and she smiled, glad of the company.

'I don't need anything tonight, thank you, Judith.'

'Very good, my lady, but I have something for *you*.' The maid held out a strip of red silk. 'You said that today is your birth date. I found this amongst Lady Cille's belongings. I thought she'd want you to have something.'

'It's beautiful.' Aediva ran her fingers along the ribbon admiringly.

'In your best colour too. It'll go perfectly with the russet gown.'

'It will. Thank you, Judith.'

'You should try them on together. The dress might need adjusting.'

'It won't. Cille and I are the same size.'

'I'd like to make sure.'

'Now?' Aediva tilted her head, bemused by Judith's persistence. 'Can't it wait?'

Judith lifted her shoulders evasively and then dropped them again. 'I thought you might like to wear it for Sir Svend.'

Aediva dropped her gaze quickly. 'I doubt he'll be back tonight. It's almost dark.'

'But just in case…' Judith smiled secretively. 'I *might* have told Renard what day it is…'

'Judith!'

'Only in passing. Now, please!' Judith grasped her hands imploringly. 'Let me do your hair, at least. I want to see how the ribbon looks. Then, if he comes, you'll be ready.'

'Ready for what?' She tore her hands away in exasperation. 'A polite meal? So that we can discuss the fact he's out hunting Saxons?'

'No, but you have to talk sometime.'

Aediva bit her lip. That was true. And every day they avoided each other only made it worse.

She sighed. 'Even if he does come, he might not want to see me.'

'Then why is he always looking at you?'

'He's hardly *here* to look at me!'

'But when he is he's always watching you.' Judith gestured towards the Saxon hall behind them. 'You shouldn't have moved back here. These rooms didn't bring your sister much joy either.'

'I had to.' She couldn't have stayed another night in his chamber—not after their last disastrous night together.

And she couldn't stay in Redbourn either. As much as she was starting to enjoy her new role, she'd come to realise that her remaining there was impossible. It was bad enough that she'd married her enemy, but now she knew how much she cared for him. She'd wanted to build a new life with him but he didn't want her—not like that. He desired her, but he didn't love or trust her. If he'd ever cared for her it had been when he'd thought she was Cille—before he'd found out she'd been lying, and before she'd reminded him of Maren.

What had he told her in Offley? *'The woman I loved wasn't real. I thought I could trust her, but she was only pretending to be someone she wasn't.'*

That was how he felt about *her* now. Except that she *was* real. She might have changed on the surface, but she was still the same woman underneath. The only thing she'd lied about was her name. Everything else—every kiss, every touch—had been real.

She pressed a hand to her stomach, trying to hold back the emptiness inside. Since their last night together that feeling had come back with a vengeance. No, she couldn't stay in Redbourn—couldn't live with Svend any more. If he couldn't trust her then there was only one thing she could do.

She would confront him, and then she would leave.

It was late when Svend rode back through the gates—so late that for a moment he thought he'd fallen asleep and was dreaming. The woman standing on the steps of the tower *looked* like his wife, but couldn't be. She couldn't be there simply to greet him. Something must have happened.

He dismounted quickly, tossing his reins to a groom as he hastened towards her. She was standing motionless in the torchlight, a red gown he hadn't seen before billowing in the evening breeze, moulding the fabric to her body.

'Aediva?' He tore his gaze from her legs. 'Is everything all right?'

She nodded, her eyes flickering towards the prisoners and then back again. 'You've been busy.'

He frowned, his jaw tightening defensively. 'I have orders, Aediva, you know that.'

'I know.'

They were both silent for a moment as he looked around the bailey, searching for some kind of problem.

'So nothing's the matter?'

'No.' She looked surprised. 'Why?'

His eyebrows lifted before he could stop them. 'I didn't expect to see you.'

'Can't a wife greet her husband?'

'She can.' He was already regretting his words. 'And a husband might be pleased to see her.'

He mounted the steps, still vaguely wondering if it were all a dream. He hadn't expected any welcome at all—had thought he'd have to search the bailey for her—but the evening was already going better than he'd dared to imagine.

'You look lovely this evening. Red suits you.'

'Thank you. You're filthy!'

He looked down and grimaced. 'I need a bath.'

'I thought you might. I asked the maids to prepare one when we saw your torches approaching.'

'For me?' His eyebrows shot even higher.

'And there'll be a hot meal for your men shortly. The prisoners too.' Her gaze darkened. 'If you'll allow it.'

'Of course.'

She looked mildly appeased. 'Where will you put them?'

'In one of the barns. They won't be harmed, I promise.'

She studied him intently for a moment before gesturing for him to follow her inside. 'Come, your bath is upstairs.'

Svend followed her in stunned silence. That she'd arranged a bath for him was surprising enough. That she appeared to be going *with* him was almost unthinkable.

'Here...' She opened the door to the bedchamber and pointed towards a metal-lined wooden tub by the fireplace. 'It's all ready.'

'I'm impressed.' He grinned with anticipation. The water looked steaming hot and inviting. He could hardly have asked for a better welcome—not unless she intended to join him.

Instead she perched on the side of the bed, her face studiously averted as he undressed and lowered himself into the water, groaning with pleasure as the heat reached his tired muscles.

'Is it good?'

'Extremely. I should go away more often. Is there any particular reason for this treatment?'

Seeing the look on her face, he regretted the question almost at once.

'I thought it was time that we talked.'

The relaxed feeling vanished at once. 'Perhaps you're right. Though I'd like to give you your birthday present first.'

Her head spun around. 'Renard told you?'

'Fortunately, yes. I'd be a poor husband if I missed it.'

'True.'

'So come here.'

'You have it on you?' Her eyes narrowed suspiciously.

'Don't look so alarmed. It's not a thing, it's a message, and I don't want to shout. Or are you afraid to come any closer?'

'No!' She tossed her head indignantly. 'But if you think I'm going to wash you…'

He gave a shout of laughter. 'I wouldn't be so cruel. I just thought you'd like to know that I had word from Etton this morning.'

'Etton?' She shot to her feet, almost hurtling across the room.

He smiled, savouring the moment. 'One of de

Quincey's scouts found us on the trail. Your sister and nephew will be here within the week.'

'They're on their way?'

'As we speak. And your people are home and safe. Henri found them.'

'Thanks to you.'

'*And* you.'

She crouched down by the tub, looking at him dubiously. 'I'm the one who sent them away.'

'You did what you thought was best.'

'I did…at the time.' She pursed her lips thoughtfully. 'Capturing the rebels…is that what *you* think is best?'

'Yes. The longer the fighting goes on, the more innocent people suffer. I'm trying to make Redbourn a safer place. Etton, too. It's my responsibility and I can't shirk it.'

She sighed. 'I *do* understand. I don't like it, but I understand.'

'Aediva…' He reached out towards her, oddly touched.

'I need to go home.'

'Home?' He stiffened instantly. 'You mean to Etton?'

'You said I could go if I wanted to.'

'I did. *Is* that what you want?'

She turned her face to one side. 'It's not about what I want. I only know that I can't stay here. If you don't trust me then I might as well be one of those prisoners. I know you married me against your will, but if we don't try…'

'I'll try.'

She shook her head. 'No. You cared for me when you thought I was Cille, but now you'll always compare me to *her*—to Maren.' She swung back towards him, her face clouding with anger. 'It's not fair! I lied when I said I was Cille, but that's *all*. Everything else was real. Everything I felt…'

He realised that he was holding his breath. 'Everything you felt for *me*?'

'Yes!' She glared at him fiercely. 'You're just too pig-headed to see it!'

He felt a lightening sensation in his chest, as if the last bitter knot were untwisting and he could think clearly again. She was right—she was nothing like Maren. She was the same woman he'd fallen in love with—the same woman he wanted more powerfully than ever. All along he'd been too stubborn to see the truth, trying to shield himself from the mistakes of his past, from anyone who might hurt him again. He'd built so many walls around his heart he hadn't even known they were there—not until she'd broken through them.

'It wasn't against my will.'

'What?' Her scowl turned to a look of confusion.

'I didn't marry you against my will, Aediva. I wanted Redbourn, but I wanted you more.'

'But...you don't trust me.'

'I do. Deep down I always have. I know you're not Maren.' He climbed out of the bath, standing streaming wet in front of her. 'Don't go, Aediva. I want you here, with me.'

She made a movement towards him and he met her halfway, hauling her into his arms as they stumbled towards the bed.

'Wait.' He pulled back reluctantly, every part of him aching, needing, yearning to touch her. 'Are you certain this is what you want?'

'I want *you*.' She nodded eagerly. 'I want to be your wife.'

He didn't hesitate any longer, claiming her mouth and thrusting his tongue inside. How could he want a woman so badly? He wanted to touch and feel every part of her, to bury himself in her.

'What are these?' He tore at the lacings on her gown in frustration.

'I don't know.' She squirmed against him, trying to help. 'Judith fastened it. They're all down the back. You have to— *Svend*!'

She gasped as he grabbed the fabric in both hands, tearing it down the middle.

'Aediva.' He tossed the pieces aside. 'After everything else, I'm *not* letting a dress come between us.'

He tumbled with her onto the bed, restraining himself with an effort as his fingers trailed over the soft skin of her legs and between her thighs.

He wanted to take her quickly, but he didn't want to hurt her. He had to go slowly—had to hold himself back and be gentle. Not that she was helping. She was meeting him kiss for kiss, touch for touch, her tongue twining hungrily with his as she wrapped her legs around him, pulling him closer, her desire clearly equal to his own.

He let out a groan, unable to wait any longer, and entered her in one swift movement.

She tensed at once, gasping aloud as he plunged deep inside her.

'Aediva…?' He waited, using every ounce of control he possessed not to move. 'If you want me to stop…' Somehow he forced the words past his lips.

'No.' She shifted her hips, started to move beneath him, slowly at first, then faster as her body started to relax.

'More…' she murmured against his mouth.

He gave up all pretence of restraint then, pushing himself ever deeper inside her, harder and faster, revelling in the wetness of her body as she panted and writhed beneath him. He could hardly contain himself any longer, could feel himself building to his peak, crying out as their bodies finally shuddered together.

Then he held her tight, clasping her in his arms, unable to let go even as the last ripples of feeling faded away. He'd never felt so helpless in the grip of overpowering emotion. It was more than desire—though the urgency of his need had taken even *him* by surprise.

He loved her. Whatever else he might have told himself, he'd always loved her—had married her for that reason alone. He wondered that he could ever have doubted it.

And now she was truly his wife he vowed never to doubt her again.

Chapter Sixteen

Aediva picked up the tattered shreds of material ruefully. How was she going to explain this to Judith? The gown was ruined. Not that she could regret it. She couldn't regret anything that had happened last night.

She looked down at her sleeping husband and smiled, memories of the night before making her body tingle anew. Their lovemaking had been tender and wild and overwhelming all at once, sweeping her away in a primal, tempestuous sea of desire. She'd felt powerless to resist as the waves had whirled higher and faster, carrying her along, until a sudden shuddering sensation had overtaken her, dropping her panting and breathless onto some unknown shore. She'd cried out with pleasure at a sensation centred deep down in her core, unable to stop herself from quivering uncontrollably as she'd clung to his body—the only thing left to cling on to.

Then she'd lain dazed beside him, her mind and body still struggling to find each other as ripples of feeling had continued to pulse through her veins, knowing at last that there were no secrets between them.

'Sleep well?'

She blinked, so lost in her reverie that she hadn't noticed him wake up.

'Quite well.'

'I'm glad to hear it.' He propped himself up on one elbow. 'What were you thinking about? You were smiling.'

'I was thinking that you've ruined Cille's dress.'

'Remind me to apologise when I see her.' He grinned. 'Now, come back to bed.'

'It's getting late.' She pursed her lips, trying to resist the temptation. 'Don't you have work to do?'

'Bertrand can do it today.' He leapt up suddenly, coiling an arm around her waist and pulling her down on top of him. 'I'll tell him you've worn me out.'

'You will *not*!'

'Then you'd better stay and make sure I don't start any rumours.'

She laughed, happily conceding defeat as she propped her chin on his chest. 'Was it worth it in the end?'

'It?' He chuckled softly. 'Yes, *it* was. Didn't you think so?'

'Definitely.'

'It's just a pity we've wasted so much time arguing. We've been married for two weeks.'

'Mmm...' She sighed contentedly. 'I suppose I might have been a bit difficult...'

'Difficult?' He laughed at the understatement. 'You tried to kill me the first time we met!'

'You knocked me over! Besides, I only wanted to scare you.'

'As I recall, you tried to stab me twice in the first two days.'

'The second time doesn't count. You gave me the knife, remember?'

He ran a hand through her hair, teasing the strands through his fingers. 'So I did.'

'*And* I saved your life.'

He cocked an eyebrow. 'Is that so?'

'I saved you from the rebel ambush. You could have been killed if I hadn't warned you.'

'You said something about a river. Is that what you call a warning?'

'I stopped the fighting.'

'Your horse bolted.'

'*After* I stopped the fighting.'

'Ah.' He tugged gently at her hair, pulling her face towards his. 'In that case it seems I owe you a debt. How would you like me to repay you?'

She smiled, brushing her lips teasingly against his. 'Well...there are some hay bales that need to be moved.'

She squealed as he flipped her onto her back, pinning her beneath him.

'I'm disappointed.' His mouth dipped to her throat, moving in slow circles over the skin. 'Are you *sure* you can't find another use for me?'

She drew air between her teeth. 'There's nothing I can think of…'

His head dipped lower, his lips drifting over a nipple. 'Should I go and get started, then?'

'Ye—yes…' She'd heard the smile in his voice and clamped her teeth together, trying not to pant.

'If you're *completely* sure…?' His tongue was relentless. 'Then I'll go.'

'Svend!' She gasped as he released her abruptly, a rush of cold air washing over her skin.

'You told me to go.' He grinned wickedly. 'Or do you want me to stay now? You'll have to ask nicely.'

Aediva narrowed her eyes. If he thought he could toy with her, then two could play at that game. She pulled herself upright, shaking her head so that her hair tumbled provocatively over her shoulders.

'No. I wouldn't want you to think I'm fickle.'

'Then the barn it is.' He sighed dramatically. 'It does seem a shame, though.'

'It does—but what choice do we have?'

'Perhaps if I showed you something else we could do…?' He lowered his voice seductively.

'There's more?'

'Much more. Trust me, Aediva, we're just getting started.'

She bit her lip, pretending to think about it, her pulse already racing with anticipation. 'And you think it will please me?'

'Based on last night, I think it should please us both.'

'Well, in that case…' She surrendered, wrapping her arms around his neck. 'I suppose you *could* show me.'

'With pleasure.' He caught hold of her waist, twisting her around into a sitting position on top of him.

'What…?'

'You've worn me out, remember? This time *you* can do all the work.'

'Work?'

'Nothing too strenuous, I promise. Here…' He took hold of her hips, positioning her over him.

'You want me to…?' She clasped her hands over her breasts, staring at him in shocked comprehension.

'Don't cover up.' He peeled her fingers away gently. 'I want to see you.'

'But…'

'Aediva.' He pressed her fingers to his lips. 'You don't have to do anything you don't want to, but it will be even better for you, I promise.'

'Better?' She moved her hips against him tentatively. 'You mean like this?'

He gave a sharp intake of breath. 'Like that.'

'Like the first time we met?'

'What?'

'When I tried to kill you, or so you said.' She rocked herself backwards and forwards, saw him grit his teeth. 'I sat astride you like this.'

'Aediva...'

She gave a coy smile, enjoying her power. 'Of course if I'd known you were enjoying it I might have used that dagger after all.'

He made a guttural sound in the back of his throat. 'I didn't realise you enjoyed torturing men.'

'Just you. *Norman*.'

'Wildcat.'

She bent towards him and then froze, clutching a blanket to her chest as she heard a knock on the door.

'What?' Svend's voice was a roar.

'Sorry, sir.' Renard's muffled voice sounded more than a little nervous. 'But the masons need to speak with you. There's some kind of problem with the wall. They say it's urgent.'

'Tell them to—'

Aediva clamped a hand over his mouth. From the murderous look on his face, whatever he wanted to tell them to do didn't bear repeating.

'Be nice!' she admonished him. 'If it weren't for Renard you might not have come home last night.'

Svend made a face. 'True. I'll be down in a minute, lad!' He gave her a smouldering look, then rolled off the bed and into his hose. 'It seems I owe him a debt too. But I'll think of a different way to thank him.'

She lay on her side, watching him dress. 'I suppose the barn will have to wait too?'

'It doesn't help that you look so irresistible.'

'There's always tonight.'

'Tonight? You think I can wait *that* long?' He bent over the bed, kissing her thoroughly before making for the door. 'I want to see you back here in an hour. That's an order!'

She laughed gleefully and wrapped herself up in the blanket, running to the window to watch as he strode out into the bailey. He raised a hand in salute and she waved back, unable to keep the smile off her face. Danish or Norman, whoever he was, she didn't care any more. He was her husband and she loved him.

He hadn't said that he loved her, but he'd certainly shown her how he felt. The words could wait for the moment. All that mattered was that the pit in her stomach was gone, all the loneliness and fear of the past year banished. For the first time since before the Conquest she felt safe and happy. Because of him.

She only hoped that whatever the masons wanted wouldn't take long. He'd said he had lots more to show her and suddenly she felt very eager to learn.

She leaned happily against the side of the window and looked out over the bailey, over the barns and tents and kitchens. They'd all have to manage without her today. Though maybe later she'd take Svend to one of the barns and show him their winter supplies. She could probably find a hay bale that needed lifting too…

She saw a commotion on the far side of the bailey and her face fell at once. A crowd had gathered, watching as the prisoners were moved between barns. Their hands were untied, and there were no signs of ill treatment, but the guards around them were taking no chances, swords drawn in case of attack.

She watched as they came closer. The men were unkempt and dishevelled, their faces contorted with loathing even towards the other Saxons in the bailey, but her heart still ached for them. A month ago she might have been one of them, but now… All she wanted was for the fighting and the turmoil to be over, for there to be peace again.

Her attention fixed suddenly on a sandy-haired rebel near the front. There was something familiar about him—something about his posture and the way he walked. Intrigued, she leaned over the ledge, trying to get a better look, and for a fleeting moment he looked up.

Edmund.

She drew back at once, her heart pounding violently. She hadn't seen him for months, but it was him—she was sure of it. And he'd seen her too. The look of disgust on his face had been more eloquent than words. She could hardly have arranged it to look any worse—wrapped in a blanket in a Norman's bedchamber in the full light of day. She didn't want to think about what she looked like, but it was obvious what *he* thought.

She ran a hand over her face in dismay. She hadn't expected ever to see Edmund again—hadn't wanted to—but he was still part of her past, her father's favourite. The Saxon side of her didn't want to see him imprisoned, even if the new Norman side knew there was no choice. But for old times' sake she couldn't just turn her back on him—she had to do something.

But what? She could hardly help him escape. If she deceived Svend again he'd never forgive her—not a second time. It would be the end of their marriage before it had even begun. Besides, she couldn't keep such a secret from him. Not after last night. She'd have to tell him and ask for his help instead, try to persuade him to let Edmund go even if it meant another argument.

Her stomach plummeted. She had a feeling their morning together was ruined.

Svend grinned, inhaling the fresh morning air with relish. He was in a better mood than he'd been in for… His brow creased as he considered. Could it really be *years*? He felt more at ease and contented than he could even remember. It was a beautiful day, cloudless and bright, and all he wanted was to spend it indoors, in bed, with his wife.

'So what's the issue with the masons, exactly?'

'They've had some kind of argument, sir.' Renard was still flustered, struggling to keep up with his long strides. 'One of them says part of the wall is unstable—the rest say not. So they asked me to fetch you. I thought I should, just in case the first one was right.'

'You did the right thing.'

'I did?' Renard sagged with relief. 'Thank you, sir.'

'Am I such an ogre, lad?'

'No, sir, but I didn't want to interrupt…anything.'

Svend grinned. 'Well, *I* forgive you, but you know Lady Aediva has a fearsome temper. It's not me you need to worry about.'

He started to laugh at Renard's panicked expression and then stopped, distracted by a noise coming from the building site—a low rumble followed by voices raised in alarm. He looked towards the sound and then broke into a run. Part of the wall was leaning precariously, the scaffolding beside it teetering over with men still trapped on top. As he watched two of them jumped clear, but a third man was too high, and the wooden planks were wobbling dangerously beneath his feet.

'Climb down!' Svend bellowed, charging towards the scaffolding and ramming his shoulder up against a beam, trying to stabilise the frame.

Already he could tell that it was too late. Other men were rushing to help, but the weight of the wall was pushing him down to the ground and the wood was already starting to crack, fragmenting into a thousand small pieces around them.

The last man clambered down a level and then jumped, landing just clear of the wood as it finally splintered apart. There was an eerie creak followed by a bass rumble as the wall started to disintegrate alongside them, large blocks of stone teetering at first and then tumbling down in a torrent of boulders.

'Get back!' Svend shouted, taking the weight by himself as he heaved the remains of the scaffolding aside. He made sure everyone else was clear before he jumped backwards himself, disappearing beneath a cloud of dust and rocky hailstones as the rest of the wall finally collapsed around him.

Chapter Seventeen

Svend forced his eyelids open. They felt leaden and heavy, as if they were trying to drag him back down into sleep, back to troubled dreams of noise and chaos. It was dark, though the flickering light of a candle told him he was back in his bed in the tower.

He flexed his sword arm, then winced as pain shot down his side, black dots dancing in front of his eyes like coal dust. A series of disjointed memories came back to him. The bailey wall collapsing…the scaffolding buckling under the weight of stone…a shower of dust and rock.

What had happened next? What was he doing here?

He waited for the dizziness to subside, then tested his other muscles more carefully. He felt battered and sore all over, though he seemed to have avoided serious injury. Only his chest felt heavy—as if there were a horse sitting on top of it.

He heard somebody else's breathing and turned his head carefully, his heart lurching as he saw Aediva curled up in a chair by the bedside. Instinctively he tried to sit up, and then fell back with a grunt of pain, his shoulder collapsing beneath him.

'Svend?'

He heard her whisper his name but couldn't answer, his senses still reeling. Then he felt fingers, soft and tender, moving in circles over his chest, loosening the tight muscles. From the smell he guessed she was rubbing in some kind of ointment. It felt warm and sticky, not unpleasant despite a slight stinging sensation. He fought back a growl, inhaling sharply as her fingers brushed across his injured shoulder.

'Can you hear me?' She stopped at once.

He could feel the warmth of her breath on his skin, could tell that she was leaning over him. Her hair was trailing across his chest like a silken blanket, filling his senses almost to breaking point. She was close now—so close that if he reached out she'd have no chance of escape.

He moaned, luring her face down to his.

'Svend?'

Quickly he coiled his good arm around her neck, bringing her mouth down to his, and was caught off guard by the depth and fervour of her response. Her lips surrendered immediately, her mouth soft and sweet and irresistibly delicious, deepening the kiss with every passing moment. If they went on like this…

She pulled back abruptly, squealing in protest. 'Brute! You tricked me! How long have you been awake?'

'Not long.'

He tried another groan and she started forward again in alarm.

'Have I hurt you?'

'Not yet. Care to try?'

'Stop teasing me!' She stamped her foot angrily. 'It's not fair.'

He grinned. 'You are too good to resist.'

She glared at him, perching on the side of the bed just out of arm's reach. 'And how do you feel?'

'Like a wall has fallen on me.'

'Renard says they were rushing to finish and the mortar wasn't dry.'

'Is everyone all right?'

'One of the masons broke a leg, but everyone else escaped. You must have been the slowest.'

He caught the mischievous glint in her eye. 'Getting old, perhaps?'

'Probably. It's amazing that you didn't break any bones. Wait!' She sprang forward as he started to sit up. 'What are you doing?'

'The old man wants to get up.'

'You need to lie still.'

'I'm not staying in bed like an invalid.'

'Yes, you are.' She put her hands on her hips.

'And you needn't look at me like that. I'm not afraid of you, Svend du Danemark.'

He lifted an eyebrow. 'Not at all?'

'I've held a knife to your chest before. Don't think I won't do it again.'

He laughed painfully. 'I believe you.'

'I haven't finished yet, anyway.' She reached for the ointment again. 'Now, lie down and be still.'

He fell backwards, heaving a sigh. 'So this is marriage? Very well, then, wife. Do your worst.'

She gave him an arch look, trailing her hands along the sides of his ribcage.

'Will I live?'

'You'll survive.'

'Somehow I can't tell if you think that's a *good* thing.'

'It's bearable.'

He smiled. 'Surely you can't deny me a small walk around the chamber?'

'No! Look what happened the last time I let you out of bed.'

'In that case you'd better join me. I won't make the same mistake twice.'

He heard her breathing quicken, before she shook her head emphatically. 'It's definitely too soon for *that*.'

'Aediva…' He gave a low growl. Despite the pain, he could feel himself getting aroused. 'Either let me out of this bed or get in.'

She hesitated for another moment before climbing up and nestling down by his side.

'You scared me. Don't do it again.'

He twisted towards her, surprised by the quiver in her voice. Up close, he could see that her eyes and cheeks were swollen, as if she'd been crying.

'I promise never to be crushed by a wall again.'

'Stop making light of it! You could have been killed!'

'It'll take more than that.' He reached out, stroking the side of her face with his fingertips. 'I'm not so easy to get rid of.'

'So I'm learning.'

'I'm sorry you were scared. So was I, if it helps. One night with you is nowhere near enough. The thought of not having another was terrifying.' He pressed his lips into her hair. 'Speaking of which…that position I showed you would be perfect for a situation like this.'

She batted a hand at him. 'I'm not being held responsible for you relapsing.'

'I'll take my chances.'

'You need to rest.'

'I can't think of a better way to help me sleep.'

'Svend!'

He laughed at her ferocious expression. 'All right. But soon…'

'Soon,' she agreed. '*Very* soon.'

* * *

Aediva looked up from the bed, pressing a finger to her lips and smiling as Bertrand bent his head under the doorframe. A month ago she would have felt uncomfortable in the presence of such an alarmingly large, archetypal Norman, but now she was genuinely pleased to see him.

'Lady Aediva…'

He looked embarrassed to find her on the bed and she took pity on him, wriggling away from her sleeping husband and onto her feet. It wasn't her fault that Svend insisted on her lying beside him all the time. His men probably thought she was some kind of wanton.

'What is it?' She smiled encouragingly.

Bertrand lowered his voice. 'I have some questions about tomorrow, my lady, but I'll come back later.'

'Tomorrow?'

'We're taking the prisoners to the Earl for sentencing.' He saw the look on her face and cleared his throat awkwardly. 'I'm sorry, my lady, I thought you knew.'

'No.' She tried to keep her voice from shaking. 'I didn't.'

'Those are the Earl's orders.'

'Oh.'

'I'll come back later.'

He backed out of the room hastily and she sank down onto the bed, stricken with guilt. She'd been so preoccupied with Svend over the last two days that she'd hardly thought about the prisoners at all. She hadn't even considered what was going to happen to them. Her whole world seemed to have contracted to this one room.

She gazed down at him lovingly, dipping her fingers into the soothing ointment the wicce had given her, then rubbing them gently over his bare skin. His chest moved up and down beneath her touch, warm and smooth and sprinkled with a fine layer of soft white-gold hair. She took a deep breath, trying to keep her mind on the task. Even covered in red and purple bruises, his body still had a powerful effect on her senses. The thrill of running her hands over his hard, taut muscles was as strong and distracting as ever.

Should she tell him about Edmund? She'd intended to, but that had been before the accident. She didn't want anything to disrupt his recovery, but she couldn't bear to think of Edmund being dragged in chains before the Earl either. No matter what he'd done to her, she didn't want that.

'You should get some air.' Svend's voice was sleepy. 'You don't have to tend to me all day.'

'I'm not leaving you.' She smiled, amazed at the power his blue eyes held over her. Just one look from them made her insides feel weak. 'Not until I can trust you to stay put.'

'And I hoped it was because you might care...'

'That too.' She took hold of his hand and squeezed it, feeling a rush of tenderness.

When they'd carried him in on a stretcher she'd felt as though it was her own body that had been crushed. She'd spent a night of anguish waiting for him to wake up, and spent every day since falling more deeply in love with him than ever.

On the other hand, he was the worst patient she'd ever known—trying to get out of bed twenty times a day and wanting to know everything that was happening in the castle. To quell his impatience she'd arranged for Renard to bring almost hourly reports, but it was becoming increasingly difficult to keep him in bed. There was only one sure method she could think of, and that was the one thing she had to avoid—no matter how tempted she was to succumb. Injured or not, nothing seemed to dampen his ardour.

She forced her mind back to the present. 'Bertrand was here. He wanted to ask about tomorrow.'

'He told you about that?'

'Only by accident. He said the prisoners are going to be taken for sentencing.'

'Those are the Earl's orders.'

'That's what he said.' She took a deep breath, steeling her nerve for her next question. 'What's going to happen to them?'

'If they surrender and swear fealty there's a chance they might be pardoned, but FitzOsbern's losing patience with them. In all honesty, I don't know.'

'Isn't there another way? Couldn't you just… send them away? Let them go?'

'No.' His voice hardened. 'I can't let the Earl think I have any sympathy with them.'

'*Do* you? Have sympathy with them, I mean?'

'They're fighting for their home—I can understand that—but they knew what they were doing when they joined the rebellion. They chose their side.' He sighed. 'I have to follow my orders, Aediva.'

'Because FitzOsbern will blame *me* if you fail?'

He looked surprised and she shrugged.

'He told me so at our wedding feast.'

Svend's jaw tightened revealingly. 'I won't take any risks—not where you're concerned.'

'What would he do? Annul our marriage?'

He didn't answer and she tilted her head, peering at him quizzically. 'Svend?'

'That would be the best we could hope for.'

'Oh.' She held back a shudder. That was that, then. She had her answer. There was no point in asking Svend to release Edmund. But she still had to admit that she'd seen him. Somehow it felt disloyal not to.

'I saw the prisoners on the morning of your accident. One of them…it was Edmund.'

'Edmund?' His whole body seemed to tense. 'Did he see you?'

'Yes.'

'And…?'

'He looked angry.' She felt her cheeks flush. 'I was only wearing a blanket at the time.'

'So that's why you're asking me all this? Because you want me to let him go?'

'Yes—but not because I care for him.' She hastened to explain. 'I never did. I was always more scared of him than anything.'

'Scared?' He frowned. 'Why?'

She hesitated. She didn't want to talk about this—didn't want to remember it—but she had a feeling that Svend wasn't simply going to drop the subject.

'He was…rough. When he kissed me it hurt. And…he tried to make me do other things.'

'And you want me to let him *go*?' Svend's face was a mask of restrained fury.

'Yes.' She put a hand on his chest quickly. 'I know it sounds strange. Part of me hates him, but I don't want revenge—not like this. He was part of my life once, and he's Saxon. It doesn't seem right for me to be so happy when he's lost everything.'

'So happy?' Some of the anger ebbed from his face. 'Is that what you are?'

'*Very* happy. I thought that all men were like Edmund until I met you. I thought I never wanted anyone to kiss me again. But now…' She pressed her lips against his. 'Now I can't seem to kiss you enough.'

'Temptress. You should have told me all this before.'

'It's not easy to talk about.'

'No, but if I'd known…'

She smiled at his anxious expression. 'You're nothing like Edmund, Svend. I've *always* wanted you to kiss me.'

'Always?'

'Most of the time anyway.'

'I wish I'd known that sooner too.'

He seemed to consider for a moment before shaking his head.

'No, I can't let him go. Even if I wanted to—which I don't—I can't make exceptions. I trust my men to keep their own counsel, but de Quincey's men are another matter. If word ever got back to the Earl… I won't expose you to that kind of danger.'

'Can I speak to Edmund, at least?'

'That's not a good idea.'

'But I could tell him what you said—that he should surrender. I could tell the others too.'

'No.'

'Svend, they're my countrymen. I'll be perfectly safe with Bertrand.'

'No!' His eyes flashed a warning. 'Prisoners are desperate men and that makes them dangerous. Don't argue with me on this, Aediva. I won't change my mind. The further you stay away from the rebels, the better.'

Chapter Eighteen

Aediva climbed out of bed carefully, wrapping a cloak around her shoulders and tugging the hood forward to disguise herself. Then she stole down the stairs, past the hall and out into the dawn, trying to concentrate on each passing footstep and not on what lay ahead. If she stopped to think about what she was doing she might never be able to go through with it.

A pale grey mist hovered over the bailey as she made her way towards the barn where the prisoners were being held, its silvery droplets of moisture lending the scene an unreal, dream-like quality. She felt as though she were in a dream herself, moving against her own volition, even against her own wishes, scarcely able to believe the risk she was taking. Common sense urged her to turn back, but conscience drove her onwards. She couldn't go back—not yet…not until she'd spoken to Edmund. If surrender was his best chance of survival she had to tell him so to his face.

She glanced up at the tower guiltily. Behind the shutters Svend was still asleep. With any luck he'd never know she'd been gone. Not that she was violating his trust—not exactly. He'd said that speaking to Edmund was a bad idea and told her not to argue, but he hadn't actually forbidden her. And she'd made no promise—wasn't breaking her word. She *was* acting against his wishes, but she only intended to talk to Edmund, that was all! She wasn't betraying Svend. She had every intention of telling him what she'd done later—*much* later.

Even so, if he were to wake up now…

She had a feeling it would make all their other arguments seem like friendly discussions. He'd probably lock *her* up too. But it was a risk she had to take. If she didn't do something she'd feel like a traitor to her people for ever.

She straightened her shoulders as she approached the guards at the barn door, trying to look as though her arrival ought to be expected.

'Lady Aediva?' One of them stepped forward, exchanging a pointed look with his companion. 'Can I help you?'

'Matthieu, isn't it?' She flashed her brightest smile. 'I need to speak with the prisoners. I have a message for them.'

'It's very early, my lady.' He looked visibly perturbed. 'My orders are to let no one in.'

She let her smile fade deliberately slowly. 'I'm the warden's wife. Are you refusing me permission?'

'No, my lady, but the orders came direct from Sir Svend. Perhaps if I could speak to him first...?'

'My husband is asleep and my message is urgent.' She feigned affront. 'But perhaps you'd like to wake him up and ask him if I'm lying? I'm sure he'd be pleased to hear your good opinion of me.'

'Pardon, my lady, I meant no offence.' The guard cast a pleading look towards his companion before backing away.

'Good.'

She averted her gaze, amazed that he couldn't read the guilt on her face. She hadn't been at all certain that her bluff would work, but he was already lifting the locking bar, beckoning her forward with the look of a man who wished he were anywhere else in the world.

She took a deep breath and stepped inside. Light spilled in through the open door to reveal the dark silhouettes of at least twenty men lying on the floor.

'Edmund?' She whispered his name, almost afraid to disturb the eerie hush.

'What are *you* doing here?'

She recognised his voice at once, though she couldn't distinguish his face.

'Edmund, where are you?'

'I said, what are you doing here?'

A shadow at the back stood up and started to move towards her, slowly and steadily, like a predator stalking its prey.

'Have you come to gloat?'

'No! Of course not!'

He stepped into a patch of sunlight, revealing a handsome face made ugly by hatred. 'Then what do you want, Aediva?'

She lifted her chin, resisting the urge to back away, looking around the room as she spoke. 'I want to help you. You're going to be taken east today to the King's deputy for sentencing. If you surrender and swear fealty he might show mercy. You could still be set free.'

'To live under *Norman* rule?' Edmund's expression was scathing.

'It's your only chance.'

'We're not *all* as keen to surrender as you.'

She flushed angrily. 'I haven't surrendered. I've come to terms with the Normans, that's all.'

'Is *that* what you call it? I saw you in the tower. Your father would have been ashamed of you.'

'He would *not*!' She held her ground, recognising the truth as she said it. 'My father wanted to protect Etton, but he wanted peace too. So do I.'

'By whoring yourself out to a Norman?'

'By giving myself willingly to my husband.'

'Husband?'

Edmund raised his fist and she sprang backwards, catching hold of the doorframe just as one of the guards came around it.

'My lady.' He took one look at the scene and raised his sword. 'It's time to go.'

She nodded her head. From the look on Edmund's face there was no point in trying to reason with him. There had been no point in coming. She'd risked antagonising Svend for nothing. And suddenly all she wanted was to be back with him again.

'I thought you didn't *like* men.' Edmund's voice was sharp-edged with malice. 'Now I see I was just the wrong kind. How many Normans have you slept with, *my lady*?'

The scuffle started so fast she hardly knew how it had happened. The guard at her side made a lunge towards Edmund just as half a dozen men leapt up from the floor, surrounding him in a mob. The other guard pushed past her, charging into the fray with a shout of alarm. She heard grunts, followed by a sickening cry and a thud, and then Edmund's hands were around her throat, circling her neck like a noose, gripping so tightly she could hardly breathe, let alone scream.

'We want horses.'

Edmund's voice was a snarl in her ear, but he wasn't talking to her. One of the guards was being pinned to the floor with his own sword, now wielded by one of the Saxons. Desperately she sought the other, but there was no sign of him—only a bloody patch on the floor.

'What have you done?' She stared at the blood in horror.

'What all Normans deserve!' Edmund spat into the rushes, aiming a kick at the guard's stomach. 'Now, get horses and open the gates!'

'Don't do it!' She struggled furiously, but Edmund's grip on her throat only tightened.

'Do it. Or your commander loses his lady.'

The guard nodded and staggered to his feet, hobbling out of the prison and towards the stables as if expecting to feel a knife in his back at any moment.

She watched him go with a sickening feeling. Why wasn't he raising the alarm?

'You won't get away with this!' Somehow she managed to croak out the words.

Edmund let go of her neck and spun her around, grabbing her breasts as he pulled her roughly against him. 'I think I will. And then I'll find out what all the Normans have been enjoying.'

'Just one Norman.' She brought her knee up, catching him hard in the groin. 'And he's worth a hundred of you!'

'Whore!'

Edmund's fist hit her square in the jaw, so forcefully that she flew backwards, skidding to a halt beside the door. For a moment the world seemed to go dark, and the barn spun around her as she tried to hold onto consciousness. She couldn't let Edmund escape…couldn't let him get away it…

'It's all ready.'

The guard's voice seemed to come from a long way away. She looked up, trying to see through a swirling fog. How could he be back so soon?

'Horses?' Edmund grabbed her arm, hoisting her roughly to her feet.

'Outside. I've tied up the door warden. No one will stop you from leaving.' The guard lifted his arm suddenly, brandishing a new sword. 'But you have to let her go.'

She felt a flicker of hope—quickly extinguished as Edmund shoved her forward abruptly, so fast that the guard was forced to lower his weapon. Too late she saw the flash of a dagger as another Saxon lunged towards them, stowing the point under the guard's ribs.

'No!'

She started to scream, but a hand clamped itself over her mouth, an arm coiled around her waist and she was carried out of the barn towards the gates.

What had she done?

She was almost too horrified to think. She'd only wanted to help her countrymen, but instead she'd allowed them to escape and kill innocent Normans. She craned her neck, trying to see behind her, but all she could make out was the crumpled body of the guard. She didn't even know where the other one was.

Her stomach heaved with guilt. She'd tricked them, but she'd never intended for them to get hurt. She'd have rather Edmund had stabbed her instead.

'Scream again and I'll kill you.' Edmund let go of her mouth, throwing her over the back of a horse like a sack before mounting quickly behind her.

'Let me go!'

He ignored her, pinning her down with a hand on her back as they galloped out through the gates. Blood rushed to her head in a deafening roar. Who *was* he, this man who seemed to hate her? The Edmund she'd known had been rough and insensitive, but this man was a cold-blooded monster. And yet she found her fear of him was gone, replaced by icy loathing. She wasn't afraid of anything he might do to her any more. She hardly cared. After what she'd done to the guards she deserved everything she got.

And Svend would think so too.

She retched, and her stomach emptied itself at the thought. When he woke up and they told him what had happened—that the prisoners were gone and her along with them—he'd think that she'd betrayed him again. He'd see the slain guards and think she'd had a hand in it.

Her own words from the evening before would incriminate her. She'd actually *asked* him to free them! What if he thought she'd simply been biding her time, trying to manipulate him into letting them go before taking matters into her own hands? Who would believe that she wasn't a rebel now?

'Edmund, you're free! You don't need me any more!' She tried to lift her head, but he forced it back down again.

'I might if your husband decides to follow us.'

'He won't!'

She shouted the words with conviction. Svend was in no condition to follow anyone. And even if he was, it wouldn't be to rescue her. The only reason he'd come after her now was for revenge. And as for his men… Bertrand might try to recapture the prisoners, but he wouldn't rush to save *her*—not if he thought she was a rebel.

No, this time she wasn't going to be rescued. If she were going to survive she had to save herself. But how? Surely it was easier just to give up, to let Edmund punish her as she deserved.

Her head hurt and she felt dizzy. Even face-down, and being jolted from side to side, the urge to close her eyes was almost overpowering.

But if she gave up now then Svend would never know the truth. If anything happened to her he'd never know what had really happened. She had to survive so that she could tell him the truth—that she wasn't a rebel, that she hadn't wanted to leave him, that she loved him.

And that she'd never let *anyone*, Saxon or Norman, ever come between them again.

Svend's first thought was that they were under attack. He heard shouts, followed by swearing and running footsteps, then someone calling for horses and armour. He opened his eyes in alarm, surprised to find no sign of Aediva beside him. She'd been at his side almost every moment for the past three days. Where was she now?

'What is it?' He jolted upright as the door burst open, ignoring the searing pain in his shoulder.

'It's the prisoners!' Renard rushed up to the bed, followed by a hard-faced Bertrand. 'They've escaped.'

'What? When?'

'Half an hour ago. The guard at the gate was bound and gagged. He says it was just after dawn.'

'Go after them.' Svend turned to Bertrand. 'You know what to do.'

'There's something else, sir…' Renard's voice faltered.

'What?' He frowned. Something about the look on their faces made him suddenly reluctant to hear the answer.

'It's Lady Aediva.'

He felt a painful thud in his chest. 'What about her?'

'We can't find her anywhere, sir. It looks like…'

'Like what?' Svend fought the urge to grab his squire by the throat and shake the words out of him.

Renard gulped. 'Like she went with them.'

'The night watchman saw her leave the tower this morning.' Bertrand interceded quickly. 'She was alone and heading for the barn.'

'That doesn't prove anything.'

'He saw her speak to the guards before she went inside.'

'They let her in?'

'That's what he says. He thought it was strange at the time, but since they opened the door he assumed everything was in order and moved on.'

'Where are the guards now?'

'In the infirmary. They're alive, but they won't be able to tell us anything for a while. There are no other witnesses, but from all appearances…'

'She helped them escape.' Svend finished the sentence for him.

'That's what it looks like.'

He shook his head, snippets of conversation from the evening before coming back to him. She'd asked him to free the prisoners, but when he'd refused she'd seemed to understand what was at stake. She'd asked what would happen to them, had seemed upset by his answer, but that didn't mean that she'd helped them escape…did it? But why else would she have gone to the barn?

Edmund.

She'd mentioned Edmund. His insides twisted with jealousy before the rational part of his brain took over. Why would she have told him about Edmund if she'd been planning an escape? Why risk arousing suspicion? Besides, she'd said that Edmund had scared her, that she only wanted to warn him…

Hell and damnation! He swung his legs off the bed and stood up determinedly. She was just as headstrong and reckless as ever—going to warn the rebels because she thought it was the right thing to do, simply assuming she was safe because they were Saxon. Damn it all, it wasn't as if she'd ever followed his advice before. Why the hell had he expected her to start now?

'Get my horse ready.'

'Sir, you can't!'

'Now!' He fixed Bertrand with a hard stare. 'She didn't do it. She's not a rebel. Make sure the men understand that.'

'Yes, sir.'

'And tell them I'll cut the hand off any man who touches her.'

He grasped hold of the wall, steadying himself

as the others departed the chamber. Renard was right, he shouldn't be out of bed, but he had to go after her. If she'd gone, she'd done so against her will. He refused to believe otherwise.

But that meant she was in danger too.

His heart stalled at the thought. If he lost her it would be the end of everything, all his hopes and plans for the future. He had to find her. He'd told her he trusted her and he'd meant it. He was going to keep on trusting her until she looked him in the eye and told him otherwise.

And if she did that he'd never trust the evidence of his own senses again.

Aediva twisted her neck, looking for any sign of pursuit, but there was nothing—not so much as a cloud of dust on the horizon. She had no idea how long they'd been riding, but the sun was already past its zenith and the weary horses had slowed to a walk. They must be miles away from Redbourn by now—so far that she didn't even recognise their surroundings.

She heard her name and pricked up her ears to listen. One of the other rebels seemed to be arguing with Edmund about her.

'She's weighing you down. Better to leave her behind.'

She held her breath, hoping that Edmund would agree, but if anything his voice only grew harder.

'It's not far to the marshes.'

The marshes! She felt a jolt of panic. Once they entered the marshes the Normans would stand no chance of finding them. And she'd have no hope of escaping such a maze. If she was going to make a break she had to do it soon.

If...

At the moment her chances seemed slim to non-existent. Edmund's hand was still pressing down hard on her back, and even if she somehow managed to jump free of the horse without breaking her neck there was nowhere to hide. In which case…

Suddenly the marshes didn't seem such a bad idea. If she could get away from Edmund and hide amidst the reeds she'd stand a chance of escape.

Her only chance.

Tentatively she brought her knees up and braced her hands against the horse's side, looking for purchase. *There!* Now, if Edmund released her for even a second, she could propel herself forward, dive off the side of the horse and hope that its hooves landed elsewhere. She was ready…she could do it…just as soon as he let go.

The ground grew boggier at last as they entered the morass of the marshes. Tall ferns brushed her face as the horses waded reluctantly into the reed beds, kicking up splatters of muddy water as they shied and whinnied in protest. Aediva held her breath, sensing Edmund's distraction as his horse started to buck, feeling his hold on her back easing as he grappled with the reins.

Then he let go.

She didn't hesitate, heaving herself over the side of the horse and headlong into the icy swamp below. For a few terrifying seconds she was lost in a swirl of muddy, frigid water before she found her feet and resurfaced, glad of the commotion around her as she half stumbled, half swam away through the reeds.

'Get her!'

Edmund was bellowing furiously behind her, but she didn't look back, dragging her sodden dress around her waist as she thrashed on through the reeds. If she could just find a place to hide she could wait them out. The Saxons hadn't gone far enough into the marshes to be safe. If they wanted to be free from Norman pursuit they didn't have time to waste looking for her. Their own need to escape would save her.

At last she found a thick clump of weeds and forced her way inside, crouching low in the water as a family of voles scurried past. She could still hear Edmund roaring in the distance, but the other voices were receding slowly, moving further away with every second.

She flung back her head, savouring her freedom as she laughed aloud with relief. She was free! Crouched down in a bog, up to her chin in filthy water, miles away from Redbourn and safety, but *free*!

Cautiously, she waited until the sound of Edmund's ranting ceased completely, then waded out of the reeds towards the open countryside beyond. It was risky, emerging into the open so soon after her escape, but she couldn't cower in the marshes all day. It was past noon already, and she'd catch her death unless she found shelter.

She moved slowly, keeping a wary lookout as she stepped back on to dry land, following the hoof prints back up the hill. It was near hopeless, she knew. There wasn't the faintest hope of her reaching Redbourn on foot before dark, and they hadn't passed any other villages. But she wasn't going to give up. If there was any chance that the Normans were following their trail she had to head out to meet them.

Every footstep was taking her back towards Svend. That thought alone gave her strength. As long as she kept moving there was hope.

She stopped abruptly, staring at the ground in confusion as it started to vibrate and shudder beneath her feet. What was happening? She looked around, a horrified scream rising to her throat at the sight of Edmund behind her. He was riding at full tilt, bursting out of the marshes as if there were a wild beast on his tail, looking less like a man than an animal himself, snarling with rage. And there was something else—a look of such hate-filled intensity that for a moment she thought he might be going to trample her into the ground.

Her heart stopped. He *was* going to trample her into the ground. Here in the open, with no weapon and nowhere to hide, she was going to be ridden down in cold blood by the man she'd once thought to marry.

If it weren't so appalling she might have laughed. But now there was nothing to do but run.

No. She squeezed her hands into fists. There was no point in running. There was nowhere to run. And if she couldn't run she could only fight. He wouldn't expect it, and his horse was tired—wouldn't be able to turn quickly. Its eyes were already rolling, its mouth flecked with gobbets of white foam. If she could confuse it, wear it out somehow, then Edmund would be forced to dismount. And then…

Then she'd think of something else.

She sprinted forward, trying to hold her nerve as Edmund hurtled towards her, giant clods of earth spinning out of the ground as he closed the distance between them, his horse's hooves louder and heavier with each passing moment. She screamed—a war cry of defiance—waiting until the last possible moment before diving to one side, sprawling in the dirt as the beast swung madly towards her, one large hoof barely missing her chest.

Quickly she struggled to her feet, grabbing a

branch from the ground and jabbing it up into Edmund's face. As she'd hoped, he raised a hand to push it away and the horse shied, throwing him backwards through the air.

She felt a rush of triumph, and wielded the branch in front of her like a sword as Edmund staggered to his feet.

'Bitch.' He wiped a trickle of blood from his forehead. 'I should have killed you when I had the chance.'

'Why are you doing this, Edmund?' She swung the branch between them. 'You should be running away—not coming after me. Why won't you let me go?'

'Because you're *mine*!'

'I was never yours!'

'You were supposed to be. Your father was going to give me half his land too. It was supposed to be mine! Now the Normans have taken everything. I won't let them have you too!'

'But you don't want me!'

'No, but *he* does. And if I can't kill him I might as well kill you!'

He drew his sword and sliced downwards, cutting the branch in two as she staggered away.

'You can't win like this, Edmund.' She could hear the desperation in her own voice.

'Maybe not, but I can make sure that *you* lose.'

He lunged at her again and she swung the remainder of the branch upwards, blocking the blow instinctively, so hard that his sword embedded itself in the wood.

Quickly she seized the advantage, heaving the branch towards him before turning to run. His horse was now halfway up the slope. If she could just reach it before he did…

'Aediva!'

She looked up, afraid that she was imagining things as she heard Svend's shout. But it was him—really him—thundering down the hillside towards her, a band of Norman soldiers at his back.

'Svend!'

Relief gave her a fresh burst of energy. She changed direction at once, running towards him with only a swift glance over her shoulder at Edmund. He'd managed to free his sword, but seemed frozen to the spot, staring at Svend with a look of pure hatred. Silently she willed him to run, to flee back into the marshes, to escape so that she'd never have to see him again. Surely he wouldn't come after her now—not with the Normans so close. He couldn't want to hurt her *that* badly…

Then he looked at her and her stomach plummeted.

The answer was clear on his face.

It was going to be her or him.

Svend surged ahead of his men. Talbot's mane was a streak of pale grey as they flew over the ground, faster and fiercer than they'd ever ridden before.

He'd allowed the horses a few brief rests, but they were still flagging. Only Bertrand was managing to keep pace—though his attention seemed less on the pursuit than on keeping his commander alive. Svend set his jaw grimly. He'd no intention of expiring just yet—not until he found Aediva. He'd go back to Redbourn with her or not at all.

'Their tracks are heading for the marshes.' Bertrand's tone was discouraging.

'Then we go into the marshes.'

'It'll be dark in a few more hours.'

'Then go back!'

Svend shot him a savage look and Bertrand stiffened at once.

'I won't leave you, sir.'

Good. Svend tightened his grasp on the reins, fighting to stay upright. He was relying on his men's loyalty. He'd ride alone into the marshes if he had to, but if he was going to rescue his wife he'd need every fighting man he could get. He didn't care about the rebels, but he was going to rescue her even if it took every last ounce of his strength.

If he didn't…if anything happened to her…

He pushed the thought aside, refusing to consider the alternative.

They crested another hill and his blood froze

at the sound of a woman's scream. Quickly he looked around, trying to find the source. Then he saw her. She was halfway up the slope, wrestling a Saxon warrior with what appeared to be a stick.

He spurred onwards, charging down the hill just as she turned to run.

'Aediva!'

He roared her name and she looked up at once, her eyes locking with his in a mixture of amazement and relief. The Saxon looked up too, and his expression of outrage turned to one of implacable resolve as he started to follow her, swinging his sword above his head as if preparing to strike.

Svend drew his dagger and took aim—felt something tear in his shoulder as he flung his arm back.

'Move!' he shouted, hoping she would understand, and she moved, dropping to the ground as the blade flew through the air, its sharp tip embedding itself in the Saxon's shoulder.

The man bellowed and Svend leapt from his horse with a grim sense of satisfaction. *There.* That evened the odds. Now they both had only one arm to fight with. That ought to be more than enough.

'Edmund.' He pointed his sword at the Saxon's throat menacingly. 'I'll give you one chance to yield. That's more than you deserve.'

'You can't have her!'

Edmund wrenched the dagger out of his shoulder, thrusting forward as Svend stepped to one side, slapping the blade away with the flat of his sword before driving his point up towards the other man's chest. Edmund reeled backwards, parrying wildly with his sword as Svend pursued him remorselessly, closing him down with a rain of powerful blows before pummelling the hilt hard into his face.

Edmund sank to the ground, his nose streaming with blood, and dropped his sword with a grunt of pain.

'I yield!'

'I said one chance. You didn't take it.'

Svend towered over him, his knuckles white, resisting the urge to finish what the other man had started. But he couldn't do it—not in front of Aediva. She'd said that Edmund was part of her past. He couldn't kill the man in front of her—couldn't taint their future with his blood. Better to let FitzOsbern see that justice was done.

'I'll spare you for her sake.'

He lowered his weapon with a grimace. In the heat of combat he hadn't noticed the pain in his arm, but now even his sword felt too heavy.

'Tie him up.' He jerked his head at Bertrand.

'Svend!'

He turned towards the sound of her voice. She was running towards him, arms outstretched, soaking wet and covered in mud, but she looked more beautiful than he'd ever seen her. Eagerly he started towards her—then stopped as her expression changed abruptly, her mouth opening in a silent scream.

He reacted instinctively, spinning around and thrusting his sword up just in time to see Edmund run chest-first onto its point, the dagger in his hand grazing harmlessly against Svend's chainmail.

For a moment nobody spoke. There was only an uncanny silence as Edmund's body jerked and then stiffened. A red stain soaked through his tunic as he made a faint gurgling sound and then folded backwards, collapsing to the ground with a thud.

'Aediva.' Svend tossed the sword away, bridging the distance between them in two strides as she stared at Edmund in horror. 'Don't look.'

'You killed him…'

He tensed. Was she angry with him? In spite of everything, would she hate him for killing a Saxon?

'He killed himself.'

'I know.' She met his gaze finally. 'It was *all* him. He wanted to kill me too. He hated me so much…' Her voice caught on a sob. 'I thought you would too. I thought you wouldn't come.'

His chest tightened. 'I told you before—I won't let you go. I could never hate you.'

'You trusted me.' She gave him a look of wonder before her face crumpled. 'Your shoulder… it's bleeding!'

'It doesn't matter.' He pulled her into a hard embrace, wrapping his arms around her like a vice, pain forgotten as he held her tight. 'None of that matters now. Let's go home.'

Chapter Nineteen

'Ow!' Aediva started awake as someone pressed a cold compress to her forehead, letting out a shriek as she saw the identity of her nurse. 'Cille! You're here!'

Her sister beamed. 'We arrived last night—just in time as it turned out. Between you and your husband, the men had quite a struggle getting you back. You were both well-nigh unconscious.'

'Svend!' She jolted upright in panic. 'Where is he? Is he all right?'

Cille raised a finger to her lips, gesturing towards a chair by the fireplace. 'He tore his wound open, but he wouldn't let anyone touch him until you were safely in bed. We had a hard enough time getting him into that chair.'

Aediva gazed at his sleeping face, her heart swelling with love. 'He saved me.'

'He loves you.'

'I love him too. I was afraid I'd never get the

chance to tell him. Even when Edmund was trying to kill me that was all I could think about.'

'Edmund…' Cille's expression hardened. 'I never liked him.'

'Father did.'

'He liked Leofric too. He wasn't right about *everything*.'

Aediva blinked, taken aback by the sudden bitterness in her sister's voice. 'Judith said you weren't happy with Leofric. Was he cruel to you?'

Cille hesitated. 'It's in the past now. It's probably best to leave it there.'

'What about de Quincey? Do you love him?'

For a moment Cille seemed on the verge of saying something, and then she appeared to change her mind. 'It's complicated. He loves our son. That's what matters.'

Aediva took a sharp intake of breath. Until that moment she hadn't fully believed that the rumours were true. 'So he's really the father?'

'Yes.' Cille looked down at her knotted fingers. 'I know I should have told you before. I wanted to, but I couldn't.'

Aediva shook her head in amazement, so many questions crowding her mind she hardly knew where to start. 'But you ran away from him!'

Cille's gaze slid to one side evasively. 'I wasn't thinking straight. When I found out I was expecting a child he'd already left for Normandy. It was only a few months after Leofric's death and I was afraid of what everyone would think. I didn't know what to do, so I ran.'

'But why didn't you tell me?'

'How could I? After what happened to Father you were so angry. So was I—but I couldn't hate all Normans the way you did. I thought if I told you you'd hate me too.'

Aediva bit her lip guiltily. She knew how that felt—not feeling able to tell someone the truth. 'I'm sorry, Cille. I let you down.'

'No! You didn't fail anyone—least of all me. You did everything you could to protect me. Just promise that the next time you pretend to be me we'll talk first.'

'I promise.' Aediva smiled sheepishly. 'At least we're talking now. We haven't done that in a while.'

'I know.' Cille's face clouded over again. 'There were things I couldn't talk about. I wasn't myself for a long time.'

'And now?'

'Now I feel like I'm waking up again.'

'Because of de Quincey?'

Cille nodded and Aediva squeezed her hand. 'So you want to go to Normandy?'

'Yes. It'll be a fresh start for us and—' Cille bit her tongue, her face suddenly crumpling with laughter.

'What? What's so funny?'

'We've changed our son's name. Leofric didn't seem appropriate any more.'

'Oh? So what's my nephew called now?'

'William.'

'William?'

'After everything that's happened we thought we might need to curry favour with the Earl *and* the King.'

'Do you think it will work?'

'Philippe thinks so, and I trust him.'

Aediva smiled. Judging by the look on her sister's face as she said the Baron's name, she didn't need to worry about her any more.

'If you truly want to go to Normandy then I'm happy for you, but what about Etton?'

'I think you and your husband are more than capable of taking care of Redbourn *and* Etton. Speaking of your husband…' Cille stood up determinedly. 'I promised to tell him the minute you woke up. And I certainly don't want to be on the wrong side of his temper.'

'Wait!' Aediva put out a hand to stall her. 'I must look a mess!'

'No more than usual.' Cille smiled affectionately, putting a hand on Svend's good shoulder. 'But I don't think he cares. I think he loves you the way you are.'

'Just let me comb…' She caught her breath unsteadily as a pair of blue eyes sprang open.

'I'll leave you two alone.' Cille gave an enigmatic smile as she drifted towards the door. 'I have a baby to tend to.'

Neither of them spoke as Svend heaved himself out of the chair and walked to the end of the bed, looking down at her with an expression like granite.

Aediva watched him nervously. When he'd held her in his arms on their journey back from the marshes she'd thought that he understood what had happened. Now she wasn't so sure.

'How's your shoulder?'

'Worse than before.'

'Oh.' She swallowed hard, quailing beneath his accusatory stare. If he'd been torturing her for information she couldn't have felt more uncomfortable. 'I wasn't trying to help them escape.'

'So the guards said.'

'They're alive?' She almost cried with relief.

'Badly wounded, but they'll survive. They're none too pleased with *you*, though.'

'No…' Her insides twisted. 'I tricked them into letting me see Edmund. I only wanted to tell him what you'd said—that if he surrendered he might be pardoned—but it all went wrong. I thought I could reason with him, but…' She gave an involuntary shiver. 'He wasn't the man I remembered.'

Svend looked distinctly unsympathetic. 'I told you…war changes men.'

'Women too. I'm sorry—truly.'

'You'll have to tell the guards that.'

'I will. Are *you* angry with me too?'

'Angry doesn't begin to cover it.'

'But do you forgive me?'

He held out for another moment before heaving a sigh, sitting down on the end of the bed. 'Yes, for my sins, I do. I just don't have to be pleased about it.'

She watched him with trepidation. He was sitting out of her reach, as if he didn't want to come within touching distance. 'What will FitzOsbern do when he finds out?'

'He won't be pleased.'

'Maybe if I tell him…'

'You'll tell him *nothing*!' Svend rounded on her fiercely. 'You'll stay as far away from William FitzOsbern as possible.'

She caught her breath. He looked severe, but there was something else in his expression too—something she'd never seen or expected to see there before. *Fear.*

'I need you to promise me, Aediva.' Svend set his jaw firmly. '*I'll* talk to FitzOsbern.'

'I promise.' She was almost afraid to ask her next question. 'Will he punish you?'

'Perhaps.'

'But…he won't take Redbourn away?'

'Possibly.'

'No!' Her throat tightened on a sob. 'Svend,

I'm so sorry. I never meant for you to lose your reward. I know what it means to you.'

'What?' He stared at her for a long moment. 'Hell's teeth, Aediva, do you *ever* listen to a word I say? I don't care about my reward!'

'You don't?'

'I want a *home*! That means with you. If I had half of England it wouldn't mean anything without you. *You're* my reward!'

She clambered over the bed, her heart brimming with happiness, but he held his hands up as if to fend her off.

'It's too late for us.'

'What?' She sat down again abruptly, her blood turning to ice. 'You said that you trusted me.'

'I did. I *do*. I knew you didn't go with Edmund willingly, but you still went to him when I had asked you not to.' He shook his head. 'I thought we could build a future together, but we have different allegiances. Yours almost got you killed. I've lost everything before, but when I thought I'd lost *you*… I can't go through that again. We should go our separate ways.'

She stared at him hopelessly, shuddering at the note of finality in his voice. He was bidding her farewell—sending her back to the old life he thought she still wanted. Except that she *didn't* want it. Not any more.

And how dared he tell her that she did? How dared he give up on them so easily?

'So you're sending me away because you're afraid of losing me?'

'I can't live with you when I don't know whose side you're on.'

'Yours! *Ours*!' She felt a rush of anger. 'I only went behind your back because you gave me no choice. You wouldn't even let me *talk* to Edmund. If you had then none of this would have happened.'

'So it was *my* fault?'

'Yes, in part. I'm Saxon—you know that. You can't expect me to turn my back on my people just because you say so. I'm not one of your soldiers to be ordered around, and you can't make decisions for me. We need to work things out together, find a new way—somewhere between Saxon and Norman.'

'There isn't—'

'Why did you come after me if you were just going to give up? Why did you almost kill yourself to save me?'

'Because I *love* you! But that's not the point!'

'Yes, it *is*! If you truly love me then you won't give up, no matter what. If we give up now then it's all hopeless. Edmund will have won. And if you think—'

She didn't get any further as he swept her into

his arms, closing her mouth with his with a fervour that took her breath away.

'Aediva.' He broke the kiss finally. 'You're the most infuriating woman I've ever known.'

'I know—but I love you. I don't want to go back to Etton. Not any more. If you want me to go then you'll have to drag me there in chains.'

His lips twitched. 'I never wanted you to go. I doubt I'd have been able to go through with it anyway. I'll just have to stay one step ahead of you in the future.'

'You won't have to. From now on we'll make decisions together.'

'Together. Speaking of which…' His eyes flashed wickedly. 'Everyone keeps telling me I ought to be in bed. If it hadn't been for your sister I'd have been there already.'

She smiled eagerly, wriggling aside to make room as he lay down beside her.

'I wouldn't be surprised if we had to stay here for days.' He pressed his lips against the curve of her throat. 'Recovering, that is.'

'Days?' She felt her pulse start to race.

'Unless you have anything better to do?'

'Nothing at all. Except appeasing an earl, maybe.'

'We'll find a way. There's still time to recapture the rebels. If not…' He shrugged. 'So long as I'm with you, I don't care. We'll find somewhere else, or maybe go back to Danemark. I've been in exile long enough. I'd like to see my family again.'

'I'd like that too.' She nestled beside him with a sigh of contentment. 'I love you. *Norman*.'

'And I love *you*. Wildcat.'

* * * * *

MILLS & BOON®

EXCLUSIVE EXTRACT

Prince Rafiq must save his desert kingdom's pride in a prestigious horse race. But he's shocked when his new equine expert is introduced… as *Miss* Stephanie Darvill!

Read on for a sneak preview of
THE HARLOT AND THE SHEIKH
by Marguerite Kaye

Prince Rafiq could be wearing tattered rags, and still she would have been in no doubt of his status. It was in his eyes. Not arrogance but a sense of assurance, of entitlement, a confidence that he was master of all he surveyed. And it was there in his stance too, in the set of his shoulders, the powerful lines of his physique. Belatedly garnering the power to move, Stephanie dropped into a deep curtsy.

'Arise.'

She did as he asked, acutely conscious of her disheveled appearance, dusty clothes, and a face most likely liberally speckled with sand. Those hooded eyes traveled over her person, surveying her from head to foot with a dispassionate, inscrutable expression.

'Who are you, and why are you here?' Prince Rafiq asked, when the silence had begun to stretch her nerves to breaking point. He spoke in English, softly accented but perfectly pronounced.

Distracted by the unsettling effect he was having on her while at the same time acutely aware of the need to impress him, Stephanie clasped her hands behind her back and forced herself to meet his eyes, answering in his own language. 'I am here at your invitation, Your Highness.'

'I issued no invitation to you, madam.'

'Perhaps this will help clarify matters,' Stephanie said, handing him her papers.

The Prince glanced at the document briefly. 'This is a royal warrant, issued by myself to Richard Darvill, the renowned Veterinary Surgeon attached to the Seventh Hussars. How do you come to have it in your possession?'

Stephanie knitted her fingers more tightly together, as if doing so would stop her legs from trembling. 'I am Stephanie Darvill, his daughter and assistant. My father could not, in all conscience, abandon his regiment with Napoleon on the loose and our army expected to go into battle at any moment.'

'And so he saw fit to send his daughter in his place?'

The Prince sounded almost as incredulous as she had been, when Papa suggested this as the perfect solution to her predicament. The enormity of the trust her father had placed in her struck her afresh. She would not let him down. Not again.

Give a 12 month subscripti
to a friend today!

Call Customer Services

0844 844 1358*

or visit

millsandboon.co.uk/subscriptic

*** This call will cost you 7 pence per minute plus your phone company's price per minute access charge.**